P9-DDB-784

DETROIT PUBLIC LIBRARY

3 5674 05291304 4

Losing It

CHASE BRANCH LIBRARY
17731 W. SEVEN MILE RD.
DETROIT, MI 48235
578-8002

Losing It

Zaria Garrison

www.urbanchristianonline.net

Urban Books, LLC
78 East Industry Court
Deer Park, NY 11729

Losing It Copyright © 2010 Zaria Garrison

All rights reserved. No part of this book may be reproduced
in any form or by any means without prior consent of the
Publisher, excepting brief quotes used in reviews.

ISBN 13: 978-1-60162-870-1
ISBN 10: 1-60162-870-6

First Printing October 2010
Printed in the United States of America

10 9 8 7 6 5 4 3 2 1

*This is a work of fiction. Any references or similarities to actual
events, real people, living, or dead, or to real locales are intended to
give the novel a sense of reality. Any similarity in other names, char-
acters, places, and incidents is entirely coincidental.*

Distributed by Kensington Corp.
Submit Wholesale Orders to:
Kensington Publishing Corp.
C/O Penguin Group (USA) Inc.
Attention: Order Processing
405 Murray Hill Parkway
East Rutherford, NJ 07073-2316
Phone: 1-800-526-0275
Fax: 1-800-227-9604

Losing It!

Zaria Garrison

This book is dedicated in loving memory to
Michael Joseph Jackson
August 29, 1958 – June 25, 2009
The greatest entertainer of all time

Acknowledgments

As always, I have to begin by thanking God, who is the head of my life and the true author of all of my books. Without Him, I not only would not be a writer; I truly would be nothing at all. I give Him all of the honor, glory, and the praise.

To my family: thank you for your support in all that I do. Family is strength and power, and I thank God for the family He's given me.

Ebony Farashuu, Kelli Little, and Sandra Poole, my friends and business partners, thank you for being a part of the process from the beginning to end. Your encouragement helps me keep going even when I want to give up. Thank you for being a part of my life.

Rhonda McKnight, author of *Secrets and Lies*. Thank you for reaching out to me and becoming a true friend. I appreciate all of your great advice. Most of all I appreciate the beautiful person that you are.

Michael Hubbard, Danita Jackson, and Cornellius Robertson, thank you for taking the time to be my advance readers. Your feedback and comments helped make this story all that it is. I appreciate each of you.

Last but certainly not least, I must thank my other family, the members of Soul City. If you read closely, you will see yourselves within these pages. Always remember that imitation is the sincerest form of flattery. I have love and respect for each and every one of you.

Chapter One

As she walked down the studio hallway to her dressing room, Sharmaine Cleveland felt elated. Entering the large plush room, decorated completely in pink per her request, she sat down at her dressing table and smiled at her own reflection. Although heavily made up and wearing a lace front wig for her performance, Sharmaine's smooth brown skin glowed. She'd just filmed the most physically draining scenes of her latest movie, involving an emotional and demanding funeral. Her character's mother passed away, and Sharmaine was required to bring back memories and grief she'd long since buried; however, she was pleased with the job she'd done.

It was well past midnight, and she didn't feel the least bit tired. In fact, she felt exuberant and ready for more. As she slowly wiped the thick stage makeup required for her scenes from her face, she couldn't help but reflect on her wonderful life.

Sharmaine's middle-aged parents had believed they would never conceive, but Sharmaine came into the world only a few months shy of her mother's forty-second birthday. After years of unanswered prayers, they vowed to give her life back to God. A covenant was made with Him; Sharmaine had been told that as long as she was faithful, her life would be led by His hand. Her parents took her to church on Sundays and made sure that Sharmaine had a personal relationship with God.

Hearing a knock at her dressing room door, Sharmaine slowly turned around and called out, "Come in. It's open."

"Hey, I've called around for the limousine, and he'll pick us up at the rear door in a few minutes," Keisha said as she walked into the room. Keisha Williams was Sharmaine's manager, publicist, personal assistant, and best friend.

"Thanks, Keisha. Have you spoken to Marshall? Was he pleased with my work today?" Sharmaine asked.

"As usual, he was very pleased with your performance. He said he's never directed anyone who was such a natural, and he has become a fan."

Sharmaine beamed. It hadn't been easy convincing an A-list director to sign on for a Christian movie with a predominantly African American cast. Sharmaine's previous two movies premiered at number one across the country and were fan favorites; however, even with that success, A-list directors still considered religious movies too risky. *Pearls of Righteousness* was Sharmaine's third starring role in a Christian movie, and she could have had her pick of many talented directors, but she would only accept the best. With that goal in mind, she had asked Keisha to personally contact Academy Award–winning director Marshall Vitowski and invite him to lunch.

Sharmaine had handed him the script while dining on shrimp and pasta prepared by her personal chef. He was hesitant at first, but within a few weeks, he was convinced this movie would be a major blockbuster. As usual, Sharmaine received top billing, but with Marshall Vitowski on board, she had been able to snag an Oscar-nominated co-star. Marshall's influence persuaded former professional football player and three time Golden Globe winner Chase Vinton to sign on. They were under budget, on schedule, and she happily looked forward to a fabulous opening Christmas weekend of the following year.

"What time am I scheduled to be on the set tomorrow?" Sharmaine asked.

"You are not shooting any scenes tomorrow. Marshall says it's a wrap. He still has to do some exterior shots and things with the extras."

"Really? We're done already?"

Keisha nodded her head.

They'd been shooting on location and in the studio in Atlanta for more than six months. Sharmaine enjoyed her work so much that it seemed like only days. Feeling just a bit melancholy, she realized she would miss the entire cast and crew.

"So what's on my agenda for tomorrow?" Sharmaine asked.

"Absolutely nothing. You are not scheduled to work again until your CD tour begins at the Georgia Dome on the first of next month. You have rehearsals and sound checks a few days prior, but that's not for a few weeks. Go home and get some rest."

"I'll go home, but I won't rest." Sharmaine laughed. "When do I fly to New York for the interview with Tyra?"

"That's two weeks from Thursday to coincide with your CD release on the following Friday. Until then, you have some much needed free time."

"Wonderful! I can hardly wait to tell Leon and the kids that they will have me all to themselves for a few days."

Sharmaine put her arms into her jacket as Keisha gathered her purse and belongings from the dressing room. Feeling content, Sharmaine followed closely behind Keisha as they navigated the studio hallway. After several moments, they finally arrived outside, where a limousine awaited to take them home.

Although she had several houses around the country, including a condo in Los Angeles, a beach house in Florida and an estate in Encino, California, her house in Atlanta's Buckhead neighborhood was the one Sharmaine referred to when she said the word "home." With seven bedrooms and six and one half baths, it was modest when compared to other mansions in the area. But she and her husband, Leon, had fallen in love with the spacious estate the moment they saw it. Sharmaine had been pregnant with their oldest daughter, Camille, at the time, and felt it was the perfect place to build their family. She had traveled all over the United States and internationally to many countries, but she was always grateful when the time arrived to return home.

After a peaceful hour drive, the limousine pulled into her front gate and made its way up the long circular driveway. Sharmaine said her usual prayer of thanks to God for allowing her to return to her family safe and sound.

"It's late, Keisha. Why don't you spend the night here and have breakfast with us in the morning?" Sharmaine said as the driver opened the limousine door for her to exit.

"No, this is your family time. I wouldn't want to intrude."

"Oh, please, girl. You are family."

Keisha and Sharmaine had been best friends since the third grade. When she decided to pursue a career in music, Sharmaine possessed the talent, but she had no idea how to proceed. Keisha volunteered to be her guide, and their journey began toward a successful career. Sharmaine was thankful that she had never considered hiring anyone else for the job.

Keisha had expertly guided Sharmaine's career while also being there for every major life-changing event. She was maid of honor at Sharmaine and Leon's wedding. She'd been in the delivery room for the birth of all three of Sharmaine's children, and held her hand and consoled her as she buried first her mother then her father. Sharmaine honestly did not know what she would do without Keisha by her side.

"You know what I mean. This is your time, Sharmaine. Enjoy it. You'll see plenty of me once the tour starts," Keisha answered.

"Well, if you won't spend the night, at least promise me you'll stop by tomorrow. I can hardly believe the warm January we are having. It's not warm enough for swimming, but we can have a barbecue out by the pool."

"That sounds like fun. I'll be here."

Keisha stepped out of the limo with Sharmaine and gave her a long hug. "Have a good night," she said as she waved good-bye and then got back inside the limo.

Sharmaine casually walked into her foyer, laying her purse and other belongings by the doorway for the maid to put away. She looked over at the clock and realized it was almost two A.M. As her family slept peacefully upstairs, Sharmaine decided against climbing the stairs and possibly disturbing them; instead, she went into her expansive office.

As she entered, she always stared in awe at the numerous awards and accolades that hung on the walls and sat on the shelves. It had been Leon's idea to decorate the office with her memorabilia, and each time she entered the room, she felt thankful and deeply humbled by her success.

As the only gospel recording artist to write and star in three major motion pictures, Sharmaine's face had graced the cover of every prominent magazine in the country. Her recordings, although fully religious, received airplay on most secular stations. This caused her hits to continually hold a spot in the nation's top five songs. Sharmaine had released eight solo albums, and each of them had gone platinum within the first week. In the last three years, every one of her new singles premiered at number one on *Billboard* magazine's top 100 charts. Sharmaine took pride in the fact that she'd accomplished all of that without ever compromising her Christian values or changing her religious lyrics. She loved Jesus, and she loved to sing his name in praise. Her latest recording, simply titled *My Praise*, was due for release at the beginning of February. Critics and experts were predicting the same type of sweeping success.

Slowly, Sharmaine knelt down in front of her huge brown leather sofa and softly prayed. She thanked God for everything He'd blessed her and her family with, and praised Him for his presence in her life. When she was done she rose, went to the closet, and retrieved a leopard-print faux fur blanket and a fluffy pillow. She lay down on the sofa, curled underneath the warm fur, and gradually drifted off to sleep.

A piercing scream awoke her early the next morning.

"Mom, come quick! You're on the news."

Groggily, she turned over and stared at her eldest daughter, Camille. "What's the matter with you, girl? I'm always on the news." Sharmaine rolled over and stretched.

"No, this is different. Come quick. You have to hear what they are saying," Camille answered. She rushed from the room and screamed upstairs for her father.

Sharmaine rose from the couch and casually strolled into the family room. Her seventeen-year-old daughter, Camille, was known for being overly dramatic, so Sharmaine was expecting to see a news report regarding her upcoming CD release, or the filming of her movie. As the reporter spoke, though, Sharmaine's mouth fell open as she stared, stunned, at the screen.

"Early this morning video tapes began arriving at news stations throughout the city, as well as popping up all over the Internet. We will attempt to show small clips on air; however, please be reminded these tapes are explicit in nature, and parental discretion is advised."

Sharmaine watched as her face appeared on the screen. At least she thought it looked like her face. The woman was the same dark caramel color, with big, round brown eyes. She had a crooked nose just like Sharmaine's nose, which was the result of a biking accident as a child. Her lips were full and thick; again, just like Sharmaine's. The woman's hair was cut short in a classic pixie style that just barely covered her small ears. It was identical to Sharmaine's jet black hair with light brown highlights. Staring at the screen, Sharmaine realized the resemblance was uncanny; however, the things the woman was doing made Sharmaine sure that this woman was not her.

"Turn it off. Turn it off right now," she ordered. "You know we don't watch that type of thing in this house."

"But, Mom, the news reporter says that woman is you," Camille answered before pressing the off button on the remote.

"That's ridiculous. She may look like me, but she definitely is not me," she said as she noticed Leon joining them in the room. She greeted him with a hug and a kiss.

"What's going on down here? Camille, what's this big news story you wanted me to see?"

"Mom made me turn it off." Camille sulked.

"It wasn't me anyway. It was a woman who looks like me. Camille, forget about the television. Go call your brother and sister down for breakfast," Sharmaine replied.

Half-heartedly, Camille stood up and trotted up the stairs. As soon as she was gone, Sharmaine turned to her husband.

"Leon, you won't believe what I just saw. I've got to get Keisha on the phone immediately. We have to do something about this," she said, rushing back to her office to retrieve her BlackBerry.

"Honey, wait. What did you see?" Leon asked, following closely behind her.

Once inside her office, she closed the door so that the children coming down the stairs would not overhear. Sharmaine and Leon were the parents of three children: Camille who was seventeen; Jeanna, who'd just turned fourteen; and ten-year-old Rodney.

"There's some sort of tape circulating the news stations and the Internet. They say the woman on the tape is me. It's crazy," she said. She grabbed her BlackBerry and frantically dialed Keisha's number.

"I've already seen it. I'm on my way over," Keisha replied as soon as she picked up her phone.

"What is going on? Who is that woman?" Sharmaine asked.

"I don't know any details yet, but several news stations have called me for a comment."

"What did you tell them?" Sharmaine paced back and forth with the phone.

"Nothing. I told them no comment. Calm down. I'm in the car, and I will be at your place in less than five minutes. Don't worry. I will handle this."

"Okay, just please hurry." Sharmaine hung up the phone, and then suddenly remembered her husband was still in the room.

"What's going on? What's kind of tape is it?" he asked.

"The woman on the tape, she was naked, in bed with a man, and . . . and she's . . . and they . . . Oh, I can't even say it. Leon, it was unbelievable."

"Are you telling me it's a sex tape?" His eyebrows shot up and his eyes widened.

Sharmaine slowly nodded.

Leon sat down on the sofa and shook his head. "I don't believe this. What did the woman look like?"

"Me. I told you. She looked exactly like me." Sharmaine continued pacing back and forth, wringing her hands.

"I can't believe they actually showed that on the morning news."

"They tried to strategically block things out, but it was obvious what they were doing."

Leon looked over at a distraught Sharmaine still pacing back and forth. "Come sit with me. I'm going to see if I can find it and see this for myself." He picked up the remote to her office TV.

"No, I can't stand to see it again," she answered.

Just then, Keisha arrived and rushed breathlessly into the office. "My phone has been ringing off the hook all morning," she said. "The whole city of Atlanta is talking about this sex tape, and it's rapidly going nationwide."

Moving her short, petite frame quickly across the room, Keisha took a seat in front of Sharmaine and Leon and opened her laptop.

"Tell me the details, Keisha. I didn't see the news report," Leon said.

"There is a sex tape with a woman and a man having sex. The woman has been identified as Sharmaine. There's no word on the identity of the man. So far this morning, there have been over five thousand views of the clips online, and it's been featured on every news network," she answered.

Leon sighed. "Can't you do something to get it pulled from the Internet?"

"I could try, but it would probably pop right back up again in a couple of hours. People download and save those types of things. There's no way to get all of them," Keisha answered.

"So what's your plan of action?" Sharmaine asked.

"I guess our best course of action is to deny. No one can prove that it's you, so we'll just deny it. I mean, it's not you, is it?" Keisha looked up from her laptop at Sharmaine.

"Are you out of your mind? Why would you ask such a thing?" Sharmaine glared at her.

"I'm not accusing you of anything, but that woman looks amazingly like you," she replied.

"Keisha, surely you don't believe my wife would be involved in anything like this?" Leon asked. He looked back and forth between the two of them.

"I'm not saying that she is. All I'm saying is we are all human, and we make mistakes. If it is Sharmaine, you can tell me, and it won't leave this room." Keisha looked at Sharmaine expectantly.

"I don't believe you, Keisha! That is not me. I have never and would never make a sex tape. The only man I've ever slept with in my whole life is Leon, and our first time was on our wedding night. You know that." Sharmaine folded her arms across her chest in frustration and anger.

"I know. I'm just asking the same questions everyone else will be asking. Please don't take offense. I'm sorry, but I had to ask," she said. Keisha looked away and began typing rapidly on her laptop keyboard.

"What are you doing now?" Sharmaine asked.

"I'm preparing a statement to send to all the major news outlets, denying any involvement in the tape. It should all blow over in a few days," Keisha replied.

"Is that all? You are just going to say it's not her and that's it?" Leon asked.

Keisha looked up and pushed her glasses up on her round face. "Basically, there's not much else to do. Sharmaine is America's sweetheart. I'm sure once we release a statement, things will calm down. Don't worry."

Sharmaine and Leon's maid, Consuela, tapped on the office door and opened it without waiting for an answer. "Breakfast is ready, Mr. and Mrs. Cleveland. The children are waiting in the kitchen. Will you be in soon, or should I serve you in here?" she asked.

"We'll be there in a minute," Leon answered. "Oh, and keep the TV off in the kitchen and the family room," he added.

"It's too late, Mr. Leon. The children have already seen the news." She glanced sadly over at Sharmaine.

"Okay, just make sure they don't see any more of it. We'll be right in," Leon told her.

Consuela quietly backed out of the room and closed the door.

"I wonder if the people who are behind this ever gave a

thought to what would happen when my ten-year-old son saw this." Sharmaine struggled to fight back tears.

"It's a crazy world we live in, honey. We've never allowed Satan's power in our lives, and we won't start now. We'll get through this together." Leon took her hand into his and patted it. He smiled broadly at her.

Sharmaine silently thanked God for Leon and his strength.

The two of them had met when they were kids, but it wasn't until after he'd graduated college that Sharmaine even gave him a second glance. By that time, he'd grown to be over six feet tall and was quite handsome. Leon had been a geeky teen with pasty light tan skin, the result of being biracial, with a Caucasian mother and African American father. His face was covered with moles and zits, as he had been losing the battle with acne. His light brown hair, and that of all of his siblings, was wild and unruly because their Caucasian mother had no idea how to style it for them.

Keisha and Sharmaine had spent many teenage afternoons laughing at Leon and his brothers; however, when he returned from college, he'd cut and styled his hair into a neat fade, his skin had cleared up, and Sharmaine had to admit their three-year age difference no longer mattered.

They'd been married for eighteen years, and she loved him more every time she looked into his face.

"You're right. Let's just go talk to the kids." Sharmaine turned to Keisha. "I want to read over that statement before you send it out. Come on and have some breakfast. We can finish this when we're done."

The three of them left the office and joined the children in the kitchen. Consuela had already placed breakfast on the table.

"Camille, you are such a liar. That was not Mom," Sharmaine's son, Rodney said. "Stop saying it or else," he threatened.

"Lower your voice, young man, and don't threaten your sister," Leon said as soon as he entered the room.

"Dad, Camille is saying awful things about Mom. Make her stop it," he whined.

"Listen, your mother and I want to talk to all of you about what you have seen. Stop arguing right now," Leon said.

Their younger daughter, Jeanna, spoke up. "I didn't see anything. I came down here and these two were arguing about what they saw. Is there really a sex tape with Mom on it?"

Sharmaine sat down next to Jeanna. "No, there is not. There's a tape with someone on it that resembles me," she answered.

"See, Camille, I told you!" Rodney stuck out his tongue at his sister.

"Then who is the woman on the tape?" Camille asked, ignoring her baby brother.

"We have no idea, and frankly, it doesn't matter." Leon looked back and forth between his three children as he spoke. "What does matter is that you three understand that it's not your mother. She would never be involved in anything like that."

"No problem," Jeanna said. She cut off a huge piece of waffle with her fork and stuffed it into her mouth.

Sharmaine looked over at Camille. "Are you okay, honey? I know what you saw this morning has to be confusing to you."

"She looked exactly like you, Mom," Camille answered.

"Do you remember last year when we went to that church down in Valdosta, Georgia, and they hosted a Sharmaine

Cleveland lookalike contest? Some of those women came pretty close," Sharmaine said.

"That was just all in fun, Mom. None of them really looked like you at all. Not like this woman does."

"You know, Camille, with computer graphics, and things like that, people can do a lot of things with a video camera and a computer. It's probably just an elaborate photoshop job," Keisha said.

"Right, honey, they could have put my head on someone else's body. People do that all the time to celebrities," Sharmaine answered.

"Why would someone do that? It doesn't make any sense," Camille asked.

Sharmaine was running out of excuses and explanations to give to her daughter. She looked over at Leon for help.

"It doesn't have to make sense, honey. Some people, like the ones who did this, do things for reasons that don't make sense. Your mother and I have led our lives for Christ. We've told you before that being people of God makes you a target sometimes," he answered.

"I know, but—"

"Don't worry about it, Camille," Sharmaine said. "It's going to all be over in a few days, and this will just be a bad memory. Listen, I'm off work for a while. We wrapped shooting on the movie last night. After you guys get in from school this afternoon, we are going to have a poolside barbecue, and tomorrow we can go shopping, just us girls."

"That is a great idea!" Jeanna chimed in. "Mom, I saw this gorgeous pink outfit I wanted at Nordstrom's. I could wear it to your concert."

"Shopping? What about me?" Rodney asked.

"I'm not finished. On Sunday, we're going out to Lake La-
nier and do some fishing. I'll pick you up a new rod while the
girls and I are shopping." Sharmaine grinned at her son.

"Great! I can hardly wait," he said.

Feeling just a little better, Camille finally began to eat her
eggs, and within a few moments, the entire family and Keisha
were laughing and talking.

Sharmaine sat back in her chair and watched her family
as the morning's events seemed to float away into the air.
"Thank you, God," she whispered.

Chapter Two

"So, I guess you've heard the news about Sharmaine Cleveland. Her publicist is denying any involvement, but it doesn't look good for her."

Shawn Reeves, entrepreneur and CEO of Raga Records looked up from the folder he was reading at his wife Brenetta. She sat perched on the edge of his desk, filing her long fingernails.

"Yes, I've heard it, and I'm a bit concerned," he replied. "We have a CD release in a couple of weeks, and a forty-city tour coming up. This could potentially have a negative effect on sales."

Brenetta suddenly stopped filing her nails and stared at him. "What do you mean, potentially? Who do you think wants to buy a gospel CD by a porn star? You need to cancel the release."

Shawn shook his head. "She's no porn star. It's just a tape. I'm just going to wait and see how this all plays out. Sharmaine Cleveland has been the most successful act we've ever signed. I'm not going to let some unauthenticated Internet tape cancel out all that." Shawn turned his attention back to the material in his folder.

"It didn't take much more than that to get my CD cancelled," Brenetta huffed.

Shawn looked over at his wife sitting in front of him, obviously peeved. "Now, you know that's not true. Your past legal troubles had very little to do with my decision not to release *Sexy Saint*. I just didn't agree with the whole project. The production fell behind schedule, and you were way over budget. It was a business decision."

"None of that would have happened if you'd gotten me the production team I wanted. You had me in the studio with amateurs, while Sharmaine had the opportunity to work with Russell Dent. He's one of the best producers in the country."

Shawn sighed. He loved his wife dearly, but her musical talent was limited. During their marriage, he had spent thousands of dollars on voice and diction lessons, but she still sounded like a chicken caught in a blender when she sang. She had begged and pleaded to have a singing career, so he had tried everything to make her recordings successful. He'd even tried to pull a "Milli Vanilli" and have someone else sing for her. It almost worked, until she barged her way into the recording studio one afternoon and discovered them. Without the help of the voiceovers, he had no other choice but to cancel the project.

"Brenetta, you have to understand that Sharmaine earned the right to those producers. She's brought millions of dollars into this company. People love and respect her."

"She's a fraud. The tape proves that." Brenetta rolled her neck and eyes.

"I'm surprised at you. We've attended the same church as Sharmaine and Leon for ten years. We've had dinner in their home on numerous occasions. She's supposed to be our friend. You know she's a righteous woman of God. That tape has to be a fake."

Brenetta flipped her long, auburn-colored weave behind her left ear. "What if it isn't? If that tape is real, you have to cancel the CD release."

"Maybe," Shawn answered. He slowly rubbed his chin; then he brushed his fingers across his mustache and goatee.

"What does that mean?"

"It means that regardless of what you may think, I'm a businessman above all else. As long as Sharmaine is making money for this company, I don't care what kinds of videos she makes on her own time."

"You just said it yourself: she's a righteous woman of God. What kind of woman of God would make a video like that? She's the queen of gospel music and Christian movies. How can you say that you don't care?"

Shawn closed the folder he'd been trying to read and stood up from his desk. "As a businessman, I honestly don't care. Sometimes scandal sells records."

Brenetta put down her nail file and stood up also. "Scandal sells rap records. It does not sell gospel records."

"You may very well be right, but it's too soon to know that. Like I said, I am a bit concerned. Let's just leave it at that." Shawn reached for his jacket and put it on.

"I still think you need to go ahead and cancel the release."

"And I think that you are not going to let me get any work done, so we might as well go to dinner," Shawn answered.

Brenetta grabbed her purse and stuffed her nail file inside. Reluctantly, she followed him out of his office into the reception area.

His secretary stopped him as soon as he stepped outside his office door. "I was just about to buzz you, Mr. Reeves. *The Tyra Show* called. They've cancelled the interview with Sharmaine Cleveland."

Shawn looked surprised. "Cancelled? Did they give a reason?"

"They sent the list of questions to Keisha for Sharmaine to go over, and she has refused to discuss the sex tape. The show decided not to go forward without some discussion of it."

"You're kidding me, right? What did they expect her to say about it?"

"The producers felt that it should not be ignored. Sharmaine could have denied any involvement in it; however, they were insistent that it be discussed and edited clips be shown. Sharmaine refused to do that."

"Get her on the phone now!" he bellowed. Shawn stormed back into his office with Brenetta right on his heels.

"I told you so. I told you so," she gloated.

"Not now, Brenetta. I've got to get that interview back. Go ahead and get the driver to take you to the restaurant. I'll meet you there when I'm done."

"No, I want to hear all of this. I'm not going anywhere," she said, planting herself firmly in a chair facing his desk.

Ignoring her, Shawn answered his office phone as his secretary buzzed him. "I have Keisha on the line, Mr. Reeves. She says Sharmaine is out of town with her family and is unreachable. Do you want to speak with her?"

"Put her through." Shawn took a seat at his desk, then picked up his Bluetooth headset and put it on his ear. "What is wrong with Sharmaine? How could she refuse Tyra?" he demanded.

"Hi, Shawn, it's nice to hear from you," Keisha answered.

"Don't try to doubletalk me, Keisha. You need to inform Sharmaine to get her butt home so that she can get ready for this interview."

"She didn't cancel the interview, Shawn; they did. What do you expect her to do?"

"I expect her to answer the questions they ask her. She can't go on a national television show and completely ignore the existence of this sex tape. That's crazy. All she has to do is allow one question, deny being the woman on the tape, and move on to discussing the CD. What's wrong with that?"

"Frankly, I agree with you, but Sharmaine feels it's best to simply ignore the tape. She also flat out refuses to be there if they plan to show clips of it. Her husband and children will be in the audience. She says it's not negotiable."

Shawn slammed his fist against his desk out of frustration, and to scare Brenetta, who was busy making faces at him and mouthing *I told you so* over and over. He pointed a finger of warning at her before returning to his conversation. "What else do we have lined up before the release?"

Keisha hesitated before answering. "That's what I've been working on all day."

"You must be kidding me. You waited until now to start lining up publicity and interviews. Keisha, you are usually on top of these things. I never check up on it, because I know you will handle it. What's going on with you?"

"I did handle it, Shawn. The problem is the tape. Since it came out, the secular shows want to discuss it, and Sharmaine refuses. The religious shows don't want her or the controversy. All of the TV shows I had scheduled have pulled out. The only things left are the magazine interviews, because they've already gone to press."

Shawn sat back in his chair, stunned. "I had no idea this tape thing was so big. I'd seen it on the gossip blogs, but I wasn't concerned. This is really going to cause major problems."

"Shawn, it's huge. That's why she left town. The headmaster from the kids' private school asked her to pull them out for a while because their presence was causing too much of a disruption."

"That's ridiculous. That school is full of celebrities' kids. What's the problem?"

"The other children were harassing the kids about the tape. Rodney got into a fight and came home with a black eye. After the headmaster asked them to leave school, she and Leon decided to get out of town until the tour starts."

"Keisha, you are her right arm. You've got to reason with her and get these interviews rescheduled."

"Trust me, Shawn, I have tried. The worst part is Sharmaine thinks she can pray it away. Every time I try to talk about it, she says that God is in control and He's handling it." Keisha sighed deeply into the phone.

"That sounds like Sharmaine. She's a firm believer that her success is attributed solely to God. I'm not surprised that she'd take that attitude in this situation, but does she really expect us to do nothing?"

"Yes. She says that I worry too much, but things are going crazy. She and the girls were mobbed last week at the mall, and they had to leave without completing their purchases. I stayed behind and paid for everything then delivered it later."

"That's a good thing, Keisha. If the fans were excited to see her, then—"

Keisha interrupted him. "No, it wasn't fans. It was former fans. It was people pointing fingers and calling her names. She was accused of being a hypocrite and much worse. Camille and Jeanna were in tears. It was awful. She had to get away from it, Shawn."

"Wow. I guess I need to keep a close watch on this going forward. I have to tell you that after hearing this, I am seriously considering canceling, or at the very least postponing the release." Shawn looked over at Brenetta as he said it, watching a huge smile spread across her face.

"Shawn, no, you can't do that! Sharmaine would be crushed."

"I feel for her, but we've put a lot of money behind this project. I can't afford to lose it all. You need to have her call me so we can discuss this."

"I will, Shawn. I promise you. Please don't make a final decision until we've spoken again."

Shawn hung up the phone without replying. He looked over at a smug Brenetta staring at him. "I'm not in the mood, Brenetta," he said before she could speak.

"Cancel the release, Shawn. This scandal is going to cost you a lot of money if you don't," she answered.

"It's going to cost me either way. If we cancel, I lose everything I've put into it. If I move forward and it flops, I lose as well. This is not good either way."

"I've got an idea," Brenetta said, perking up.

Shawn eyed her suspiciously. "What is it? I'm really not in the mood for nonsense. This is serious."

He listened intently as Brenetta outlined her plan of action. He wasn't sure if it would work, but he was running out of ideas.

"That's something I'll have to mull over for a while. It's too risky to bring up right now. Let's go to dinner. I'm starved."

In Florida, Sharmaine stretched leisurely as she lay on the beach. She watched the clouds float by, feeling peaceful and content. The home she and Leon purchased there was in a secluded area with a private beach. Seagulls flew over her as she marveled at God's majesty in the sound of the waves.

Her cell phone suddenly began ringing in her backpack, disturbing the calm atmosphere. Reluctantly, she pulled it out and answered. "Hello."

"Have you lost your ever loving mind, Sharmaine?" she heard a familiar male voice ask.

"Chase?"

"Yeah, it's me, Chase. Now answer my question."

Sharmaine sat up on her multi-colored beach towel. "I don't know what you are talking about. What's wrong?"

"Don't play the innocent act with me, Sharmaine. I only signed on to do that stupid movie in the first place because of Marshall Vitowski. How dare you pull a stunt like this?"

"Like what? Chase, slow down and just tell me what you are talking about."

"The studio is postponing the release of the movie. Don't sit there and pretend you didn't know."

"What? No, I'm on vacation with my family. I had no idea."

"Right, you are on vacation while my career is plummeting to the ground because of you," he yelled.

"Why are they postponing? I always release during Christmas weekend. It's a tradition. Besides, I always win the numbers."

"Are you dense or what? The studio execs have seen that sex tape you made. You know, that's why I don't believe in religion. You fake Christians really get under my skin."

Sharmaine cringed at the mention of the tape, but she was more annoyed by Chase calling her a fake Christian.

"That's not me on that tape, Chase. You have to bel—"

Chase cut her off before she could get out the word *believe*. "Sharmaine, please, I spent months with you and I've seen the video. It's definitely you. How could you be so careless and stupid?"

Sharmaine's heart began to beat faster and she felt nauseated. If her own co-star believed she was in the video, how could she convince anyone else otherwise? She took a deep breath and tried to reason with Chase. "Listen, I know what it looks like, but my reputation should speak for itself."

"I don't care about your reputation. My Dad was a Baptist minister with six kids spread out all over the city that he didn't have with my mother. But that never tarnished his reputation. At least he was smart enough to keep his skeletons in the closet until after he died. All of you religious types are the same. You live one way in the public eye, but behind closed doors you are worst of all."

His words cut deep, and Sharmaine felt tears stinging her face. "Chase, I'm sorry that you got caught up in this. I promise you this will all blow over soon, and I'm sure by next year the studio will change their minds."

"Blow over? No, you need to get on the phone and convince them to move ahead with this now. You are not gonna kill my career because of your stupidity."

"Why won't you calm down and just listen to me?"

"Tell them it was a mistake. Tell them you were drunk. Or tell them aliens inhabited your body. I don't care. Just fix this, Sharmaine!" Chase screamed then violently hung up the phone.

Sharmaine sat stunned for several minutes, trying to calm down. She wiped at her tears, but they continued to flow. Suddenly, she grabbed her backpack and towel from the beach and rushed back to the house.

As she approached the house, Leon sat playing Scrabble with the kids by the pool.

"What is I-D-K? That's not a word," Rodney said to Camille.

"It's an abbreviation for *I don't know*," she answered.

Leon laughed at them both. "Sorry, but you have to use real words, honey," he said. His attention shifted from the game as he noticed Sharmaine rushing by. "I'll be right back," he said to the kids.

He followed the sound of Sharmaine's sandals clicking across the hardwood floors, up the stairs, and into their bedroom. He found her lying across the bed in her red swimsuit. He watched her body convulse back and forth as she silently cried.

Slowly, he sat down on the bed and gently reached out to her. "What's wrong?" he asked quietly.

Sharmaine sat up to face him. In between sobs she managed to relay the information of the phone call with Chase. "This is not all blowing over, Leon. First Keisha says Shawn wants to cancel the CD release; now the studio has postponed the movie. What am I going to do?"

"It's a long time before next Christmas, honey. Chase is overreacting."

"Maybe you're right. He did seem a bit overly theatrical when I worked with him. I just thought it was the mark of a good actor."

"This is his first leading man role, honey. He's a bit anxious, that's all. You'll see once you start the tour; your fans will remind you why you are so successful."

"My fans hate me. Have you forgotten about the incident at the mall?" She sniffed loudly and wiped at her tears. "Don't let the actions of a few ignorant people sway you. Shawn agreed to go ahead with the CD release. He has faith in you. I know that once you get onstage and those songs of praise start floating up to heaven, none of this will be important anymore. I'm sure of it."

Sharmaine rested her head on Leon's strong shoulder. "Thank you for believing in me. I don't know what I'd do without you."

"You'll never get a chance to find out either."

The next morning, Sharmaine, Leon, and the kids boarded a plane and flew back to Atlanta. A mob of reporters greeted them at the airport, screaming questions and flashing cameras. Sharmaine and Leon shielded the kids from the paparazzi as best they could. Finally, Keisha arrived with a limo, allowing them to escape the frenzy as they returned to their Buckhead estate. A media circus was set up outside the sprawling gates as the family arrived. The limousine carefully navigated the circular driveway, finally bringing them to a place of solitude in front of their home.

Later that evening, after they'd all shared dinner together, Sharmaine and Keisha retreated to her office for business.

"How are things looking for the tour?" Sharmaine asked as she sat down on her sofa.

"The good news is that the tour is still on. None of the promoters have cancelled your dates. Shawn's influence had a lot to do with that."

"Why did Shawn have to get involved at all? He said he wasn't cancelling the release."

Keisha hesitated before responding. "Tickets sales are way down, and some places have been forced to give refunds. None of your dates have sold out the way they have in the past."

"What about the interviews? Did Tyra's show change their minds?"

"No, honey, I'm sorry, but they didn't. Don't worry. I'm waiting to hear back from Billy Wayne's gospel hour. I think they will agree to feature you."

"I hate to sound elitist, but they are so small. They are not seen in any markets outside of Atlanta. Are you sure you couldn't book me on a bigger name show?"

Keisha sighed. "There are plenty of shows that want to book you, but you know the stipulations."

"I am not going to discuss that tape. Have you tried to reach *106 and Gospel* or the *Bobby Jones Gospel* show? I would think the body of Christ would support me at this time."

Keisha put her head in her hands for a brief moment to try to think. She'd placed phone calls to every major and minor show she could think of. It wasn't as easy as Sharmaine thought. She sat quietly for several moments before speaking again. "Listen, Sharmaine, the gospel shows are afraid to feature you. They are afraid of how their audience will react. You haven't made any statements except a press release to deny, and that is not working. Please, won't you at least consider discussing it?"

Sharmaine stood up from the sofa and began pacing around the room. "What do you want me to say, Keisha? It's not me. What else is there to say?"

"It's not what you say, Sharmaine, but how you say it. I think if you went on one of these shows and made a passionate plea of your innocence, it could help."

"Keisha, I am innocent. Why do I have to make a plea?" She stopped pacing and stared at her friend, waiting for an answer.

"I just think if the fans could look into your eyes and your face when you say it's not you . . ." Keisha paused briefly. "I think that they would believe you."

Sharmaine walked over and stared out of the window onto the grounds of her estate for several moments without answering. She wondered if proclaiming her innocence in front of cameras was the right thing to do. In her mind, she imagined the audience hanging on to her every word and giving her a standing ovation. Then she imagined the crowd turning ugly and attacking her. She imagined people spewing insults and accusations at her. She saw the screens flashing the images of the woman in the sex tape over and over again.

She suddenly turned around to face Keisha again. "No, I can't do it. I just can't do it. You have to think of something else."

Keisha sighed heavily. "I'm trying. I promise you. I am trying."

Sharmaine reached out and gave her friend a long hug. "I know you are, sweetie. Thank you."

That evening, Sharmaine kissed each of her children good night before sending them upstairs to their beds.

"I'm going to check my phone messages before turning in," she yelled over her shoulder to Leon. She turned to walk toward her office.

"Oh, no you are not," he said. He grabbed her playfully around her waist.

"But, honey, I need to. I might have some important calls."

Leon did not answer; instead, he began to shower her face and neck with sensuous and loving kisses.

"I have rehearsals really early—" Her words were cut off as his lips enveloped hers. Sharmaine gave up the fight and silently followed Leon upstairs to their bedroom. Leon was the only lover she'd ever had, but as they melded together in passion, she instinctively knew there could be none better.

The next morning when she awakened, Sharmaine was surprised to find that she was alone in bed. She looked around the room for Leon, and assumed he'd gotten up already and gone downstairs. She grabbed her robe from the foot of the bed and put it on; then she strolled out into the hallway. Outside her bedroom she stopped, suddenly frozen with fear. She saw large splatters of something red on her beige carpet, trickling down the hallway leading to the stairs. Frightened, she followed the spots until she found their source. At the bottom of the stairs she saw Leon lying face down with his body covered in blood. She screamed and ran to him.

"Leon, are you all right? Leon!" She screamed louder.

The front door suddenly opened and Consuela walked in.

"Call 911 now!" Sharmaine screamed. She cradled Leon's head in her arms as she cried frantically. Praying, she waited for help to arrive and wondered what had happened.

Several hours later, as she sat in the police interrogation room, Sharmaine still could not make sense of the morning's events.

"Why did you shoot your husband, Mrs. Cleveland?" the police detective asked.

"I didn't shoot him. I've told you that over and over. I woke up this morning and found him at the bottom of the stairs like that." Sharmaine sat in the cold steel chair feeling frightened and confused.

"Mrs. Cleveland, we found the gun in the trash can outside your home. It has your fingerprints all over it. Why did you shoot him?" the detective asked again.

"Stop saying that! Did you find my children? Why aren't you looking for my children?"

"I think you know where your children are Mrs. Cleveland."

"No, I don't. I told you they were not in the house. Someone broke in and shot my husband, then took my children. Why won't you believe me?" Sharmaine pleaded.

"This is getting us nowhere, and frankly, I'm tired of it. You spoiled, rich celebrities seem to think you can do anything and get away with it. Well, not in my district. I just hope your husband survives so he can fill us in."

Sharmaine put her head in her hands and wept with relief that Leon was still alive. "Is he going to be all right?" she asked through her tears.

"You better pray that he is; otherwise you're facing murder one charges." The tall black detective stood up and opened the door. "Jeff, go ahead and book her. She's not willing to cooperate," he said to the uniformed officer who was standing outside. He gave Sharmaine one last disgusted look, then walked out of the office.

Somberly, Sharmaine followed the officer out of the room to the booking area. Quietly, she handed the attendant her clothing, underwear, jewelry, and dignity. She felt humiliated after being asked to strip naked, and then every cavity of her body was searched. After being dressed in a prison jumpsuit, she was photographed, fingerprinted, and placed into a holding cell.

Sharmaine immediately noticed a payphone hanging on the wall. She ran to it and dialed Keisha's number. The operator allowed it to ring over and over, but there was no answer. Dejected, she sat down on the floor and waited.

Sharmaine spent the next three days in the dirty, cold cell crying and praying. As desolate as she felt, she had to believe that God had not forsaken her, and somehow He would work it out. In her mind, she recited the words of the apostle Paul as he sang in prison, trying not to be consumed with the hopelessness of her situation. She tried repeatedly to reach Keisha with no success. Finally, late Sunday evening, Keisha picked up the line.

"Where have you been? I've been calling you all weekend," Sharmaine screamed into the line.

"Sharmaine, I'm sorry. I just got back into town. Are you okay?"

"No, I'm not. Think about it, Keisha. I'm in jail, and they think I shot Leon. I don't know where my kids are. Of course I am not okay."

"I'm sorry. I just meant are you okay physically. I know that you can't be okay in there. Oh, and the kids are in North Carolina with Leon's parents," Keisha answered.

"They are? How do you know that?"

"I took them myself. Leon asked me to after what happened

at the airport. You were still asleep when I picked them up, but I assumed he told you."

"What are you talking about, Keisha? When did you pick them up?"

"Early Thursday morning. Leon said you had to be in Atlanta for work, but he felt it wasn't good for the children with everything that's going on. I'm sorry. I thought you knew."

"I didn't know, but thank God they are safe. The police didn't believe me when I said they were missing. Thank you, Keisha. I've been so worried. Thank you so much. Hurry and get my attorney on the line. I don't think I can take another night in this place."

"I spoke to Victor as soon as I heard the news. He told me that you have a bond hearing tomorrow morning. There's nothing we can do until then." Keisha paused. "Sharmaine, what happened? Did you and Leon have a fight?"

"I don't know what happened. I came downstairs and Leon had been shot. You have to believe me." Sharmaine started to cry. "This whole situation is unbelievable."

"Calm down, honey. I believe you," Keisha said.

"How is he? They won't tell me anything in here."

"He was shot four times at close range. His condition has been upgraded from critical to serious. That's all I could find out." Keisha heard Sharmaine weeping loudly into the phone. "Listen, just try to relax and get some sleep. Victor and I will be there first thing in the morning to get you out of there. Everything's going to be okay."

The next morning, Sharmaine felt as if she were in a nightmare as she stood before the judge and listened to the charge against her. She stood silently as the judge stated she'd been charged with the attempted murder of Leon Terrence Cleveland, and her heart skipped a beat. The judge then set bail at one hundred thousand dollars. Sharmaine stood quietly while Keisha paid the bond and Victor asked for special permission for her to be released into his custody, without going back to the jail for processing. After several moments, she was finally free to go.

"We have to take you out the back way," Victor whispered when he noticed Sharmaine headed toward the exit.

She peeked through the tiny windows in the door and saw a mob of reporters outside the courtroom. Each one strained to get a glimpse of her. Feeling uneasy, Sharmaine turned and followed Victor and Keisha out of the courtroom door and down the back stairs.

The trio stepped out the back door into the bright Atlanta sunshine.

"Where's the limo?" Keisha said. She looked around the parking lot, then immediately pulled out her cell phone to make a call. After a brief conversation, she hung up the phone. "He's stuck out front," she said. "He can't get past the reporters."

"Now what are we going to do?" Sharmaine whined.

"We can take my car. It's over there." Victor pointed to the left of the parking lot. "I'll be right back," he said.

Several moments later, he pulled his late model BMW to the curb where the ladies were standing. Keisha opened the back door, and she and Sharmaine climbed into the car. As she settled into the back seat, Sharmaine breathed a sigh of relief; then she screamed in terror as she felt the car suddenly rocking. A throng of reporters had spotted her and surrounded the car, blocking their exit. Sharmaine ducked down as the flashbulbs went off.

"Do something, Victor, before they turn the car over," Keisha shrieked.

Victor pressed the gas and revved the engine loudly, and then he rolled down the window. "Move or I'll run you over," he yelled.

He revved the engine again to emphasize his point. The group of reporters immediately parted like the Red Sea. Several continued trying to snap photos while scrambling out of the way onto the curb. Victor pressed his foot onto the gas and sped away as quickly as possible.

Sharmaine peeked over the seat to see if all was clear, and then slowly sat up. "Take me to the hospital. I want to see Leon," she said.

"Sharmaine, you can't. It's a condition of your bail," Victor answered.

"He's my husband. I need to see him."

Victor glanced over the back seat at her. He turned his attention back toward the traffic before speaking. "Listen to me. Do you understand that you've been charged with his attempted murder?"

"I know it, but I still don't understand why they think I did it."

"There was no forced entry into the house, and your prints are all over the gun. It's also registered to you, Sharmaine," Victor answered.

"What? I don't own a gun. I've never owned a gun."

"We'll have our day in court, but until then, you can't see

Leon. I'm sorry, Sharmaine. It's for the best. When he gets better, he'll tell the police what happened, and then you can see him. Please, try to understand."

"If you want, I'll go by and check on him for you later," Keisha offered.

"He's not alone at the hospital, is he?" Sharmaine asked.

"No, his brothers are with him. His parents wanted to come, but they felt taking care of the children was more important."

Sharmaine breathed a sigh of relief. Leon was the youngest of six boys, and she knew that with his five brothers surrounding him in love and prayer, he would be safe.

"Keisha, I want you to go get the children and bring them home. We need to be together as a family during this time. Let me use your phone. I want to talk to them."

Reluctantly, Keisha handed over her cell phone and watched as Sharmaine dialed the number.

"Jeanna, it's me, Mom. How are you?" Sharmaine said. A broad smile covered her face as she spoke.

"Mom, you are all over the news. They say you shot Dad," Jeanna responded.

"No, honey, I would never do anything like that. It's a big misunderstanding. Listen, I want you and your brother and sister to come home." Sharmaine stopped speaking as she heard muffled voices on the other end of the phone, then someone began speaking.

"How dare you call my home," her mother-in-law yelled. "My baby boy is lying in a hospital fighting for his life, and you have the nerve to call here."

Sharmaine cringed. She and her mother-in-law had always enjoyed a great relationship. She could not believe that she honestly thought she'd shot Leon.

"Mother Cleveland, I didn't do this. You can't believe everything you hear on the news. I love Leon. Please, put Jeanna back on the phone."

"Don't you tell me what to believe. That's the same lie you told about that nasty movie you made. Leon has been a good husband to you. He didn't deserve the embarrassment of that movie, and he certainly didn't deserve to be shot."

"Please, listen to me. I would never hurt Leon. You know that I love him dearly. I don't know what's going on. Someone made that tape and someone shot Leon, but you have to believe it wasn't me. Please, let me speak to Jeanna."

"You are not going to speak to or see my grandchildren. You should be behind bars where you belong. Don't call my home again."

"I'm their mother. You can't keep them away from me."

Keisha tugged lightly on Sharmaine's sleeve. "Don't fight with her. Maybe it's best if the kids just stay there for a while," she whispered.

Sharmaine shook her head and returned to her conversation. "Listen to me, Mother Cleveland. Those are my children. You have no right to keep them from me. I'm coming to pick them up tomorrow."

Keisha interrupted her again. "You can't leave the state," she whispered.

"What?" Sharmaine put her hand over the phone and stared at Keisha.

"You are charged with attempted murder. You cannot leave the state until after the trial. If you do, you will forfeit your bail and end up back in jail."

"Then you go get them," Sharmaine ordered.

"Sharmaine, just let them stay there. I'll try to figure out a way to convince her to let you talk to them, but don't fight her on this. It only adds fuel to the fire."

Sharmaine sighed loudly. As much as it pained her, she realized Keisha was right. The last thing she needed was a battle between her and Leon's mother. She took a deep breath and went back to the conversation. "Mother Cleveland, I did not shoot Leon, and that is not me in that tape. I don't care if you believe me or not, but don't poison my children's minds against me."

"I don't have to take orders from you," she answered.

Sharmaine softened her tone. "I'm not telling you what to do. I'm asking you to please just give me the benefit of the doubt. The children can stay with you for a while, but please at least let me talk to them."

"This is the last time I'm going to say this: Don't call here again."

Sharmaine heard the phone slam down in her ear. Keisha reached over and slowly took the cell from her. Weeping, she collapsed into Keisha's arms.

Chapter Three

"I'm sure you didn't sleep well in that cell. Take this and go upstairs to relax." Keisha held her hand out with two white pills inside. Keisha and Sharmaine had just arrived at Sharmaine's home, so Keisha offered Sharmaine a sedative; then she suggested she go to her room and lie down.

Sharmaine took the pills and swallowed them dry. "I can't go up there to our bed. I just can't sleep in that bed without him."

"I understand. Are you hungry? The food in there must have been horrible. I can ask Consuela to fix you something to eat."

"You are right. The food was horrible, but I don't have an appetite." Sharmaine slowly trudged into her home office and slumped sadly onto the couch.

"Tell you what; I'll go run you a hot bath. That will relax you, so you can get some rest. Maybe you'll feel hungry later."

"No, I don't want a bath. I don't want any food. I don't want any sleep. I want my family back," she suddenly screamed.

Keisha gave her a side-eyed glance then slowly backed away from her. "Sharmaine, I know you are upset. I'm only trying to help."

"Well, you are not helping at all! Why did you take my children up there in the first place? They should be here."

"I told you; Leon asked me to take them," Keisha answered.

"You don't work for Leon. You work for me," Sharmaine snapped.

Keisha looked strangely at Sharmaine. "I thought I was here to help both of you. You've never objected to me following his requests before."

They were interrupted by the chime of the doorbell.

"Consuela, get the door," Sharmaine screamed then turned toward Keisha. "I want my children home. I don't care what Mother Cleveland has to say about it. I'm not taking orders from her. I want you to go and pick them up first thing tomorrow morning."

"That's not a good idea, Sharmaine," Victor said as Consuela showed him into her office.

"I thought you'd left," Sharmaine answered, turning around to face him.

"I tried. I couldn't get out of the driveway for the reporters. Apparently a crowd of them followed us from the courthouse. They've got the whole street blocked," Victor answered as he sat his pudgy frame down on the leather sofa. He unbuttoned his suit jacket to allow his burgeoning stomach some freedom. "I thought I'd go ahead and get a head start on working on your case. Maybe they'll disperse later."

"I guess we may as well," Sharmaine answered. She folded her arms across her chest and sighed heavily.

"As I was saying, it's not a good idea to bring your children back home. There's a media circus going on out there. They are much safer where they are." He opened his briefcase and pulled out the morning's newspaper. He handed it to Sharmaine.

She sat in stunned silence as she looked at her mug shot on

the front page of the *Atlanta Journal Constitution*. Slowly, she read the article that was underneath:

Grammy award–winning singer and actress Sharmaine Cleveland has been arrested and charged with the attempted murder of her husband, Leon Terrence Cleveland. Deputies were called out to her spacious mansion in Buckhead early Thursday morning following a frantic 911 call from the couple's maid.

When police arrived on the scene, they found Mrs. Cleveland slumped over her husband's body in tears. Leon Cleveland was taken to Piedmont Hospital, where he is listed in serious condition. Mrs. Cleveland was taken to the Atlanta police department for questioning about the incident. Subsequently, she was charged with attempted murder.

Police have declined to provide further details, due to an ongoing investigation. An anonymous source within the police department has advised that the gun allegedly used in the incident is believed to be registered to Sharmaine Cleveland. It was found on the premises following the shooting.

Sharmaine Cleveland is a Grammy award–winning gospel songstress who has also made a name for herself as an actress. She has starred in several highly successful Christian films produced by her husband's company. Her latest movie, Pearls of Righteousness, wrapped shooting earlier this month. Cleveland was in the news prior to this incident when a video tape of her performing sex acts was discovered and released. Cleveland is expected to be released later today following a bond hearing.

Sharmaine crumpled up the paper and threw it across the room. "This is crazy. I can't believe any of this is happening. I did not shoot Leon," she screamed.

Victor looked over at a worried Keisha.

"I gave her a sedative. It should kick in soon," Keisha said.

"Shut up, Keisha. I told you before I don't need anything but my family. I need to erase the last few weeks of my life and start all over. Everything has gone absolutely crazy, and you stuffing pills down my throat is not helping at all!" Sharmaine screamed.

"Maybe I should just leave you two alone," Keisha offered. She stood up and solemnly walked toward the door. She stopped with her hand on the knob and turned toward Sharmaine. "I'll leave my cell on in case you need me later."

"Keisha, wait," Sharmaine said. She walked over to the door to stop her. "I'm sorry. None of this is your fault, and I'm taking my hurt and anger out on you. I'm sorry. I'm so sorry." Sharmaine began to cry, and Keisha pulled her into her arms to soothe her.

Keisha held her for several moments as she wept, then she led her to the couch to sit down. Victor handed Sharmaine some tissues, and the three of them sat in silence, waiting for Sharmaine to regain her composure.

When he felt she was calm, Victor spoke. "Sharmaine, I need you to tell me everything that happened the morning that Leon was shot."

Sharmaine sniffed loudly before answering him. "I woke up about nine-fifteen. We'd just gotten back from vacation the day before, and I was tired, so I slept a little later than usual."

Victor turned to Keisha. "What time did you pick up the kids and leave for North Carolina?" he asked.

"It was about six-thirty when I arrived. I let myself in using my key and woke the kids. I helped them pack, and we left the house about seven," she answered.

"Okay, according to the police report, Leon was shot sometime between 8:30 and 9:30 A.M., so it's safe to say no one else was in the house when it happened except you, Sharmaine, and your maid. Is that right?"

"No, Consuela arrived later. She came in just as I found Leon on the floor. I told her to call nine-one-one."

Victor pulled a notepad from his briefcase and began to scribble notes on it. "Let's back up, Sharmaine. What happened when you woke up?"

"I was alone in bed, so I grabbed my robe and left the room. I saw blood in the hallway, and I followed it to the stairs. Leon was lying at the bottom. So, I rushed to him. As soon as I got to him, Consuela walked in."

"Does Consuela have her own key?" he asked.

Sharmaine nodded her head.

"Okay, who else has a key to your home?" Victor inquired.

"Pierre, my personal chef, has one also, but his only fits the kitchen door because he doesn't work every day. We don't have anyone else working inside the house, so other than Keisha, that's it."

"What about your limo driver, the security guard, or your gardener?"

"No, they don't need access to the house."

Victor sighed very loudly and scribbled more notes on his pad.

"What's wrong?" Sharmaine asked.

Victor brushed an unruly blonde strand of hair behind his ear before answering. "This doesn't look good for you. You and Leon were alone in the house; there's no sign of forced entry, and your prints are all over the gun. Frankly, I'm having trouble thinking of a viable defense for you."

"My defense is that I'm innocent. You don't need anything else."

"The jails are full of people who claim to be innocent. Unfortunately, that's not enough. Did you hear anything that morning? Was there a car driving away, or maybe a door slamming? Did you even hear the four shots that hit Leon?"

"No, I was asleep. I'm a sound sleeper, Victor. Is that a crime?"

"Of course it's not a crime, but it's going to be very difficult to get a jury to believe you slept through someone breaking into your home and shooting your husband four times."

Sharmaine leaned back on the sofa and shook her head. "I know that. We've got to just hope and pray that Leon can tell them something." She suddenly sat forward. "Keisha, call the hospital and find out if he's awake, talking or something," she said.

A few moments later, Keisha hung up the phone after speaking with the duty nurse.

"I'm sorry. I couldn't find out much. His family has given strict orders not to give out information over the phone, because so many reporters have called. All they would tell me is he's alive," she said.

Sharmaine stood up and went over to her desk. She rummaged through the top drawer then pulled out an address book. She thumbed through the pages one by one, until she found what she was looking for. "Here's Jack's cell phone number. See if you can reach him at the hospital. He probably won't talk to me, but maybe he'll tell you something." She handed the book to Keisha.

Keisha dialed the number and waited through four rings

before Leon's oldest brother, Jackson Cleveland, picked up the line.

"Hey, Jack, it's Keisha Williams. I was just calling to see how Leon is doing."

"Unless you've quit working for his wife, I really don't think I want to talk to you, Keisha," he answered.

"Come on, Jack. You know Sharmaine wouldn't do this. She's worried sick about him."

Jackson hesitated before answering. His family, as well as Keisha and Sharmaine, had grown up together in the small rural town of Fort Valley, Georgia. They'd attended the same elementary and high schools, although Jackson was several years ahead of them. He honestly could not remember when he didn't know either of them personally. It was hard for him to believe Sharmaine had shot his brother, but the police were confident she was guilty.

"Is she there with you now?" he finally asked.

"Yes, she's right here."

"I want to talk to her. Put her on the phone," he demanded.

Sharmaine tentatively took the phone and put it up to her ear. "Hey, big brother, how's Leon?" she said, using her nickname for Jackson.

"He's in pretty bad shape, but the doctors are hopeful that he'll pull through."

"Oh, thank God. And thank you too. I really appreciate you talking to me. I've just been so worried. Mother Cleveland wouldn't let me talk to the children, and I just thought everyone was against me."

"Don't thank me. Tell me the truth. Did you shoot my brother?"

"Jack, I swear to you I did not shoot him. I love Leon.

Something really strange is going on. I wish I could explain it, but I can't figure it out."

"I talked to him a few days before the shooting. He didn't believe it was you in that video, but he never bothered to watch it. Sharmaine, I saw it. I gotta tell you, it looks like you."

"I know it does, but it's not me, Jack. Someone is trying to ruin my life. That's the only possible explanation for any of this."

"Yeah, whatever. I'll keep you posted on his condition. I think that's the least I can do for now. But if we find out you are responsible, there's not a rock you can hide under. You won't get away with it."

"Thank you, Jack; I appreciate that," Sharmaine said before realizing he'd hung up the phone already.

Chapter Four

Jeanna snuck out of the bedroom she and her sister shared at her grandparents' home, and made her way to the telephone hanging on the wall in the kitchen. She picked up the old-fashioned receiver slowly and carefully, in order not to make a sound. It was almost three o'clock in the morning, and everyone else in the house was asleep.

On the other end, the phone rang and rang, but there was no answer. Dejected, she finally hung up and turned to walk down the hallway that led to her bedroom.

"What are you doing up at this hour?"

Jeanna was startled by her grandmother's voice. "Grandma, did I wake you?"

"I'm old, honey. If you live long enough, you'll find out that the older you get, the less you sleep. Now answer my question. What are you doing up?"

"Um, I was thirsty. I wanted a glass of water," she answered.

"Funny, it looked to me like you were trying to make a phone call."

Jeanna pulled out a chair and sat down at the kitchen table. "I was trying to call Mom. I miss her," she confessed.

"I told you that I don't want you talking to her."

"I know, but I don't understand why. She didn't shoot Dad. I know she didn't. I don't care what the newspapers say.

I don't care what the police say. I know Mom. She didn't do it."

"Jeanna, you're too young to understand what goes on in a marriage between a man and a woman. Sometimes things get out of control."

"I'm fourteen years old, Grandma. Mom and Dad hardly ever disagree about anything. There's no way she got mad enough to shoot him."

Angela Cleveland pulled out a chair and sat down across from Jeanna. Without speaking, she grabbed a rubber band from the table and pulled her fiery red hair into a ponytail. When she was done straightening it out, she turned to Jeanna. "Honey, when your daddy was growing up, he and your uncles never saw me and your grandpa argue. We made sure of that. But I can tell you that doesn't mean we didn't have our fights."

"Okay, so they disagreed. Mom is a Christian woman; she'd never shoot anybody. She would get angry and walk away or something. Give me one good reason why she'd shoot him."

Angela rolled her green eyes at the mere thought of Sharmaine. She'd never had an issue with her, but she'd always believed that one day she'd go "Hollywood" and change. Angela felt that day had finally come. "Do you know about that sex tape your mother made?" she asked.

"That's not her in that tape. She and Daddy both told us that it's just somebody who looks like her."

"Jeanna, I don't want to turn you against your mother, honestly I don't, but she's not being truthful with you. Any fool can tell that's her face in that video tape."

Angela stood up and went to her kitchen drawer. She pulled

out a copy of the *National Enquirer* with Sharmaine's picture on the front. She flipped it open in front of Jeanna.

"Now, I'd never show this to your little brother, but I showed Camille, and now I have to show you too. Look at that face, and honestly tell me it's not your mother," she said.

Jeanna turned her head, refusing to look at the newspaper. "I don't care what that paper says," she replied.

Angela picked it up from the table and shoved it in front of Jeanna's nose. "Look at it, girl. Just look at it," she said.

"That's not my mom." Jeanna began to cry, but still refused to look at the paper.

"It is, honey. I think your father realized that too. I believe when he confronted your mother about it, she shot him." Angela took the newspaper and returned it to the kitchen drawer. Jeanna put her head down on the table and continued sobbing.

"Quiet down, child. You are going to wake everyone up," Angela said.

"Just leave me alone. I want to be alone," she answered.

"All right, I'm going back to my room, but don't stay up much longer." Angela walked over to the phone and pulled the receiver from the base then unplugged it. She took the phone receiver and returned to her bedroom.

Brenetta Reeves walked briskly down the hallway of Raga Records as she left her husband's office. Her heels clicked on the manicured floors, echoing throughout the halls. She stopped at the end of the hallway and pressed the button for the elevator. The doors opened, and she was just about to step on when she heard her name being called.

"Mrs. Reeves, can you wait just a minute?"

Brenetta turned around and saw her husband's secretary, Stephanie, running after her. Patiently, she waited by the elevator for her to catch up.

"Mr. Reeves asked that you bring this folder of information along with you to the meeting," Stephanie said.

"Thank you, Stephanie. Please call my husband and tell him I'm on my way," she said then stepped on the elevator.

Brenetta whistled as the elevator descended. She was elated that her husband had asked her to go along with him to see Sharmaine Cleveland. Shawn planned to tell Sharmaine that although he'd released her CD, he was planning to pull it from the shelves very soon, unless she could come up with a good reason to stop him. Brenetta held in her hands the proposal they planned to offer Sharmaine, and she felt confident she'd accept it. It was the first time Shawn had seriously allowed her to be a part of his business dealings, and she intended to make him proud.

When Brenetta finally arrived on Sharmaine's street, the limo driver stopped several houses down the block. The street was filled with reporters and news crews camped outside Sharmaine's home.

She pressed the button, rolling down the window that separated her from the driver. "This is madness. Is there any way to get through?" she asked.

"Yes, ma'am, it's just going to take a bit longer," he answered as he inched the limo forward.

Several reporters and camera men ran toward them, trying to catch a glimpse of who was inside. Finally, after spending twenty minutes only yards from Sharmaine's front gate, the driver was able to pull in and make his way up the circular driveway.

Shawn was waiting outside Sharmaine's home in his Lexus. He stepped out as soon as he noticed them driving up. "I've been waiting over an hour, Brenetta," he said.

"I'm sorry, but the traffic on this street is ridiculous. Reporters are everywhere."

"What did you expect when you arrived in a limousine?" He turned to her driver. "You can go now. Mrs. Reeves will ride back with me." He handed him a fifty dollar tip; then the two of them approached Sharmaine's door and rang the bell.

"Mr. and Mrs. Reeves, come in. Mrs. Cleveland is expecting you," Consuela said as she greeted them warmly. She stopped to offer each of them a drink, which they declined, before ushering them into Sharmaine's home office.

Sharmaine was seated on the sofa, dressed casually in black pants and a pink blouse. Shawn immediately noticed how tired she looked. He felt sorry for what she was going through.

Brenetta, on the other hand, had no such emotions. "Dang, you look awful," she commented. "Have you been sleeping?"

"Actually, I haven't slept very well at all, Brenetta," she answered. "It's been four weeks since the shooting, and Leon is still in a coma. Excuse me for not putting on a Cover Girl face for you." She rolled her eyes at Brenetta.

"I'm sorry for that remark," Shawn said, apologizing for his wife. "May we sit down?" he asked politely.

"Of course. Excuse my manners. Please have a seat, both of you," Sharmaine answered.

"I'm not going to beat around the bush with you, Sharmaine. I don't have good news, but hopefully we can work together to do something that will benefit all of us," Shawn said. He crossed his legs and leaned back in his seat.

"I've seen the reports. I know the CD is not doing well at

all. I think if I could get out and do some promotions it would help. Victor is working on getting special permission for me to travel for tour dates."

"That won't be necessary." Shawn hesitated. "We're pulling the CD, Sharmaine," he said solemnly.

"I was afraid of something like this. Is there a possibility that you'd reconsider?" Sharmaine pleaded.

"Are you crazy? How can you expect Shawn to put his entire career and company on the line for you?" Brenetta asked.

Surprised, she looked over at Brenetta. "Why are you here anyway?" She turned to Shawn. "Since when is Brenetta involved in these types of things?"

"I brought Brenetta along because she's come up with a solution that may help us recoup some of the money we've lost on this CD and tour. Since it was her idea, I thought it would be best to let her present it to you."

Sharmaine raised her eyebrows in disbelief. She then turned to look at Brenetta. "Fine. What is your solution?" she asked.

Brenetta opened the folder that was on her lap and pulled out a stack of pornographic photographs. She handed one to Sharmaine. "Do you know who this is?" she asked.

"No, and frankly I don't care. Those photos are disgusting," Sharmaine sneered, then turned to Shawn. "What is this all about?" Sharmaine asked.

"Just let her finish," he answered.

"Fine, but take this filth away from me." Sharmaine handed the picture back to Brenetta.

"Since you don't know, I'll tell you. This picture is of Dirk Northridge of TV's classic show *School's In.*"

"Didn't he play the blonde teen hero on that show?" Sharmaine asked.

"Yes, but after it was cancelled, he had trouble finding work again, because he was typecast. A sex tape of him and his girl-friend was accidentally released after his laptop was stolen. But it sold millions of copies. After that success, he decided to start doing porn films, and he's become a multi-millionaire doing so. The porn industry is one of the most lucrative in the country right now."

Sharmaine scrunched up her face and looked back and forth between Brenetta and Shawn, trying desperately to fig-ure out what she was getting at.

"Snoop Dogg is another musician who is making porn movies," Brenetta continued. "Shawn and I believe there is money to be made here."

"Are you suggesting I start making pornographic movies?" Sharmaine asked.

"No. We are suggesting that you admit it's you on the sex tape. You don't have to make any new movies. We just want to make a profit on the one that is already out," Brenetta answered.

"Sharmaine, Raga Records' DVD division is prepared to back this fully and anonymously under one of our partnering companies. I've managed to get my hands on some really good copies of the tape. We'll cover the packaging and distribution cost after you sign off on it," Shawn added.

"You are out of your mind. You both are out of your minds. That is not me on the tape. Besides that, I am a woman of God. I'm not going into the porn business," Sharmaine shrieked.

"Sharmaine, we are not asking you to go into the business. I've prepared a statement to be released to the press where you simply admit that it's you on the tape. You would state that it was done a long time ago, but you've put that part of your life behind you." Shawn reached over to Brenetta to retrieve the statement and handed it to Sharmaine.

Slowly, she read over it before answering. "You want me to lie and say it's me. Leon and I have been married eighteen years. Just when do you propose that I pretend I made it?"

"The details are not really important. Sharmaine, everyone has skeletons. Remember when Kirk Franklin admitted his porn addiction? His wife even helped him talk about it on some talk shows. Your fans will understand that you made a mistake. We won't publicly do any promotions, but I believe that it will really sell. You'd be amazed at the number of hits it's received online." Shawn smiled at her and then at Brenetta, satisfied with their presentation.

"This whole idea is absolutely crazy. I cannot believe that the two of you would come here with this nonsense. I'd expect as much from Brenetta, but, Shawn, not you. We've known each other for years. How did you let her talk you into this?" Sharmaine crumpled up the press release and tossed it in Shawn's direction.

He picked it up off the floor before speaking. "No disrespect, Sharmaine, but I think this is one of the best ideas Brenetta has come up with. Let's face it; things don't look great for you right now. The tapes are minor compared to this attempted murder charge. I respect your faith. Honestly, I do. But you've got to meet us halfway on this thing."

"Do you understand what you are asking me to do, Shawn? You are asking me to go against everything I believe in. Never mind the fact that it's not me in those tapes, but as a Christian, the last thing I want to do is be responsible for putting more porn out there. I'm sorry. I won't do it." She paused before continuing. "I can't do it."

Shawn stood up and motioned for Brenetta to join him. "I'm sorry to hear you say that, Sharmaine, but you've left me no choice. Raga Records is officially cancelling your contract with us. We are not only pulling this CD, but we are ceasing production on everything you've recorded in the past."

Sharmaine stood up to face him, and her eyes grew wide with surprise. "What? You can't be serious. I'm the most successful act on your label."

"No, Sharmaine, you were the most successful. With your current status, I'd be lucky to get five dollars for a bootleg of your CD! If I continue producing your CDs, I'm only going to go deeper in debt. It's over and done."

Sharmaine was surprised to hear Shawn raise his voice, and somewhat frightened as he continued to yell.

"I've spent millions on promotions, only to see it all go up in smoke when that video was released. I could have saved some money if I'd cancelled the CD then, but I trusted you. I believed you when you said it wasn't you. Then on the morning of your CD release, your husband ends up shot four times." He paused and slowly shook his head. "I had to cancel a forty-city tour, and not only did I lose money, but a huge chunk of my integrity is gone as well. I have no other choices, Sharmaine. Our business relationship is over."

"I told you Victor is working on getting me approved to tour," Sharmaine said quietly.

"It's too late for that. I couldn't get you booked at a kid's birthday party at this point. The tape was bad enough. The shooting and attempted murder charge made things a thousand times worse."

"Are you suggesting I shot Leon? Is that what you believe,

Shawn?" Sharmaine stared at him intently, waiting for an answer.

He averted his eyes, not wanting to answer her question. Instead, he shrugged his broad shoulders.

"Well, I believe it," Brenetta said smugly. "All of the evidence leads right to you."

Sharmaine's heart sank. Although they clashed at times, it hurt to hear that Brenetta believed she was guilty. She returned to the sofa and sat down, slowly shaking her head. "I thought you were more than the owner of my record label, Shawn. I thought you . . . I thought both of you were my friends," she said quietly.

"We are your friends, Sharmaine. That's why I wish you'd sign these papers," Shawn replied.

"No, you are not. A friend would never ask me to do this," she answered.

Brenetta suddenly stepped closer to the sofa between Sharmaine and her husband. She pointed her long, thin finger at Sharmaine's nose. "Shawn came here to try and help you in your time of need. This is the thanks he gets. How dare you sit here acting righteous and sanctimonious with no regard for what this is costing anyone else? You are a selfish woman, Sharmaine." She looked at her husband. "Shawn, let's go." Brenetta turned on her heels and quickly left the office.

Shawn laid the folder down on the sofa and took one last pleading look at Sharmaine. "I wish I could help you, but you've made it impossible. Your life is going straight down the toilet. I'm sorry, but I don't plan to end up in the sewer with you. My attorneys will be in touch," he said. Quietly, he followed Brenetta out the door.

Sharmaine buried her face in her hands. She fought back

tears, realizing that she seemed to cry daily lately. Hearing footsteps in her office, she looked up.

"Ms. Sharmaine, you have a phone call. It's Mr. Jack calling from the hospital," Consuela said.

Sharmaine jumped up and grabbed the phone from her hands. "Big brother, what's going on with Leon?" she asked.

"He's awake, Sharmaine. He's still a bit groggy, but he's opening his eyes, and he recognizes everyone."

"Thank you, Jesus!" Sharmaine said as the tears of joy flooded her face. She did a quick happy dance of praise around her office before continuing. "Jack, has he said anything? Does he remember what happened to him?"

"Yes, he remembers everything."

"That's wonderful news. I want to see him. Give me a few minutes to get dressed, and I'll be right over."

"Don't come here. I won't allow you anywhere near him."

"Jack, I don't understand. If he remembers everything that happened, he'll want to see me. He can tell the police I'm innocent."

"The police have already interviewed him, and that's not what he said."

Sharmaine sat down on the couch, bewildered. "What did he say, Jack? Please, you have to tell me."

"I promised I'd let you know his condition. I've done my part. Just stay away from the hospital and away from my brother."

"Jack, please. Don't hang up on me. Just tell me what he said. After that, I promise I won't bother you again."

Jack held the phone silently for several moments then finally, he spoke. "He said he woke up that morning and you were not in bed. He heard the shower running, so he went to the bathroom door to surprise you. When he walked in, the bathroom was full of steam, and he couldn't see anything, but he felt the first shot. He turned around and tried to run, and he felt another shot in his back. He made it the top of the stairs, and he remembers falling down them. After that, he blacked out. I guess you pumped the other two bullets into his back after he was on the floor."

"No, that can't be true. I was in bed. I got up and I found him."

"Shut up, Sharmaine. He said you were not there. Why don't you stop with these lies?" Jack yelled.

Sharmaine started to cry yet again. "I don't understand what's going on. This whole thing is crazy," she sobbed.

"No. You are crazy if you think anyone is buying your innocent act. Leon is on the mend, and the doctors believe he will be released in a few weeks, so this is your two-week notice."

"What are you talking about?"

"I want you out of my brother's house. You'd better not be there when I bring him home."

"You must be joking. This is my home. You can't make me leave."

"No. That's my baby brother's house. When Leon and you moved in, you had one record playing locally on Atlanta radio stations. He paid for that house with money he earned before you were his wife. Maybe you've forgotten that Leon is no Stedman. He is a millionaire in his own right without you."

"It's still our home. Leon and I have shared this home with our family. It doesn't matter where the money came from."

"Let me make myself perfectly clear, Sharmaine. You can either leave the house peacefully, or we'll have you evicted.

Either way, I want you gone. If I bring my baby brother there and you are on the premises, it won't be pretty."

Sharmaine wiped her tears on the backs of her hands. Her sadness was suddenly cut short by her anger. She gripped the phone tightly. "Jack, has your whole family gone loco? Your mother won't let me speak to or see my children. Now you think you can put me out of my own house."

"You tried to kill him, Sharmaine!" he yelled. "If I were not a Christian man, I'd be over there right now showing you just how angry and loco my family truly is. Get out of my brother's house. We don't ever want to see or hear from you again."

Two days later, Consuela opened the door to a U.S. marshal. Frightened, she quickly summoned Sharmaine to the door. The marshal served Sharmaine with eviction papers, advising that she needed to be out of the house in ten days. At the bottom of the summons, she was shocked to see Leon's signature. Weeping, she ran to the phone to call Keisha.

Chapter Five

Leon Cleveland sat quietly in the police interrogation room alongside his brother Jackson as they waited for the detective to interview him. After spending four weeks in a coma and another three weeks recuperating, he'd finally been released from the hospital a week earlier.

"Jack, this whole thing is ridiculous. I don't believe Sharmaine is the person who shot me. I'm tired. Let's just go home," he said.

"From what you've told me, and the evidence the police already have, there's no other possible explanation. I know you love her, man, but you have to face the fact that maybe she isn't who you thought she was."

Leon sighed. He and Sharmaine had grown up together on the same street. He'd been smitten with her as long as he could remember. When he was fifteen, he mustered up the courage to ask her out on a date. At the time, Sharmaine was an eighteen-year-old college freshman. She laughed in his face as he professed his undying teenaged love. That didn't discourage him. He had decided that afternoon she would one day be his wife. Up until the shooting, he thought he knew everything there was to know about her. His mind refused to accept that she'd suddenly become a different person.

"Mr. Cleveland, thank you for meeting me. I just need to

get the final details of your statement. This case should go to trial in a few months," Detective Saunders stated as he entered the room and took a seat.

"Detective, I will tell you up front that I don't believe my wife did this. My brother has explained to me that she's been charged. I've read the evidence report. But there has to be some type of mistake," Leon answered.

"This is just an interview, Mr. Cleveland. It's not the trial. We just need to get all the facts together, okay?"

Leon nodded his head in agreement.

The detective continued. "In your statement, you said you went to join her in the shower, and that's when you were shot."

"No. I said I thought she was in the shower. I never saw anyone."

"Who else do you think would have been in the shower in your master bedroom, Mr. Cleveland?"

"Whoever intended to shoot me and frame my wife," Leon answered flatly.

"Leon, come on, man. With your testimony, the police can put Sharmaine away for a long time. She did this. Just accept it and cooperate," Jackson urged.

"I'm here, aren't I? I'm cooperating, but I won't implicate Sharmaine. Go ahead and ask your questions, but don't try to tell me how to answer," Leon replied.

Jack sighed and looked over at the detective, who was flipping through his folder of notes. He flipped through several pages before continuing. "Mr. Cleveland, tell me how you felt when you saw your wife having sex on that video tape that is circulating." The detective leaned forward in Leon's direction. "I'm a man. I know it didn't feel good to see your loving wife in such, shall we say, compromising positions. Did you two argue about that?"

"That's not my wife in that video. You guys know that with computers they can make anybody appear to be having sex with anybody else. It's not her. There was nothing to argue about."

"I guess of all people you would know, Mr. Cleveland. I'm just wondering if the thought that it could have been her ever entered your mind as you watched it."

"I never watched it," Leon responded.

The detective looked surprised. "You mean to tell me you've never seen the video tape or photos that have been in the news since January?"

"My wife and my daughter saw the news reports. I'm well aware of the content. I don't need to see it," he answered.

The detective stood up quickly and walked out of the office. Leon and Jack looked at each other, wondering what was up. He returned a few moments later carrying a laptop computer. After finding the file he was looking for, he set it down in front of the two men. "I think you should at least watch it, Mr. Cleveland," he said.

"Why do I need to watch it? Are you hoping I will get angry at my wife and say she shot me? No way. I'm not falling for that. Take it away."

The detective ignored him and allowed the video to start. Leon shifted his chair and turned his back to the video screen.

"That's real funny, Detective, but I still don't want to see it."

Continuing to ignore him, the detective turned the volume up as loud as it would go.

Leon heard moans that sounded exactly like his wife. He

covered his ears. "Stop it. I don't want to see this video," he protested.

"What are you afraid of, Leon?" Jackson asked. "If it's not her, what harm will looking at it do? Turn around."

"I'm not afraid of anything. I don't watch porn," he answered.

Jack stood up and walked in front of his brother. He pulled his hands from his ears and looked him directly in the eyes. "Just look at the video, Leon. Stop acting like a three-year-old and just watch it," he ordered.

Grudgingly, Leon turned around and finally looked over at the screen. He watched for several minutes before finally pushing the laptop away. "Turn it off. I don't want to see anymore. Turn it off," he demanded.

The detective stopped the video then picked up the laptop and left the room. Jackson looked over at his brother with his fists clenched. He was visibly shaken. Jackson put his hand on Leon's shoulder but Leon brushed it off.

"I know it was hard to watch. Just calm down, man," Jackson said.

Leon stood up and began pacing around the room. He paced back and forth, mumbling incoherently to himself. Then he suddenly became aggressive. He slammed his fist over and over against the wall, trying to smash his way through. Jack went to him to try to calm him down, but it was no use. He fought the wall until he couldn't stand it anymore, then he slid down onto the floor in tears.

"I'm sorry, Leon. If I'd known it would affect you this way, I wouldn't have insisted you watch," Jack said.

"It's her," Leon whispered through his tears. "It's Sharmaine."

Jack knelt on the floor near his brother. "Are you sure?" he asked.

Leon wiped his face, trying to regain his composure. "I'm positive. She has a birthmark on her left cheek the size of a dime."

"I've never seen a mark on Sharmaine's face."

Leon shook his head at his brother. "It's not on her face. It's on her bottom cheek. They didn't put anyone else's head on her body. That is Sharmaine's body." His voice shook with emotion and he wiped his face again.

Jack reached into his pocket and handed Leon his handkerchief to dry his tears. He wanted to scream "I told you so!" but realized it just was not the time. Instead, he waited without responding and calmly listened to his brother.

"I trusted her. How could she do this to me, Jack?" Leon asked.

Jack shook his head and shrugged his shoulders. He knew better than to speak, or the anger he felt would come spilling out. He was infuriated with Sharmaine, but he knew his brother felt even worse. It was difficult, but he kept his emotions inside. He realized he had to be the support for Leon. He couldn't get through it without him.

When he felt Leon was finally calm, Jackson quietly stood up and left Leon sitting on the floor of the interrogation room. He walked down the hall in search of the detective. When he found him, he advised him that no statements would be given that day. "My brother's not feeling as well as we thought. I'm going to take him home, but he'll give you a statement on another day," he said. Without waiting for a response, he returned to the room to get Leon.

They rode in silence as Jackson maneuvered through the

busy Atlanta traffic. Leon stared out of the window of the car, trying to figure out how he'd been so wrong about his wife. Prior to his release from the hospital, he allowed his brothers to convince him to file paperwork evicting Sharmaine from the house. He was reluctant to put her through it, but he felt that it would make things easier on all of them. As a condition of her bail, they could not be together, and he wanted his children to be able to return home. It was only temporary, he'd told himself. He felt once the trial was over, she would return home, and everything would be the way it was supposed to be. Now he realized that things had changed forever. His wife had lied to him about the tape. Worst of all, she'd cheated on him. He felt nauseous as the images from the video flashed through his mind over and over.

Suddenly, he turned to his brother. "Jack, where can I get one of those—" He paused. The words were on his tongue, but refused to leave his mouth.

"What is it, baby brother? You wanna stop for something to eat?" Jack tried to guess what he was trying to say.

Leon took a deep breath and forced the words to fall from his lips. "I want a copy of the sex tape. Where can I get it?"

Jack look surprised. "You've seen it. Why would you want a copy?"

"I just do. Can you get it for me?"

"It's all over the Internet. Just Google her name and it will pop up."

"We told Keisha to have it pulled. I'm guessing the only copies left are not good quality. Is it available anywhere else?"

Jack looked at Leon, puzzled. "Why do you want that tape? Don't torture yourself, man."

Leon stared at him for several silent seconds; then finally he spoke. "I guess you're right. I'm sorry I brought it up."

They rode the remainder of the way home in silence.

Chapter Six

Sharmaine waited patiently in the church vestibule for her pastor. She didn't have an appointment, but that had never been an issue in all of the years she'd attended New Life Outreach Center. Bishop Jimmy Snow was more than her pastor; she and Leon considered him to be a dear friend.

He greeted her warmly as he stepped into the hallway. "Sharmaine, it's a pleasure to see you," he said.

Sharmaine stood up and hugged his broad frame tightly. "I'm sorry to just show up like this, but I really needed to talk to you."

"It's no problem. Come into my office and have a seat."

Feeling better already, Sharmaine grabbed her purse and followed him inside. She took a seat in a plush leather chair, while he sat behind his desk.

He casually leaned back in his chair. "What's on your mind, Sharmaine?" he asked.

"I don't know where to begin. Everything just seems to be going out of control since that awful sex tape showed up."

"I've seen the news reports. You don't have to go into details if you don't want to. Just tell me how I can help you."

Sharmaine let out a long, slow breath of relief. "You don't know how wonderful it feels to hear you say that. Everyone I know and love has turned their backs on me. Well, except for Keisha, of course."

"The world is fickle. They will turn their backs on you without hesitation, but the church is not supposed to be that way. I'm here for you."

Sharmaine smiled broadly. "Thank you, Bishop. That means a lot to me."

"You're welcome. Now, tell me how I can help."

She hesitated for a moment, trying to get up the courage to ask. "I want to sing during service on Sunday. I need to sing God's praises and minister with my voice. It's what makes me feel alive. I know it's a lot to ask, but I really want to do this."

He looked taken aback. "Even with the renovations, the church will only hold about eight hundred people. That's not even a fraction of the crowd you are used to singing for. Besides, most Sundays we are not filled to capacity. It would be only around five hundred people here."

"I don't need a crowd, Bishop. All of my concerts have been cancelled, and the CD pulled from store shelves. I'm not even sure that anyone wants to hear me. I just really want to do it. I want to stand before God and sing His praises. Please, may I do that here on Sunday?"

Bishop Snow smiled. His chestnut brown face dipped in as his dimples made their mark on his cheeks. "Sure, we'd be honored to have you."

When she arrived at the church the following Sunday morning, Sharmaine went through the back entrance to the church at Keisha's insistence. Several parishioners recognized her as they drove up, and Keisha was uncomfortable with the looks they gave Sharmaine. There were numerous stares and lots of whispering.

"Let's just go find Bishop Snow," Keisha suggested.

Once inside the building, the two ladies took seats in the long hallway outside the pastor's office and waited for Bishop Snow. For the first time in years, Sharmaine felt butterflies dancing around in her stomach. Her heart was racing and her palms were sweaty. She resisted the urge to dry them on her dress. They'd only been waiting a few moments, but to Sharmaine, it felt like hours. She took long, easy breaths, trying not to hyperventilate.

Keisha looked over at her and noticed how anxious she was. "Are you okay?"

Sharmaine shook her head. "I've changed my mind. I can't do this. My throat is dry and scratchy. I can't sing this morning. I need to get out of here. Take me home."

Before Keisha could respond, the office door opened and Bishop Snow walked out and greeted them warmly.

"Good morning, ladies. I'm feeling so blessed to have you here," he said.

"Bishop, I was just telling Keisha I don't think I can do this. I'm sorry, but I think I'm going to just go on home."

Without answering her, Bishop Snow took Sharmaine's hands into his and he began to pray earnestly. He thanked God for Sharmaine and her gift of song. He praised God for allowing her to safely arrive. He prayed that someone would be blessed by hearing her voice. Bishop Snow prayed and thanked God for nearly five minutes. He held tightly to Sharmaine's hands as he spoke. When he was done, Sharmaine's eyes were misty with tears.

"Now, are you ready to go inside?" Bishop Snow asked.

Sharmaine nodded her head. She and Keisha followed the bishop into the sanctuary. Once inside, he led the two ladies to a pew in the front of the church. He gave each of them a hug and a reassuring smile; then he went to the pulpit and took his seat.

Behind them, Sharmaine heard voices rumbling and whispers. She couldn't make out everything they said, but none of it was flattering. Ignoring them, Sharmaine focused her eyes and her attention on Bishop Snow as he began service. It was the first time Sharmaine had attended church service since the tape scandal began almost four months earlier. Suddenly, she deeply regretted not coming sooner. She'd read her Bible and fellowshipped at home, but she realized that wasn't nearly enough.

As she sat listening to Bishop Snow, the weight of the past several months seemed to slowly lift from her shoulders. Before she knew it, she found herself yelling out "Amen" and "Hallelujah."

By the end of his sermon, she was on her feet, clapping and rejoicing in praise. She was so caught up in praise that she'd completely forgotten she was going to be singing that morning, and was surprised when he called her name.

"Church family, we have an extraordinary treat today. Our own Sharmaine Cleveland is here this morning, and she's going to sing. I know we are in for a huge blessing. Sharmaine, come on up here," he said.

She froze as her anxiety returned.

Keisha gently nudged her. "Go ahead, Sharmaine."

Sharmaine looked at Bishop Snow as he extended his hand to her. She took a deep breath and slowly walked toward the front of the church. Her hands were trembling and the sweat returned to her palms as she took the microphone from him. She kept her back to the congregation for a few moments as she silently prayed. Finally, she turned to face them. As she looked out at her congregation, she noticed frowns and grimaces on some of their faces. Others were leaning and whispering to their neighbors. Keisha gave her a big smile and the thumbs-up sign.

"Good morning, everyone," Sharmaine said. "Um . . . I asked Bishop Snow to allow me to minister this morning in song. I know you've all heard some things about me, which are very unflattering. I'm not here to address any of that. I just . . . I just want to sing God's praises." Sharmaine stopped speaking as she noticed several parishioners getting up from their seats. They glared at her, then turned and walked out of the church. She looked over at Bishop Snow.

"Go ahead, Sharmaine. Don't let the devil stop you from praising," he said.

"Um, this song is called 'Going Through' and um . . ." Sharmaine paused again as she noticed a commotion in the congregation. Brenetta Reeves was standing up to leave and causing a stir as she tried to drag her husband, Shawn, with her. He protested, trying not to make a scene until it was obvious that all eyes were on them. He looked toward Sharmaine and shrugged his shoulders; then he followed his wife out of the church.

Bishop Snow suddenly stood from his seat and stepped to the podium. "God sent Sharmaine Cleveland by this morning to bless us in song. None of us here has any right to judge or condemn her for the things going on in her life. She is our sister in Christ, and we should welcome her with open arms." He paused and looked out over his congregation. "Now, if there is anyone else who wishes to miss out on that blessing, then I want you to go ahead and leave right now. I will not tolerate any more rumblings or interruptions." He motioned toward the ushers. "Open the doors so that all who choose may go right now."

Sharmaine watched as a few parishioners got up and walked toward the open doors. She sighed as several more followed those. Finally, her head dropped in sorrow and shame as four more parishioners made their way to the door. She was heartbroken as Leon walked out, followed by her kids.

When Bishop Snow took his seat again and motioned for Sharmaine to continue, only half of the congregation was left. Tears streamed down her face as she nodded to the musician to begin playing. Closing her eyes, Sharmaine opened her mouth and let the song of praise flow out over the congregation. As she sang, she heard the congregation becoming involved in her song. They began clapping along with the music and nodding their heads. Several stood to their feet and praised God with her. She heard several people call out to her, "*Sang*, Sharmaine, *sang* the song, girl!"

As she reached the end of the song, Sharmaine finally opened her eyes. Filled with awe, she watched the small group rise to their feet and burst into thunderous applause.

After service, several parishioners hung around and greeted her warmly. Sharmaine stood in the front vestibule and greeted each one as they left the sanctuary. Some were fans wanting autographs and photo opportunities. Then there were others who offered words of encouragement and hugs. Sharmaine welcomed them all with a warm and friendly smile.

"Thank you, Bishop. I can't tell you how much singing this

morning meant to me," she said as she and Keisha stood near the front door preparing to leave.

"Thank you, Sharmaine. I know it was difficult, but with God's help, you got through. I hope I'll see you again next Sunday."

Sharmaine hesitated. "I cleared out half of the congregation this morning. I'll try to be in service, but I don't think I should sing again."

"God gave you a gift, Sharmaine. Your voice is anointed to sing His praises. Don't let others dictate your relationship with God. What about the half of the congregation that stayed?"

"Don't get me wrong, Bishop. I greatly appreciate those who stayed to hear me sing and then offered their support. I just . . . um . . . I just . . . Well, when I saw my family . . . I . . ." Sharmaine struggled for the right words.

Keisha spoke up to help her out. "It hurt too much watching Leon and the kids walk out on her like they did. The others were not as important, but I think that took a lot out of her."

Sharmaine nodded her head in agreement. "My family has always supported me in everything, and it's been difficult without them these past few months, but nothing was as difficult as watching them walk out today. I don't think I could go through that again, Bishop."

"I understand, Sharmaine. Please come back next Sunday. This week I want you to pray about it. Ask God if He wants you to sing again. If you feel led to next Sunday, just let me know." He reached out and gave her a hug before turning to walk back inside the sanctuary.

As Keisha and Sharmaine descended the front steps of the church, Sharmaine's driver, Gilbert, ran up to them. "I'm so sorry, Mrs. Cleveland. I fell asleep while you were inside. Don't worry. I've called the company, and another car is on the way," he said.

"What are you talking about? What's wrong?" Keisha asked.

Suddenly, she saw the limousine they'd ridden in. She and Sharmaine both stood with their mouths standing open, unable to believe it. The side, front, and hood of the limousine had been spray-painted in red letters with the words *Whore* and *Slut* all over it.

Chapter Seven

Camille sat on her bed sending text messages to her friends. They were not conversing about anything important, but she enjoyed the interaction. It kept her busy and her mind from wandering.

She looked up when she heard a knock at her bedroom door. "Come in," she called out.

"Can I talk to you?" her younger sister, Jeanna, asked.

"Make it quick." Camille laid her cell phone down on the bed and looked over at her sister. She waited for several seconds as Jeanna stood by the door, fidgeting with her hands. "What do you want?" Camille demanded.

"I just wanted to talk to you. I'm scared and I'm worried."

"What are you worried about?"

Jeanna walked into the room and picked up one of her sister's teddy bears. She sat down on the bed and leaned her chin on top of the bear's head. "I'm worried about our family. Things are not the same without Mom around here."

"So, things change," Camille answered.

"I know, but it's just weird. I wish things could go back to the way they were before."

Camille shook her head at her little sister and picked up her cell phone. She sent a text message to one of her friends. "Jeanna, things are never gonna be the way they were before.

Don't you remember Grandma told us that things would never ever be the same?"

"Grandma doesn't believe Mom's innocent; but I do."

"Whatever," Camille answered as she sent another text message on her cell phone.

"I love Grammy and Poppa, but I was tired of being there with her constantly putting Mom down and calling her names. I was so glad we were coming home, until I found out Mom wasn't going to be here."

Camille didn't respond. She laughed at her latest text message then sent another one to her friend. Jeanna put the teddy bear down on the bed and stared at her sister. She watched her sending and receiving text messages for several minutes before speaking again. "Do you think Mom and Dad are going to get a divorce?"

"Yes," Camille answered flatly.

"Why? They love each other so much. They are always hugging and holding hands. Mom said he was the best husband in the whole world."

"That wasn't real. It was acting. Your mother is a great actress, Jeanna."

"That's not true. When she does a movie, she never even kisses the men."

"Whatever," Camille answered.

Jeanna got up off the bed and walked over to her sister's dresser. She picked up a mauve-colored nail polish and brought it back to the bed. She sat down beside Camille, shaking the bottle.

"Don't open that. It's new and you can't use it," Camille said without looking up from her phone.

Jeanna placed the bottle on the nightstand. "Didn't Mom

look beautiful at church this morning? I wish we could have stayed to hear her sing," she said.

Camille sighed and rolled her eyes. "I don't. Didn't you see all those other people walking out? Even Shawn Reeves and his wife left." She tapped the keypad on her cell phone, typing out another message.

"Will you stop playing with that phone and talk to me?" Jeanna huffed.

Ignoring her, Camille laughed at her latest text message before typing a reply.

"Camille, are you listening to me? We are her family, and we should support her like Bishop Snow said."

Camille looked at her sister strangely. "Are you that naïve or just being stupid? I expect this from Rodney; he's just a little boy. But, Jeanna, you're fourteen. You should know better."

"Better than what?"

Camille sighed again, louder this time. "Your mother is a big liar and a hypocrite. She tried to kill Dad, and she lied about that sex tape. Of course they are going to get a divorce. Just accept it. Mom's a fake, and now everybody knows it." Camille's cell phone buzzed again, and she began typing another reply to her friend.

"How dare you say those things about Mom?" Jeanna screamed. "You are not even listening to me." She snatched the phone from her sister's hands and threw it across the room. It shattered against the wall.

Camille's eyes suddenly grew wide with rage. "You broke my phone. I'm gonna kill you, you little witch!" She lunged at her sister, smacking her across the face. She grabbed a handful of Jeanna's braids and pulled hard.

"Let me go!" Jeanna screamed. She fought back, slapping Camille and scratching her arm. The two of them fought aggressively on the bed for several minutes before falling to the floor.

Leon reached the top of the stairs and rushed into the bedroom. "Camille, Jeanna, stop it!" he yelled.

They ignored him, continuing to swing their fists and pull each other's hair. Exasperated, he stepped in between them, dragging them apart.

"What is going on in here?" he asked when he finally had them on separate sides of the room.

"She threw my phone against the wall and smashed it, Dad. I didn't do anything to her," Camille answered. She reached down onto the floor, picking up the pieces. "Look. It's ruined."

"Jeanna, did you do this to your sister's phone?" Leon asked.

"Yes, but she—"

Leon interrupted her. "It doesn't matter what you think she did. You had no right to destroy your sister's property. You're grounded for the next two weeks."

"Ha!" Camille said. She looked smugly at her sister.

Leon turned to his other daughter. "You are grounded also. We don't settle things in this house by fighting. I can't believe you two were rolling around on the floor like a couple of wrestlers in here."

"That's not fair! She started it! I was in here minding my own business when that little brat came in and threw my phone," Camille protested.

"But, Dad, you didn't hear the horrible things she said about Mom," Jeanna said.

"You are stupid. Dad knows that everything I said is true. Mom is a hypocrite, and he's glad she's out of our lives!" Camille screamed.

Leon looked at Camille stunned. "What did you say?" he asked, unable to believe his own ears.

"Mom lied, and she shot you. Tell her it's the truth. That's why you made us leave church this morning. You can't stand the sight of her, and neither can I. Tell her, Dad!" Camille insisted.

Jeanna looked expectantly at her Dad. Leon slowly pulled the chair from under Camille's desk and sat down. He turned the chair to face his daughters while he searched for the right words. "No, that's not why we left. I . . . um . . . I just thought it was best, that's all," he stammered.

"I don't understand, Dad. If Mom is innocent, why can't she come home? Why did you make us leave the church? I miss her," Jeanna said.

"It's um . . . complicated," he answered.

Camille sat on the bed and began fiddling with the broken pieces of her cell phone. "I don't see anything complex about it. Just tell her the truth, Dad. It will make it easier when Mom goes to jail."

Leon stared at his eldest daughter. He suddenly realized the anger she felt wasn't directed at her younger sister, but at Sharmaine. "Camille, do you think your mom is guilty? Do you think she's going to jail?" he asked.

She looked up at him suddenly. He thought he saw a tear forming in her eye, and then she suddenly dropped her head again. She tried fitting the pieces of the phone back together. "It doesn't matter what I think. Jeanna and Rodney just need to accept the truth. I have. "

Leon suddenly realized he'd put off discussing Sharmaine and the entire situation with his children for too long. He'd tried telling them as little as possible, as he was still baffled about the entire situation himself. Now he could see that his daughters were upset and confused. He could only imagine what ten-year-old Rodney was feeling.

"Jeanna, go get your brother. I need to talk to all of you. Meet me downstairs in the den," he said then slowly left the room.

When his children arrived downstairs, they all looked at him expectantly, waiting for answers. He'd spent the previous few moments alone, praying that God would give him the right words to say.

"Sit down, all of you. I think we need to discuss what's going on with our family. I promise to tell you the truth, and I'll do my best to answer any questions that you have," he said.

Rodney spoke up first. "Did Mom do all those horrible things that they are saying on the news? Did she shoot you, Dad?"

Leon hesitated. He didn't expect such direct questions. "Um . . . the truth is I don't know if your mother shot me or not. I remember getting shot, but I couldn't see who did it."

"She didn't do it, Dad. I just know it. She didn't. When can she come home?" Jeanna asked.

"Your mother was released from jail on bail with certain conditions. One of those conditions is that she can't live in the same house with me. It's because she's accused of shooting me. We discussed this before. I asked your mother to leave so that we could all stay here as a family. It was easier."

Jeanna nodded her head. "I know, but when will it all be over?"

"She has a court date set for the fifteenth of next month. We just have to wait and see what a jury decides," he answered.

"What about that dirty movie? You said it wasn't Mom, but all the kids at school . . . they say . . . they call her awful names. They said it's her," Rodney said. He stared at his hands as he waited for an answer.

Leon's mind flashed back to the video tape he viewed in the detective's office. He knew in his heart that it was Sharmaine in the video. *How do I tell a ten-year-old?* he wondered. Thinking quickly, he changed the subject. "Listen, the video tape is not important. I just want you kids to understand why your mother is not living with us and what could happen in the future. If she's convicted, she could be sent to jail for a very long time."

Jeanna gasped. "You can't let that happen, Dad. You have to tell them that she's innocent. You have to," she pleaded.

"I have told the police everything that I can remember. I'm sorry, but the police have a lot of evidence against her. I wish I could make this all go away, but I can't." Leon slowly shook his head.

Camille suddenly stopped brooding and joined in the conversation. "So what if she doesn't go to jail, Dad? She's still not coming back here, is she? That's what the fight was about." She turned to her younger sister. "Why don't you ask him yourself, Jeanna." She folded her arms across her chest, waiting for either of them to respond.

"Ask me what, Jeanna?" Leon asked.

"Are you and Mom getting a divorce? Don't you still love her?" Jeanna asked quietly.

The knot that began twisting in Leon's gut the moment he saw Sharmaine in church suddenly returned, twisting itself even tighter around his intestines. He took a deep breath before answering his daughter. "Your mother and I are not planning to get a divorce. We won't make any major decisions like that until after the trial is over. Let's just take it one step at a time."

"Then why did we have to leave church? I wanted to hear her sing. I love it when Mommy sings," Rodney said.

Leon knew he'd walked out for his own selfish reasons. The past several weeks had been difficult for him without Sharmaine. After seeing the video tape, he was torn between loving her one day and completely loathing her the next day. Each day it was an up and down battle within himself. He'd tried talking to Jackson, but the pain he felt was so deep he couldn't share it with anyone but God. When they'd arrived at church, he was hoping to find some solace and some relief from the constant hurt. Since they were late, they had taken seats in the back, and had no idea Sharmaine was there also. When Bishop Snow called her name, he felt his chest tightening and he couldn't breathe. If he had remained in the pew, he was sure he would've died right there from a broken heart. So, he did the only thing he could think of. He followed the crowd and walked out, taking his children with him. Now he realized that in his pain, he'd completely forgotten about their relationship with their mother. He'd never stopped to consider that by staying away from Sharmaine, he was also keeping them from her as well.

"I'm sorry, guys. I wasn't expecting to see her this morning, and I guess I overreacted," he finally answered.

"Can we see her? I miss Mom so much," Jeanna said.

"Me too. I want to see her. Can we call her and have her come to dinner today?" Rodney chimed in.

"No, I'm sorry. Your mother can't come to the house." Leon sighed. "I tell you what. I'll call Keisha and find out where your mother is staying. I don't think there's anything wrong with you three going to visit her."

Jeanna and Rodney jumped up and ran to Leon, almost knocking him over with their hugs. "Thank you, Dad!" they squealed in unison.

"No, no, no! I don't want to see her. I don't want to ever see her lying face again!" Camille screamed, suddenly standing up.

Leon turned to her. "Camille, honey, just calm down."

"No! You can't make me go. I hate her!" she screamed.

Camille ran from the den and rushed down the hallway, through the kitchen and out the back door. She didn't stopped running until she'd reached the farthest end of their property, near the woods.

When Camille was three years old, her father had built her a lavender playhouse where she and her dolls held tea parties. It was her favorite place to play, and she'd spent hours inside. Her mother had bought her curtains, a child-sized couch, table, and chairs to decorate. The two of them had even planted flowers outside to give it a real homey look. She'd long since outgrown it, but whenever she was upset, she returned to the playhouse and the solace it provided. No one in her family knew it, but she visited her playhouse regularly. Her visits had become almost daily since Sharmaine moved out.

Now that she was over five feet six inches tall, Camille had to kneel down and crawl into the front door. Once inside, she folded her legs Indian style and sat on the wooden floor. The playhouse closed around her like a cardboard box, and she leaned against the back wall as tears ran down her face. She sat crying for several minutes.

Suddenly, she became angry with herself for being weak. *Mom is a horrible witch and I hate her. She's not gonna make me cry*, she thought. She sniffed and began looking around for something to dry her tears. On the floor she saw an old cigar box sitting near the window. Slowly opening the lid, she rummaged through the contents that included Old Maid cards and empty gum wrappers, searching for a tissue. Surprised by what she found instead, she sat back and held it in her hand, pondering for a moment.

The previous summer, her family had held a pool party for a group of teenagers from a local shelter. Bishop Snow suggested it as an outreach ministry for the teens, as well as an opportunity for Sharmaine and Leon to give back to their community. Twenty youth, who ranged in ages from fourteen to seventeen, arrived to spend the day. Sharmaine and Leon had arranged for an elaborate barbecue that included ribs, chicken, hamburgers, and hotdogs. They played holy hip-hop music for dancing, and provided lots of games for entertainment. Under Bishop Snow's watchful eye, they gave the group full access to the pool and grounds.

Camille vividly remembered Danté. She'd watched him halfheartedly step off the bus wearing Timberlands, jeans, and a black T-shirt. He reminded her of the rapper LL Cool J with his caramel-colored skin, clean-shaven bald head, and sexy swagger. Infatuated, Camille kept her eye on him. Throughout the party, she noticed that he didn't eat much or join in the games. Anxious to get a look at his body, she was disappointed that he didn't put on swimming trunks and join the others in the pool. Instead, Danté found a chair and spent most of the day just sitting by the pool, watching everyone else having fun.

Camille decided he seemed lonesome, so she strutted over to him in her royal blue bikini. She smiled and asked if she could join him. With her father being very light and her mother much darker, Camille was the color of a perfectly browned piece of toast. Danté looked up and down her teenaged body, taking note of her full B cup bikini top, smooth flat stomach, and round hips. He gladly offered her a seat and they struck up a conversation.

Camille found him fascinating. He told her his mother was in jail and the man who raised him until he was seven was dead. She was shocked when he told her he had no idea who his father was, as his mother was a prostitute who didn't know either. He'd ended up at the shelter when he ran away from the fifth foster home he'd been in. His stories of life on the street seemed a million miles away from anything she'd ever known. Camille talked with him, filled with wonder, until the end of the party.

As he was leaving, Danté held Camille's hand then gently slipped something into it. He smiled at her then joined the others on the bus. Camille had watched the bus drive up the circular driveway and out of their front gate before she opened her hand, then quickly closed it. Afraid that her parents might find out, she had hidden his phone number and the marijuana joint in the box inside her playhouse. In the months since then, she had almost completely forgotten it was there, but her thoughts of Danté were constant. She'd wanted to call or send him a text message, but she was sure her parents would not approve.

Now, with tears streaming down her face, she picked up

the joint and rolled it around in her hands. She put it down for a few seconds and rummaged through the cigar box again, until she found the matches she'd saved from her cousin's wedding. Hesitantly, she picked up the joint and lit it. With her hands shaking, she slowly took a long drag. Gagging and coughing, she considered throwing it away, but instead she took another puff, and another, then another. She sat inside her playhouse, puffing on the joint until the drugs invaded her body, erasing all of the hurt and pain.

Chapter Eight

Leon paced back and forth in his family room. He walked over to the window and looked out, but no one was there. It was almost midnight and Camille was missing. After she ran out earlier, he felt it was best to give her time to calm down. Now he deeply regretted that decision, as she'd never come back. At dusk he'd grown worried, so he called all of her friends, but no one had heard from her, since her phone was destroyed that afternoon. As darkness settled in and the full moon began to rise in the sky, he contacted his personal security officer.

"Otis, have you seen Camille? She ran out upset earlier and hasn't returned."

"No, sir. She probably just went for a walk. Her car is still in the garage."

"Maybe a friend picked her up. Have there been any other cars around?" he asked.

"I didn't notice anyone, but it's possible."

"Can you please keep a lookout? She was really upset, and I'm getting worried about her."

"Yes, sir, Mr. Cleveland," Otis answered. He hung up the phone and went back to watching basketball on his portable TV in the security booth.

Leon assured Jeanna and Rodney that Camille was fine

and would be home soon before sending them both to bed. He tried to convince himself of that also as the hours ticked by. Growing frantic, Leon finally decided to call the Atlanta Police Department. An unenthusiastic officer arrived almost two hours later. He sat on the couch, drank a bottle of water he'd requested, asked Leon a bunch of unrelated questions, then marked her as a probable runaway before leaving. Leon watched the officer drive away, feeling helpless to do anything more.

Now unable to bear waiting in the house any longer, he went to the kitchen drawer, grabbed his flashlight, and walked out into the back yard. He shined his light on the ground as he walked, searching for footprints or any sign of which way she'd gone.

After a few moments, he found himself at the back of the property near Camille's playhouse. He shined his light on it and smiled, remembering his little girl and how much she'd loved playing inside. All of a sudden he thought he saw something inside the playhouse, so he crept closer and shined his light toward the window. He was unable to make it out, so he moved closer.

Kneeling on the ground, he shined the flashlight and peered into the open front door. He let out a long sigh of relief when he saw Camille curled up on the floor, sound asleep.

He gently called out her name. "Camille . . . honey, wake up."

Groggily, she stirred and looked around. "Dad?"

She tried to stand up then realized she couldn't inside the cramped space. Instead, she rolled onto her knees and crawled outside. She stood up and stretched. "What time is it?" she asked.

"It's late. I've been worried sick. What are you doing out here?"

Camille looked around confused. "I must have fallen asleep," she answered.

"Let's get in the house. We can talk in the morning." He placed his arm around her shoulders and led her back to the house by the light of his flashlight.

Once inside, Camille went straight to the stairs, trotted up to her room, and closed the door. Leon followed behind her then went into his own bedroom. He sat down on the bed and began praying. It had been years, probably not since he was in college, but he was sure he recognized the smell of marijuana on Camille's clothes. He knelt by his bed, begging God for guidance.

The next morning, Keisha hung up the phone after speaking to Leon. She'd given him Sharmaine's new number and told him she thought it was a great idea for her to visit with the children. Now all she had to do was make sure that she was there when the visit occurred, so that she could put part two of her plan into motion.

She waited about thirty minutes, long enough for Sharmaine and Leon to speak and make plans; then she dialed Sharmaine's number. "Hey, girl, did Leon call?" she asked with fake emotion.

"Yes, Keisha. Thank you for giving him the number here. Rodney and Jeanna want to see me. He also apologized for walking out of church yesterday. I prayed and prayed after I got home last night. God is so good."

Keisha rolled her eyes as she listened to Sharmaine rambling on and on. She tuned her out, waiting to hear the information she was interested in. Sharmaine droned on and on about how excited she was.

Exasperated, Keisha finally interrupted her. "So, when's the visit?"

"It's this coming Saturday. I thought it would be nice if they spent the day with me here."

"They are children. How do you plan to entertain them at your condo?"

"That's not important, Keisha. I will just be so glad to see my babies. I'm their mother. I don't have to entertain them. I will just enjoy being with them."

Keisha sighed. "I guess you're right. Do you want me to pick them up at the house and bring them over?"

"That won't be necessary. I'll just send the car for them. No offense, Keisha, but I want to be alone with the kids."

Panicking, Keisha began talking quickly. "No, you don't want to do that. Have you forgotten what happened to the car at church yesterday? I'll go over in a cab, so no one notices me. I'll pick up the kids; then I'll bring them to you. I can hang around and take them home later. I won't get in your way at all . . . I, um . . . I just think it will be safer and easier."

Sharmaine thought for a moment. She remembered her horror at seeing the words painted on her limo and realized she did not want her children to experience that. "Okay, Keisha, you can pick them up, but you don't have to hang around here. Just drop them off and I'll call you when they are ready to leave."

She wasn't pleased, but Keisha agreed.

***

Keisha arrived early that Saturday morning to pick up Rodney and Jeanna. Consuela opened the door and politely invited her in. She stood in the front entryway and waited until she saw Leon coming down the stairs alone.

"Hi, Keisha. How are you?" he asked.

"I'm good," she answered. She was surprised that he was being so cordial. "Thanks for suggesting this visit. It means a lot to Sharmaine."

"It was the children's idea. I had nothing to do with it. I thought Sharmaine was sending her driver. Why are you here?"

"We had some issues with the car last week. Sharmaine didn't want the children exposed to that, so I came in a cab."

Leon's brow wrinkled up. "What kinds of issues?" he asked.

"Well, the car was spray-painted while we were in church last Sunday. Sharmaine has a new limo, but, well, let's just say you don't want the kids reading the words that were painted. We just felt it was best to take them by cab. This way it will not draw attention to them."

Leon shook his head. "I've changed my mind. I don't want my children anywhere near Sharmaine. It could be dangerous."

"But, Dad, you promised," Rodney said as he bounded down the stairs, carrying his backpack.

Leon turned to face him. "Rodney, I didn't know you were there. Listen, son, your mother is going through some issues. I want you children to be safe," he answered.

"Leon, I promise you nothing will happen to them. You trust me, don't you?" Keisha asked.

"I . . . I don't know about this," Leon stammered.

"That's why I'm here, Leon. We knew that riding in a limo would bring out the paparazzi and media. No one will pay any attention to the cab. They are spending the day at Sharmaine's condo. It's a gated community. I promise they will be fine." Keisha flashed a reassuring smile.

Still upstairs, Jeanna tapped lightly on her sister's bedroom door. She waited for an answer, and when none came, she pushed open the door. Camille was sitting at her desk, staring at the screen on her laptop.

"Hey," Jeanna said timidly.

Camille turned around and glared at her sister. "What do you want? Did you come to break something else?"

"No, um, I'm sorry about that, Camille."

"Yeah, whatever. What do you want?"

"Ms. Keisha's here to pick us up to visit Mom. Come with us, Camille? Please?"

Camille turned back to her laptop and began typing, ignoring her sister. Quietly, Jeanna closed the door and went downstairs where her Dad, Rodney, and Keisha were talking in the front hallway.

"Keisha, I trust you. Honestly, I do. But I'm just not sure," Leon said.

"Not sure about what?" Jeanna asked as she joined them by the door.

"Dad won't let us go. He promised; now he's going back on his word," Rodney whined.

Jeanna looked crestfallen.

"I didn't say that. I'm just having second thoughts," Leon answered. He looked at the disappointed faces of his children and sighed loudly. "Fine, Keisha, just please be careful. If there are any sign of reporters or even a teen-ager with a camera phone, do whatever you have to in order to protect my children."

Rodney and Jeanna's faces lit up with huge smiles. They hugged Leon tightly.

"You have my word, Leon. They will be fine," Keisha answered then walked them out to the cab.

They arrived at Sharmaine's condo two hours later. A frantic Sharmaine met them at the front door. "Where have you been?" she demanded.

"The kids were hungry, so I stopped at McDonald's and picked them up some breakfast," Keisha answered.

"You should have called. I was worried."

Keisha looked at her oddly. "I did call, Sharmaine. You said to bring you something also." Keisha held up the fast food bag.

"No, you did not call, Keisha," Sharmaine insisted.

Rodney and Jeanna looked at them both with worried expressions.

"What is wrong with you, Sharmaine?" She turned to the kids. "Rodney, Jeanna, you guys heard me on the phone with your mother, right?" Keisha asked.

They both nodded their heads.

"I called you as soon as I left the house. You said you were just waking up, so stopping was fine. Don't you remember?" Keisha eyed Sharmaine closely.

Confused, Sharmaine just stared at them. She didn't remember speaking to Keisha at all. She'd talked to her the night before and confirmed the time she would pick up the children. When her alarm clock went off that morning, she remembered getting up, showering, and waiting patiently for them to arrive.

This wasn't the first time in the past couple of weeks she'd been confused or bewildered. The previous Tuesday, she'd missed a meeting with her attorney because she didn't remember making an appointment. Victor told her he'd texted her to confirm and she replied. When she had checked her phone, there was the message, just as he said. As hard as she tried, she could not remember sending it.

The previous Thursday, she'd walked into her kitchen and found it full of groceries she couldn't remember buying. After putting them away, she checked the receipt and found her credit card number at the bottom.

Worst of all, just the day before, she'd lost the whole afternoon, unable to remember where she'd been and what she did. It was as if someone had completely erased the day from her mind. *What is wrong with me?* she wondered.

Quickly hiding her feelings, she smiled at them. "Silly me, I must have dozed off while I was waiting and forgot."

"Let's not stand out here and worry about it," Keisha answered. "Your kids are here. Don't you want to greet them?"

Still feeling confused, Sharmaine stepped aside so that Keisha could go inside. Then she warmly greeted each of her children. She hugged them tightly, holding on to them for several minutes. "I've missed you guys so much," she said.

At his home, Leon walked up the stairs carrying a tray full of food. He stopped in front of Camille's bedroom door then knocked.

"Who is it?" she screamed angrily.

"Camille, it's me, Dad. Open the door, honey."

Camille sighed; then she closed her laptop and walked over to the door and opened it. She stood there just staring at him for several seconds. "I'm not hungry, Dad. You didn't need to bring that up here." She reached for the door to close it.

"Wait, Camille. We need to talk." He walked in and placed the tray on her bed, then sat down beside it.

Camille walked to the other side of the room and sat at her desk. She placed her elbows on the desk and leaned on her hands with her back to Leon.

"Your brother and sister are spending the day with your mom, so we are alone in the house. I thought it would give us a chance to talk."

She kept her back to him and silently stared at the wall.

Leon took a deep breath. "What were you doing in the playhouse the other night, Camille?"

"I told you. I fell asleep."

"That's not what I mean." He paused. "I mean before you fell asleep. What were you doing?"

She finally turned to look at him with a puzzled expression on her face. "I wasn't doing anything. I just needed to get out of this house."

He scooted forward to the edge of the bed so he'd be closer to her. He looked into her dark brown eyes. "Camille . . . honey, I know that what's happening in this family with your mother is confusing. I understand it's scary, and I even understand that you are angry." He paused and took another deep breath. "But drugs are not the answer."

She turned back to the wall. "Who's using drugs?" she asked.

"Camille, I smelled marijuana on your clothes when I found you in the playhouse. Tell me where you got it."

Violently, she pushed her chair back from the desk, knocking it over as she stood up. She turned around and glared at him. "How do you know what weed smells like? Are you on drugs, Dad?"

Leon was shocked at her anger and accusations. Before all of the turmoil began, Camille had been the model daughter. She made good grades in school. She was respectful to her parents and peers. Most of all, she was happy. As he stared at her, he realized she was filled with a rage he didn't understand.

"Of course not," he finally answered.

She stalked to the other side of the room and stared out the window. "I don't know what you think you smelled, Dad, but I'm not on drugs."

He knew she was lying, but felt at a loss for what to say next. He reasoned that perhaps this problem was more than he could handle by himself. He decided he'd leave her alone until he could speak with a counselor.

"Consuela made waffles. Are you sure you don't want to eat something?" he said, turning toward the tray.

"No, I don't want it," she answered without turning from the window.

Leon picked up the tray and walked toward the door.

"Can I go to the mall?" Camille said suddenly. She turned to face him again.

"You're grounded for fighting with your sister," he answered.

"That's not fair. She's not here, and she's grounded too. Besides, that brat broke my phone."

"She's visiting your mother. You could be there too. It was your choice to stay home."

"Oh, so only people who like Mom get any freedom around here? That is so not fair. I was in my room minding my own business. She came in here and started a fight. She broke my phone, and now I'm the one suffering." She folded her arms across her chest and turned back toward the window.

Leon sighed. On the one hand, he did not want to fight with Camille any longer. He knew increasing her anger was only pushing them further apart. He felt he needed to keep the communication lines open if he was ever going to get through to her about the drugs. On the other hand, he was a strict disciplinarian, and when he handed down a punish- ment, he and Sharmaine always stuck to it. They felt wavering did not allow for structure, which could lead to their children running over them. He didn't have a third hand, but he also realized that Camille had a point. Her sister had intentionally broken her cell phone, and he had not had time to replace it.

He thought for a moment before answering. "Listen, you can go to the mall, but there are some stipulations," Leon said.

She turned around and eyed him suspiciously. "What does that mean?"

"I'll have Otis take you in my car. You can pick out a new cell phone, and then come straight home. That's it. I'll call the store and let them know to put it on my account."

"Not Otis, Dad. He's such a boring old man. Why can't I drive my own car? I promise I won't be gone long."

"That's the offer, Camille. Take it or leave it."

She rolled her eyes. "Fine. Tell that old goat I'll be ready to go in a few minutes. But make him wait for me in the car. I'd die if anyone saw me with him."

Leon opened the door before turning to answer her. "I expect you both back within two hours."

Once he was gone, Camille opened her desk drawer and pulled out Danté's phone number. She placed it inside her jeans pocket before leaving her room.

Chapter Nine

"Mommy. Wake up, Mommy." Rodney placed his hand on Sharmaine's shoulder and shook her. He waited a few seconds and then he shook her again, harder this time. He turned to his sister. "I think she's sick. Maybe we should call Dad," he suggested.

Jeanna and Rodney had spent the last half hour trying to wake Sharmaine as she lay sprawled on her living room couch.

Their visit with their mother had begun wonderfully earlier that morning. After exchanging hugs and kisses, the three of them followed Keisha into Sharmaine's condo. Rodney and Jeanna sat down on the couch next to Sharmaine, and she smiled at the children. Sharmaine was elated to finally see them again.

"Did you enjoy your breakfast at McDonald's?" Sharmaine had asked her children.

"Uh-huh," Rodney answered. "Ms. Keisha bought me two orders of pancakes and a large orange juice. It was great," he said, grinning.

Sharmaine smiled at him. Although his appetite continued to grow, she was glad Rodney had outgrown his baby fat and was now thin and trim. She couldn't help beaming with pride as she looked over at his little brown face.

"And what did you have, Jeanna?" Sharmaine asked.

"Eggs, sausage, and um . . . I had an iced coffee." Jeanna paused and dropped her head in shame when she noticed the look of disapproval on Sharmaine's face. "Ms. Keisha said it would be okay," Jeanna added. She stared at her feet.

Sharmaine turned on the sofa to look over at Keisha. She was sitting behind them in a chair near the window.

"Those iced coffees are mostly milk, Sharmaine. It's not a big deal," Keisha said.

Sharmaine turned back to Jeanna. "It's okay, sweetie. Today is special. I won't fuss about it this time."

"I tried to get Camille to come, Mom, but she's being mean and stubborn," Jeanna said suddenly.

"That's okay, honey. I'm just glad that you two are here. Maybe Camille will come next time."

"Mommy, did you do all those bad things?" Rodney asked.

Sharmaine looked over at Keisha for help. Keisha shrugged her shoulders and got up and went into the kitchen. Sharmaine turned back to Rodney. "No, sweetie, I didn't do any of those bad things. It's really hard to explain what's going on, but it will all be over soon."

Jeanna reached out and hugged Sharmaine. "I knew you didn't do it, Mommy. Grandma tried to make me believe it, but I never did."

"I'm so glad to hear that, honey." Sharmaine hugged her tightly. "I know things are confusing right now, but I promise you, with God's help, we will get through it just fine."

"Sharmaine, are you gonna eat this food I bought? It's getting cold," Keisha said as she suddenly came back into the living room.

"I'm sorry. I completely forgot. Would you bring it to me on a plate, please?"

"Sure," she said, grabbing the bag.

"Oh, and could I have a bottle of water? There are several in the refrigerator."

Keisha nodded her head and walked into the kitchen. She took a plate from Sharmaine's cabinet and laid her Egg Mc-Muffin on it. Then she went to the refrigerator and retrieved a bottle of water. Several minutes later, she returned to the living room. Sharmaine and the children were laughing loudly.

"What did I miss?" Keisha asked.

Sharmaine tried to stop laughing and catch her breath. "Rodney . . . he told us a joke . . . about a . . ." She double over laughing again.

"It was about a frog and an elephant in a bar," Jeanna said. She giggled loudly.

Keisha sat the plate and the water on the coffee table in front of Sharmaine. "I guess you had to be there," she said, looking at the three of them strangely as they continued laughing loudly.

"I'm sorry, Keisha. We are just being silly," Sharmaine answered. She smiled and winked at her kids, then turned back to Keisha. "Thank you. I haven't eaten all morning." She took a bite of her sandwich then washed it down with a gulp of water.

"You're welcome. Do you need me to do anything else for you before I leave?"

"No, Keisha. You've done so much already."

Sharmaine stood up and walked Keisha to the front door. "Thank you for bringing the kids over. I really appreciate everything you do for me." She reached out and gave Keisha a hug.

"I'll see you later." Keisha waved good-bye then walked down the steps.

Sharmaine rushed back inside to the children. She sat down and finished her breakfast while they told her about school and everything they'd done since they had last seen her more than four months earlier. They also told her about their visit with their grandparents and how upset Camille was.

Sharmaine listened intently, trying to hide her anger and disappointment. After she drank the last bit of her water, she looked excitedly at them both. "Guess what I have?" she asked them with a mischievous grin.

"What?" they answered in unison.

"A Wii! It's hooked up in the den. Who wants to play?"

"Me first," Rodney squealed.

"Come on. Jeanna, you can play me after I beat the pants off your brother," Sharmaine said. They all ran into the den.

Halfway through the game, Sharmaine began to feel woozy. Her heart was beating fast and she started sweating profusely. She fanned herself with her hands. "Jeanna, will you get me a bottle of water from the kitchen?" she asked. Sitting down on the couch, she waited for her to return.

"Here, Mom. Drink it slowly," Jeanna instructed.

She took the bottle of water from Jeanna and tried to take a few sips. She thought there must be a hole in her lip because whenever she drank, the water dribbled from her mouth and ended up all over her blouse. Exasperated, she put down the bottle.

"I'm sorry. I'm spoiling your fun. Jeanna, finish the game in my place. I just need to rest a moment," she said.

"Are you sure, Mommy? You don't look so good," Rodney said.

"Yes, I'll just watch."

Sharmaine didn't want to admit it, but she felt worse than she looked. Her stomach was churning and she felt warm all over. She tried watching the children play, but her vision was becoming blurry. The game icons danced across the TV screen as if they were taunting her.

"I won. I won!" Rodney yelled.

Sharmaine tried her best to muster up some enthusiasm to congratulate him. "That's great, honey. Let's go back to the living room for a while and just talk," she suggested. She tried to stand up, but fell back onto the couch. "Whoopsie," she said.

Jeanna reached for her arm. "Let me help you up, Mom." She noticed that Sharmaine's speech was slurred and her eyes were glossed over.

Sharmaine didn't know why, but she began to giggle as she stood. "You're a good kid," she said and then burst out laughing.

With Rodney on one side and Jeanna on the other, Sharmaine stumbled out of the den and down the hallway to the living room. *Why am I so dizzy?* she wondered. She looked to her left and saw two Rodneys. Then she turned to her right and saw two Jeannas. *I need a doctor. Call 911*, she said. At least she thought she'd said it aloud, but the words didn't come out of her mouth.

Her children stared at her with worried looks on their faces. She stared back, desperately trying to remember who they were.

As soon as they were in the living room, Sharmaine plopped on her stomach onto the couch and passed out cold.

"Is she okay?" Rodney asked his sister.

Jeanna wasn't sure, but she didn't want to alarm her little brother.

"She probably just needs to rest for a few minutes. Come on, let's just leave her alone for a while," she said.

Jeanna and Rodney reluctantly returned to the den and the Wii game. They played alone for more than an hour before returning to the living room to check on Sharmaine. She was snoring loudly.

"Let's let her sleep a while longer," Jeanna said. She took her brother back to the den and they picked out a movie from Sharmaine's collection. Periodically, Jeanna left Rodney alone while she checked on Sharmaine, who had not moved from her spot.

Finally, three hours later, they tried unsuccessfully to wake her up.

"Maybe we should call Ms. Keisha. She'll know what to do," Jeanna suggested.

"Good idea," Rodney said. He handed his sister the cordless telephone. Jeanna dialed Keisha's number, but there was no answer.

Sharmaine groaned on the couch and stirred.

"Mommy, are you awake?" Jeanna rushed to her side.

Sharmaine's eyes opened for a few seconds and Jeanna thought she was trying to say something, but she couldn't understand her. Sharmaine stared at her a moment, then closed her eyes again.

Sadly, Jeanna walked away and dialed her father's cell phone number.

Leon answered on the third ring. "She's what?" he asked.

"I think she's sick, Dad. We can't wake her up."

"Where's Keisha?"

"She left hours ago. We tried to call her, but there's no answer. Please just come and bring a doctor for Mommy," Jeanna said.

"Just stay calm. I'm on my way."

Leon hung up the phone then went to the kitchen and grabbed his car keys from the hook on the wall. He was out the back door before he remembered that Otis was still at the mall with Camille and his car. They were over an hour late returning and he was beginning to worry. Now he had to also find a way to get to Jeanna and Rodney.

He went back into the kitchen and grabbed the keys to Sharmaine's car. It had been sitting in their garage since she moved out. Leon took one look at the car, and bittersweet memories flooded his head. The 1964 vintage Mustang had been restored and painted Sharmaine's favorite shade of bubble gum pink. He'd given it to her on their tenth wedding anniversary. Vividly, he remembered the look of shock that was quickly replaced by a huge smile when he'd given it to her. He sighed loudly then returned inside to the kitchen once more.

He sat down on a bar stool at the counter and dialed Jackson's number.

He was pacing around the kitchen an hour later when he heard the front door open. He rushed to the front entryway, expecting Jackson and the kids. Instead, he was greeted by Camille and a mountain of excuses.

"Dad, the line at the cell phone store was so long. It was crazy. Then I had to wait for them to program the phone and show me how to use it. Then I came outside and I couldn't find Otis, so I went to the food court for a drink and—" Camille stopped talking when she realized her Dad was not listening. He was standing by the front door, looking out of the side windows. "What are you looking for?" she asked.

"Oh, um, your brother and sister are not home yet," he answered.

"Okay, well, I'm going to my room now," she said. She rushed to the stairs and ran up to her room, thankful that he was so preoccupied.

Leon snatched open the front door as soon as he saw Jackson's car coming up the driveway. He rushed outside to wait for them. "Jeanna, Rodney, are you two okay?" he asked as soon as they stepped out of the car.

"We're fine, Dad, but I'm worried about Mom," Jeanna answered.

"I told you she's going to be okay," Jackson said. "Come on, let's go inside."

Anxious to speak with his brother, Leon told the kids to go upstairs to their rooms until dinnertime. He assured them their mom was going to be fine. Then he hugged and kissed them both before they went up the stairs.

When they were gone, he asked Jackson to follow him into the kitchen. He got them both a soda from the refrigerator. They sat down at the counter.

"All right, Jack, tell me what's going on. How is Sharmaine? It can't be good. It's written all over your face."

Jackson popped the top on his drink and took a long sip before answering. "She wasn't sick, Leon."

"But Jeanna said—"

Jackson interrupted him. "The kids probably did think she was sick, but I can promise you that she wasn't."

"I don't understand."

"When I got there, Jeanna let me in, and I found Sharmaine passed out on the couch. The kids said she'd been like that for several hours. I asked them what happened before she—well, *went to sleep* is what I said to them." Jackson took another sip of his drink.

Leon looked at his brother with anticipation. "Well, what did they say?"

"They were playing video games when she said she wasn't feeling well. She stumbled around, laughed, and then passed out." He paused. "Leon, Sharmaine was drunk."

"You are out of your mind. Sharmaine doesn't drink."

"Sharmaine has been doing a lot of things you never thought she'd do, baby brother. I'm telling you. I was there. She was drunk as a skunk."

Leon eyed him skeptically. "Are you sure?"

"I tried to wake Sharmaine when I got there. She opened her eyes for a few seconds and they were bloodshot. The kids were so worried. I began to think that maybe she was sick, so I went to the kitchen to get a cool towel for her head." He paused again, and took another sip of his drink. "Her trash can was full of wine bottles and beer cans. I don't think she drank anything in front of them. All they remembered her drinking was some water. She was probably plastered when they arrived."

Leon stood up and walked to the other side of the kitchen. "You have to be mistaken, or there must be some other explanation. She knew the kids were coming today. She wouldn't do that. If she's nothing else, Sharmaine has always been a good mother."

"When are you gonna stop defending her, man? Sharmaine is not who you think she is. I know it's hard to accept, but the last few months are proof of that."

"I'm not defending her. This just doesn't make any sense. Sharmaine never even took a drink at parties. Now you are trying to tell me she was so drunk she passed out. I don't believe that."

Jackson stood up and joined his brother by the sink. "You didn't believe she was in that sex tape either, did you?" he asked.

Leon turned his back to him. He tried to contain his confusion and disappointment. "It's like I never knew her. All these years I've been married to a stranger," he said softly.

"I know, man." Jackson placed his hand on Leon's shoulder. "Maybe it's the wrong time to bring it up, but I hope this means you won't be sending the kids over there again."

Leon turned and looked at his brother. "I don't want to decide right now. I'm still processing this new information." He sighed loudly.

"Just take it one day at a time, man."

"I think Camille is using drugs," he suddenly blurted out.

"What?" Jackson stared at him. "No way, man. What makes you think that?"

Leon checked the back stairs and the doorway to be sure no one was nearby listening. He returned to the counter and sat down. Jackson followed him and took a seat next to him.

"The other day, she ran out of here upset because she didn't want to visit her mother. She was gone for hours. I thought she'd run away. I even called the police."

"Why didn't you call me? I would've been here in a flash," Jackson answered.

"It was late and I didn't want to worry anyone if it wasn't necessary." Leon sighed. "Anyway, I decided to look around the house and I found her out back in her old playhouse. She had crawled inside and fallen asleep. I woke her up. Then, as we were walking back to the house, I could have sworn I smelled marijuana on her clothes."

"Leon, man, are you sure? I mean, she was lying around outside. Maybe it was something else you smelled."

"The playhouse has a wooden floor. It's not like she was lying on the ground. I know what I smelled."

Jackson slowly shook his head. "What are you going to do about it?"

"I tried talking to her, but of course she denied it. I was going to ask Bishop Snow to recommend a good teen counselor we could talk to."

Jackson suddenly stood up and walked toward the back door. He grabbed the door knob. "Come on, man. Let's go search this playhouse. If she's hiding drugs out there and getting high, we need to put a stop to it now."

Leon looked at his brother. Jackson was the largest of his siblings at six feet, six inches tall. His body was all muscle, as he worked out religiously every day, but Jackson was also as thick around the middle as a large barrel.

Leon shook his head. "Neither of us is small enough to get inside that playhouse, Jackson. Besides, I don't want to violate her trust by searching through her things."

"Leon, we have to do something."

"I agree, but even if we find something, that's not going to stop her from getting more. I just wanted you to know and understand what I'm dealing with right now. Sharmaine being drunk isn't even on the top of the list."

Jackson walked back over to his brother. "You're right, man. Is there anything I can do to help?"

Leon shook his head again. "You wanna stay for dinner?

Consuela should be back from the market soon. I think she's cooking chicken tonight."

"Naw, I have some stuff to do," Jackson answered. Leon stood up and walked his brother to the front door. They exchanged a strong hug, then Jackson got into his car and left.

A loud pounding in her head awakened Sharmaine suddenly. Feeling disoriented, she sat up and looked around her living room. The drum line inside her head beat louder and louder, until she realized it was someone at her front door. She dragged herself off of the couch and went to open it.

"Jackson, what are you doing here?" she asked.

"Still sleeping it off, huh, Sharmaine?" He brushed past her and walked into the condo without an invitation.

"What are you talking about? Why are you here?" She followed him inside and plopped down on her couch.

"I think I left my cell phone here," he answered. He walked around the living room, searching, and then went into the kitchen. He found his phone lying on the kitchen counter. Picking it up, he checked the log for missed calls. There were none, so he returned to the living room and a confused Sharmaine.

"I found it," he said.

"How did your phone get here?" she asked.

"You are really out of it, aren't you?" He stared at her in disbelief, shaking his head at her. Then he spoke loudly and slowly, emphasizing each syllable. "I was here earlier, Sharmaine. I came to pick up my niece and nephew."

Sharmaine suddenly remembered that her children were

there that morning. "Oh my God, where are Rodney and Jeanna?" She looked around the room frantically.

"I took them home to their father. I guess you were too drunk to remember any of that."

"I don't drink. I'm sick. A little while after the children arrived, I felt nauseous and hot all over. Maybe I've got a bug or a virus. What makes you think I'm drunk?"

Without answering her, Jackson stomped into the kitchen and retrieved one of the empty wine bottles from her trash can. He brought it to the living room and shoved it at her. "Who drank this? Do you have poltergeist, Sharmaine?"

"Where did you get that?" she asked.

"I pulled it out of my behind," he answered sarcastically.

She stared at him, still confused.

"It was in the kitchen, in the trash with the others." He threw it on the sofa beside her.

Sharmaine was stunned. She didn't remember buying any wine, and she most certainly didn't remember drinking it. Closing her eyes, she tried desperately to recall what had happened that day. The last thing she remembered was playing video games with Rodney and feeling nauseated. The rest of the afternoon was a complete blur.

"Jackson, are the kids okay? Why did you come get them?"

"They're fine. They called Leon because they were worried about their sick mother. I can't believe you did this. They love you, Sharmaine. Even after everything else, those kids still love you. Then you go and ruin their visit by getting drunk and passing out." He looked at her with disgust.

"Jackson, I am not drunk. I don't drink," she protested.

"Tell it to someone who cares." He walked out, slamming the door behind him.

Sharmaine sat on her couch feeling lost and confused. Her mouth felt dry and pasty, so she decided to go to the kitchen for some water. When she did, she noticed the trash can and all of the empty wine bottles and beer cans. "Where did those come from?" she wondered aloud.

She opened the refrigerator and retrieved a bottle of water. Feeling woozy, she took it back to the living room and sat down on the couch again. As soon as she did, another knock came at her front door.

"Who is it?" she called out. She immediately regretted it as the sound of her voice caused a thunderstorm inside her head.

"It's Keisha."

"Come in," Sharmaine called out then lay back on the sofa, trying to ease the throbbing in her temples.

Using her key, Keisha unlocked the door and walked in. "Are the kids ready to go?" she asked. Suddenly, she noticed Sharmaine lying on the sofa. "Are you all right?"

"I don't know. I think I have a virus or something," Sharmaine answered with her eyes still closed.

"Where are the kids? Do you want me to take them home now? I'm sorry I missed your call earlier. I turned off my phone when I went into the movies."

Sharmaine sat up. "Here we go again. I didn't call you earlier, Keisha."

Keisha looked puzzled. She reached into her purse and pulled out her phone. She turned the screen to Sharmaine to show her the missed call.

"Maybe it was one of the kids." Sharmaine sighed. She lay back on the couch and closed her eyes again.

Keisha stood watching her for a moment. She noticed the

empty wine bottle lying on the sofa. "Um, so where are the kids?"

"They're gone. I got sick, so they called Leon. He apparently sent Jackson to get them."

"You didn't drink that wine while they were here, did you?"

Sharmaine bolted upright on the sofa, suddenly remembering the empty bottle. "Of course I didn't. My trash can is full of these things and empty beer cans. Keisha, do you have any idea where they came from?"

Keisha slowly shook her head. She sat down on the sofa next to Sharmaine and took her hands into hers. "Honey, I'm worried about you. I think we should get you to a doctor."

Pulling her hands back, Sharmaine stared at her. "I told you it's just a bug. Just tell me where that stuff came from."

"You honestly don't remember?"

"Remember what? Just tell me, Keisha."

"You had a party last night. My guess is those are the leftovers."

Sharmaine shook her head. "I did not. What are you talking about?"

"Sharmaine, you had a party last night. I told you it was a bad idea with the kids coming this morning, but you insisted on partying with your new friends."

"I don't remember any of that. I was home alone last night. I watched a movie. I talked to you on the phone, and then I went to bed early." Sharmaine laid her head in her hands and began crying.

"These blackouts and memory lapses are getting more frequent, Sharmaine. I think you should consider seeing a doctor."

Sharmaine nodded her head and wiped her tears on her

hands. "Will you call Dr. Ray for me on Monday and make an appointment? His number is in my address book."

"He's a family doctor, Sharmaine. I think you need to see a neurosurgeon. I know one I can call for you."

"Sure, that's fine." Sharmaine sniffed loudly. She curled her feet up under her on the sofa. "Keisha, can I tell you something? It's crossed my mind, but I was afraid to say it out loud."

"Sure, honey. What is it?"

"I've been thinking. I mean, with the blackouts, there are so many situations and days that I just can't remember. I'm doing things and going places, then when it's over, it's like I was never there."

Keisha nodded her head. "The doctor should be able to help with that. Don't worry about it. It could be a chemical imbalance that can be cured real quickly with a few pills."

"I'm not worried about me." Sharmaine paused for several moments. "What if I've forgotten other things? What if I've been having these blackouts for months and didn't know it?"

"I don't understand."

Sharmaine stared at the floor and whispered, "What if I really did shoot Leon and I just don't remember?"

Keisha reached over and pulled Sharmaine into a tight hug. Behind Sharmaine's back, a huge grin spread across Keisha's face.

Chapter Ten

"People, people, we can't all speak at once. I need everyone to just calm down for a moment," Bishop Snow stated. He sat in his chair at the large table in the church conference room. "Now, Sister Reeves, I believe you were speaking. Go ahead."

Brenetta stood up. "Thank you, Bishop, but you're not gonna like what I have to say. Sharmaine Cleveland is a disgrace to this congregation, and I can't believe you allowed her to stand in our pulpit and sing."

"Sister Cleveland asked to sing, and I saw no reason to tell her no. As I've said before, it's not our place to judge her. She and her family are going through a difficult time, and they need our support," Bishop Snow responded.

"Her family walked out of here right along with the rest of us." Brenetta looked around the room at the other faces in the conference room. She waved her finger. "All of you saw Leon take those poor children and walk out. That should tell you something right there."

Bishop Snow sat in his chair and didn't respond as Brenetta continued to rant and rave about Sharmaine Cleveland. The church council meeting had been going on for more than an hour, but so far they had not discussed anything he felt was important. As soon as he had arrived and taken his seat, he was surprised to learn that his council members had a completely different agenda in mind.

Sharmaine had not returned to church the previous Sunday, but that didn't stop them from complaining about the day that she had been there. Because of that, he had not had a chance to discuss the church's monthly budget, their upcoming ministries and programs, or the new building plans. Instead, he'd been bombarded by Brenetta and those who disagreed with him about his decision to allow Sharmaine to sing at their service. He'd wanted to exercise some understanding and tolerance by allowing them to voice their opinion, but his patience was growing thin. He waited until Brenetta finally took a seat before speaking again.

"Listen, everyone, the decisions regarding who sings during worship service are solely mine. I do my best to put forth a program that will minister to the people who come here each Sunday morning. I appreciate everyone's input, and I will take into consideration what you've all said. Now, can we move on to other business?"

"Sounds like you're trying to give us the brush-off," Deacon Mathis stated. He sucked his teeth. "I mean, just 'cause you the bishop around here, it don't mean none of us ain't got no say so."

"Of course not, Deacon. As I said, I will take everything that's been said here into consideration if Sharmaine or anyone else wishes to sing here. But someone has to make the final decision. As your elected bishop, that someone is me."

Sister Michaels stood up suddenly. "Yes, we elected you, Bishop, which means we can also vote your behind right out! Don't go throwing your power around here." She pointed a long, wrinkled finger at him. "My granddaddy helped found this church before you was even a twinkle in your momma's eye."

Bishop Snow sighed. "Sister Michaels, Deacon, I promise you both—I promise everyone—I am not trying to throw my power around. I believe God sent Sister Sharmaine Cleveland to us to sing that Sunday. Her presence was a blessing to us, and I know we were a blessing to her as well. Please, let's not argue about this any longer. As I said, if she asks to sing, I will take this meeting and everyone's thoughts into consideration before making a final decision."

"This has gone way past her singing here, Bishop. I think we need to take a vote. We need to vote right now with all of the church officers in the room and decide if we want Sharmaine Cleveland back in this church. We have the power to revoke her membership, and I move that we do just that," Brenetta said.

"Sister Reeves, let's not make any rash decisions. There is no reason to vote Sharmaine out of this church. I think things are getting out of hand. Our purpose here tonight is to discuss church business, not Sharmaine Cleveland," Bishop Snow said. He opened his folder and pulled out his notes. "First on the agenda is—"

"Sharmaine Cleveland is church business," Brenetta said, interrupting him.

Bishop Snow stood up from the table with his Bible in his hands. "All right, it seems that if we don't discuss Sharmaine Cleveland, we are not going to get anything else accomplished. We've spent the last hour arguing and gossiping. It's time that we move forward."

"Are we gonna take a vote now?" Brenetta asked. "It's been properly moved. All we need is for someone to second it."

"I second it," Deacon Mathis said.

"Then it's been moved and properly seconded that we vote Sharmaine Cleveland right out of this church," Brenetta said.

"Wait just a moment, Sister Reeves. Before we take a vote, I want to read something. Any of you who've brought your Bibles, will you turn with me to John, the eighth chapter and the first verse? I will be reading from the King James version." Bishop Snow paused and waited as a few of the church council members pulled out their Bibles and turned to the chapter. When he felt they were ready, Bishop Snow began walking around the room, reading aloud:

"Jesus went unto the mount of Olives. And early in the morning he came again into the temple and all the people came unto him; and he sat down, and taught them. And the scribes and Pharisees brought unto him a woman taken in adultery; and when they had set her in the midst, they saith unto him, Master, this woman was taken in adultery, in the very act. Now Moses in the law commanded us, that such should be stoned: but what sayest thou? This they said, tempting him that they might have to accuse him. But Jesus stooped down, and with his finger wrote on the ground, as though he heard them not."

Bishop Snow paused for a moment and looked over the faces of the people in the room. Then he continued reading and walking:

"So when they continued asking him, he lifted up himself, and said unto them, He that is without sin among you, let him first cast a stone at her. And again he stooped down, and wrote on the ground. And they which heard it, being convicted by their own conscience, went out one by one, beginning at the eldest, even unto the last: and Jesus was left alone, and the woman standing in the midst. When Jesus had lifted up himself, and saw none but the woman, he said unto her, Woman, where are those thine accusers? Hath no man

*condemned thee? She said, No man, Lord. And Jesus said unto her,
neither do I condemn thee: go, and sin no more. Then spake Jesus
again unto them, saying, I am the light of the world: he that followeth
me shall not walk in darkness, but shall have the light of life. The
Pharisees therefore said unto him, Thou bearest record of thyself; thy
record is not true. Jesus answered and said unto them, Though I bear
record of myself, yet my record is true: for I know whence I came, and
whither I go; but ye cannot tell whence I come, and whither I go. Ye
judge after the flesh; I judge no man. And yet if I judge, my judgment
is true: for I am not alone, but I and the Father that sent me."*

When he was done reading, Bishop Snow took his seat
at the head of the conference table. He laid his Bible down.
"Now, who would like to lead the vote regarding Sharmaine
Cleveland and what we should do about her?" he asked. He
waited patiently for several moments, but no one spoke up.
He breathed a sigh of relief. "All right, then I guess we'll move
on to the next item on the agenda." He picked up his notes
and began discussing the church budget.

When she returned to her home that night, Brenetta Reeves
was not at all happy. Stalking into the house, she slammed the
front door. She burst into the den, where Shawn was seated
on the couch, watching a basketball game on a forty-inch
screen. She stormed over to him, grabbed the remote control,
and turned off the television.

"Brenetta, what are you doing?" he asked disbelievingly.

She plopped down on the sofa next to her husband. "I just
came from a meeting at the church. I cannot believe Bishop Snow is going to continue letting Sharmaine attend our
church. It's not right, Shawn. It's just not right."

"Why do you even care?" He reached for the remote and turned the TV back on. He saw only a few seconds of the game before Brenetta snatched the remote and turned it off again.

"I care because it's not right. What kind of example is she for our younger members? He let her stand up there and sing as if she wasn't frolicking around on the Internet in porno-graphic movies. How can he ignore the fact that she's going on trial for attempted murder in a few weeks? I hate it," she huffed.

Shawn realized he wasn't going to be allowed to finish the basketball game until he talked with Brenetta. He turned to her. "I thought you were going to bring it up in the council meeting tonight."

"I did. There were other council members who agreed with me too. Just when I got ready to have them vote on revoking her membership, Bishop Snow had to go and pull his Bible out on us. He used that thing like a weapon."

Shawn looked at her confused. "How did he use his Bible as a weapon?"

"He read some scriptures about not judging, and casting the first stone, blah, blah, blah. He's not fooling me. He knew he was losing ground, so he had to play his trump card."

Shawn chuckled. "Brenetta, don't you think he had a point? You really should not judge Sharmaine. I mean, that's if she's even guilty. None of us are sure about that."

"Whose side are you on, Shawn Reeves?" Brenetta glared at him.

"Don't start that, Brenetta. You know I've had my doubts about Sharmaine's guilt from the beginning. You can believe what you want, but don't try to make me believe it too."

Brenetta rolled her eyes at him. She slumped back onto the couch and folded her arms across her chest. "Tonia! Tonia!" she yelled, summoning their maid.

Tonia quickly scurried into the room. "I'm sorry, Mrs. Reeves. I didn't know you were home. Can I get you a drink or something to eat?" she asked.

"I'm starving. Fix me a ham and cheese sandwich. Make sure you use the whole wheat low-fat bread and that special mayo from the farmer's market. Cut it diagonally, and put my pickle on the side. Last week you put it on top of the bread and it was all soggy. See if you can get it right this time."

Tonia nodded her head. "Yes, ma'am." She scurried out of the room to the kitchen.

Brenetta turned her attention back to her husband. "I know you want to believe in Sharmaine; that's fine. She may very well be innocent. That's not the point."

"Then what is the point as you see it?"

"Her naked booty is plastered all over the Internet. I was working with the youth group last week. You know the ones from the shelter. All of those kids have seen the video. It's disgraceful."

Shawn sighed. "Sharmaine says that isn't her in the video. We've been all through this a dozen times. I still don't understand why you seem to have this vendetta against her."

"A what?" She cocked her head to the side like a confused puppy.

Shawn shook his head. As much as he loved Brenetta, sometimes he forgot that she'd only been to the tenth grade in high school. She hated when he used words that she didn't understand, believing he did so on purpose. He tried to backpedal without upsetting her. "I mean, I don't understand why you seem to be out to get her. It's like you can't rest until everyone feels about her the same as you do. The two of you were once good friends. What's going on with you lately?"

"I just don't like fakes and phony people. I keep it real. You know that."

Tonia scurried into the room carrying Brenetta's sandwich, interrupting them. "Here you are, Mrs. Reeves," she said politely.

"What is this?" Brenetta asked. She turned her nose up at the sandwich.

Tonia's eyes darted back and forth between Brenetta and the food. "It's your ham and cheese sandwich."

"I wanted honey baked ham and provolone cheese. Can't you do anything right?" she screamed.

"Brenetta, leave the woman alone. You didn't tell her that. Eat the sandwich," Shawn told her.

Sighing loudly, Brenetta rolled her eyes at Shawn. She then turned and glared at Tonia. "Take this back and give me what I asked for," she said between gritted teeth.

"Yes, ma'am. I'm sorry, Mrs. Reeves." Tonia scurried from the room once again, returning to the kitchen.

"Brenetta, why do you treat her like that? It's not necessary. You could try saying *please* and *thank you* once in a while."

Brenetta stood up from the couch. She stomped her foot like a spoiled child. "That's exactly what I mean, Shawn. That woman is a maid. She's a servant in my house. I don't have to be nice to her, but you always defend her, the same way you always defend Sharmaine. You never take my side."

Shawn held out his hand and invited Brenetta to sit back down. Unenthusiastically, she took it and sat next to him. He laid her head on his broad shoulder. Then he spoke to her softly and gently. "Brenetta, I am your husband. I will always be on your side, but this thing with Sharmaine seems to be eating away at you. I don't understand. Tell me what's really going on."

Tears dropped down Brenetta's face. "It's just not fair. I go to church every Sunday, and I sing in the choir. I teach Sunday school, and I work with the women's ministry and the youth groups, but Bishop Snow has never let me sing a solo for the whole congregation. I always had to compete with her at the record company, but I thought when you fired her, that was all over."

"Brenetta, surely you can't still be jealous of Sharmaine."

"She had everything and she never appreciated it. Not everyone is as blessed as Sharmaine Cleveland, but did she care? No. She threw it all away."

"I don't understand what you are talking about."

Brenetta sat up and looked into Shawn's face. "Sharmaine had the perfect life. She had a beautiful home with a loving husband, an exciting and successful career, and three beautiful children. I would give anything to have had just one child." Brenetta paused and wiped away a tear. "She had three and then she tossed it all away."

Shawn pulled her to him and held her tightly. He suddenly realized that his wife's obsession was not about Sharmaine at all. It was the only way she knew how to cope. She'd used her jealousy as a defense mechanism. Hating Sharmaine helped erase her own pain of not being able to have children.

Brenetta grew up in the Bankhead section of Atlanta, and by all accounts, she had lived a rough life. When she was just fourteen years old, she'd been shot in a drive-by while walking home from school. The bullet pierced her womb, and the doctors had to perform an emergency hysterectomy in order to save her life.

Shawn kissed Brenetta on her forehead. "We'll have a baby of our own one day. I promise you that," he said softly.

Tonia cleared her throat as she entered the room, not wanting to interrupt their intimate moment. Shawn looked up at her. "Thank you, Tonia. Just leave it on the table," he instructed.

She obeyed and was turning to leave the room when Brenetta suddenly sat up. "Wait, Tonia. I'm sorry I was so harsh with you earlier. I've had a bad day," she said.

Tonia smiled at her. "That's okay, Mrs. Reeves. Would you like me to draw you a hot bath?"

"That won't be necessary," Shawn answered for his wife. "You can take the rest of the night off. We'll see you in the morning."

After Tonia left the room, Shawn grabbed a blanket from the edge of the sofa and covered both of them. For the rest of the evening, he and Brenetta sat in silence, snuggling on the couch.

Chapter Eleven

Camille walked into the family room and sat down. "You wanted to see me, Dad?" she asked.

Leon was seated across from her in his large easy chair. He crossed his legs before speaking. "Why were you late coming back from the mall last Saturday?"

"I told you, Dad. There was a line at the store, and I didn't know how to use the phone, so they had to explain it to me. It's not my fault."

"Camille, we talked about this before you left. I asked you to be home within two hours, and you were gone more than four. Otis says he had to leave the car and come inside the mall to find you."

"I told you that, too, Dad. I went outside and I couldn't find him, so I went to the food court for a drink. It was hot outside."

Leon gave her an unsympathetic look. "Camille, I gave you leniency by allowing you to go to the mall in the first place. You took advantage of that. I know that you not only bought a cell phone, but also a purse and three pair of jeans." He held up a piece a paper. "It says here you also made a cash withdrawal. Do you really think I don't read my credit card statements?" Camille looked surprised. She'd hidden the bags inside her playhouse when she returned home, and retrieved them the next day, believing her Dad would never find out she'd gone shopping.

"But, Dad, I needed those things. I didn't think you'd mind."

"Well, you got the first part right; you didn't think. But I do mind when you are dishonest with me. You are grounded for another two weeks."

"That is not fair. All I did was buy a few extra things. We can afford it. What's the big deal?" She rolled her eyes.

"The big deal is that you were told to go to the cell phone store only then return home. Not only that, but you lied about where you were."

Camille stood up from the sofa, clenched her fists, let out a loud scream, and stomped the floor over and over. Leon sat calmly, ignoring her tantrum. Exasperated, she stomped from the room, ran up the stairs and into her room, then slammed her bedroom door.

She was still sulking an hour later when her new cell phone rang. Lying on her bed, she ignored it at first. Reluctantly, she decided to at least check the caller ID. She didn't recognize the number, but she answered anyway. "Hello?"

"What up. Is this Camille?"

"Yeah. Who's this?"

"Danté. I got your message, baby."

Camille suddenly perked up. She'd called Danté from the mall as soon as her new phone was activated, but he did not answer. While she shopped, she'd tried his number several more times. She was just about to call him once more when Otis showed up and told her it was time to go home.

"Hold on," she said. Camille got up from her bed and

locked her bedroom door. She returned to the phone. "I'm back."

"So, what took you so long to call? I thought you had forgotten all about me."

"No, I didn't. I just didn't think my parents would approve of you. But I don't really care what they think anymore."

"What's that all about, rich girl? Are you mad at Mommy and Daddy?" He laughed lightly.

"You could say that."

"So, you wanna hook up? I think I can get a ride out there around ten o'clock."

Camille thought for a moment. Her dad usually went to bed at eleven, but she knew that sometimes he didn't go right to sleep. One night, she'd attempted to sneak to her playhouse, and he was downstairs in the kitchen eating a snack. She knew it had to be later.

"Can you make it twelve-thirty? And don't come to the house. I'll meet you on the corner."

"Okay, no problem. I'll be in a blue Jeep. See ya then, baby."

"Danté, can you bring some . . . um . . . do you have any weed?" she asked.

Danté was surprised. When he had given her the first joint, he had never expected she'd actually smoke it. "Um, no, but I can get some. You got money?"

"I have my Visa card."

Dante laughed loudly. "They don't take credit cards, rich girl. You need to get some cash."

"Um . . . okay, I'll have it. See ya then, Danté"

"Cool," he replied.

Camille hung up the phone and went to her desk. Opening the drawers, she rummaged around, looking to see if she had any cash she'd forgotten about. When she found none, she put her head in her hands for a few moments to think.

A plan materialized in her brain, and she got up from the desk. Unlocking her door, she left the room and trotted downstairs. Leon, Rodney, and Jeanna were in the family room, sitting together on the couch. They'd rented a movie, and it was playing on the big screen TV. Without a word, she sat down in a chair and began watching with them.

After several moments, she spoke. "Pass the popcorn, Rodney," she said.

Leon looked over at her.

"I'm sorry, Dad," she mumbled. He smiled and took the popcorn bowl from Rodney then handed it to her.

They all watched the movie together in silence. It ended shortly before eleven, and Camille dramatically yawned and stretched. "I'm going to bed," she announced.

"Can I watch another movie?" Jeanna asked.

"No, you have school tomorrow. Don't worry. Summer is coming soon. I think it's time we all went to bed," Leon answered.

"Oh, Dad, I forgot to tell you. I lost a library book at the beginning of the year. I have to pay for it or I won't get my report card," Camille said.

Leon stood up and reached in his back pocket for his wallet. "How much is it?"

Camille panicked. She'd forgotten to ask Danté how much she'd need. "Twenty dollars?" she said tentatively.

"The smallest bill I have is a fifty. Can I trust you to bring me my change?" He looked Camille in the eyes.

"Sure, Dad." She snatched the bill from his hands.

Leon walked out of the family room and followed his children upstairs. He kissed them each good night in the hallway before they went into their rooms.

Camille went to her closet and pulled down all of her extra pillows. She laid them in her bed to simulate a person. Then she pulled her blanket over the pillows and fluffed them up. When she was satisfied with how it looked, she went back to her closet and pulled out the new jeans she'd purchased and a red tank top. Laying her clothes on the bed, she went into her bathroom and took a quick shower.

After she was dressed, she checked the clock on her nightstand. It was 12:15. Reaching into her desk drawer, she found the flashlight she often used when she wanted to sneak to her playhouse at night. She cracked her bedroom door open and peeked out. The entire house was dark.

Quietly, she tiptoed down the stairs. Stopping at the front door, she shined the light on the alarm keypad, typed in the disarm code, and then she slowly opened the door and crept out.

As soon as she was outside, she broke into a jog and trotted up the circular driveway to the front gate. Just as she suspected, Otis was still awake, watching TV in the security booth. She ducked down low as she sneaked past him.

Camille knelt down even lower near the gate entrance and picked up a handful of rocks. She threw them at the gate. They hit the locks, making a clanking noise.

"Who's out there?" Otis called. When there was no answer, he got up and walked out onto the driveway. He looked around.

Camille threw another handful of rocks at the gate.

"It must be those stupid squirrels again," Otis said. He reached inside the booth and pressed the button, opening the gate. As soon as he did, Camille darted to the other side and out into the street.

Feeling content that he'd scared the squirrels off of the gate, Otis pressed the button to close it again and returned inside to his chair.

Danté flashed the lights on the Jeep as soon as he noticed Camille walking up the street. She rushed over to him and hopped inside the truck.

"Did you have any trouble getting out?" he asked.

"I told my Dad I was going to bed over an hour ago. Everyone's asleep now. It's cool."

He leaned back in his seat and looked her up and down. She was still as beautiful as he remembered. Even in the dim light he could see the outlines of her curvaceous teenaged body. His eyes fell to her cleavage, which was accentuated by the tight red tank top. Finally noticing she'd cut her hair into a short bob, he decided to compliment her on it.

"I'm feeling your haircut."

Camille self-consciously touched her head. "Thanks. Um, it was my mom's idea. I think I'm going to let it grow back out."

"No, don't. It's sexy short." He grinned at her and she grinned back.

Another car came down the street, and its lights illuminated the Jeep. They both ducked down quickly. Once the car was gone, they sat up and laughed.

"Let's get out of your neighborhood," Danté said. He started the engine and pulled away from the curb.

***

Leon awoke early the next morning and went into his bathroom to shower. After he undressed, he stepped under the hot spray and let it flow all over his head and down his body. Standing still for several moments, he quietly enjoyed the pounding of the water. Then he soaped up his entire body and was just about to rinse when he heard a loud banging at his bedroom door. Quickly turning off the water, he heard Jeanna screaming his name as she continued pounding on the door. He put on his robe and tied the sash, then rushed out of the bathroom.

"What is it?" he asked as he opened the bedroom door.

"Camille's not in her room. I went to ask her if I could borrow a scrunchie for my hair, but she didn't answer. I pushed the door open and her bed was full of pillows. She's gone, Dad." She grabbed Leon's still wet arm and pulled him to her sister's room as he dripped water all over the hallway.

Leon stood stunned, just staring into Camille's bedroom for several seconds. "Go finish dressing for school. I'll find your sister," he finally managed to say.

"But, Dad, I can help," she protested.

"I appreciate that, honey." He turned to her. "Don't worry. I'm sure Camille is close by. Just get ready for school."

Once he was sure Jeanna was inside her room, Leon went back to his room for a towel and his slippers. He hurriedly dried off. Then, without bothering to get dressed, he tightened the sash on his robe and rushed out of his bedroom. Frantically, he hurried down the stairs and out into the backyard to the playhouse.

"Camille! Are you out here?" he called as he ran. When he

reached the playhouse, he was disappointed to find it empty. *Where could she be?*

Leon ran back to the house and called Otis. "Camille is missing again. Did you see or hear anything unusual this morning or last night?"

Otis was barely awake. He yawned into the phone. "Did you check the playhouse? Maybe she's there like last time," he suggested.

"No, she's not out there. I need you to check the entire property, starting with the pool house and the woods in the back."

The confusion of sleepiness began to rise off of Otis's head and a clear thought came into his mind. "There was a problem at the gate last night, Mr. Cleveland."

"What kind of problem?"

"I'm sorry. I heard a racket. I thought it was them fool squirrels, so I opened the gate to scare them away. But now that I think about it, it could've been her. I bet that's when she left."

"What time was that?"

"It was late. I think after midnight. I don't know exactly. I'm sorry. I didn't see anybody. It was really dark."

Leon sighed. "No, it's not your fault. Go ahead and search the grounds anyway, just in case." Leon hung up the phone and called Jackson.

A half hour later, Leon was completely dressed when he walked into the kitchen. Consuela was clearing away the breakfast dishes after serving Jeanna and Rodney.

"Did you find Camille?" Jeanna asked as soon as he walked in.

"Not yet, honey." He turned to his housekeeper. "Consuela, can you take the kids to school today?"

"Of course, Mr. Leon," she answered.

"No, I want to stay here until you find Camille. What if she's hurt?" Jeanna said.

"Me too. Don't make us go," Rodney chimed in.

"Listen, both of you. I'm sure Camille is fine. There are only a few weeks of school left, so you can't afford to miss any more days. She should be here by the time you get home." He managed to muster up a fake smile.

"Go on, get your backpacks," Consuela said. She waited until the children were gone then turned to Leon. "I'm sure Miss Camille is okay. Don't worry."

"Thank you," he said.

Consuela quietly went out the back door to her car. After she left the kitchen, Leon prayed that she was right.

"Leon! I found her! Leon!" Jackson yelled from the front entryway. He held Camille by her arm as she tried to pull away from him.

"Uncle Jack, you're hurting my arm," she whined.

"Oh, thank God," Leon said as soon as he saw her. He rushed over and hugged Camille. His nose wrinkled up and he stepped back. Her hair and her clothes reeked with smoke.

Camille leaned forward and squinted at him. "Waddup, Dad?" she slurred.

"She's high as a kite," Jackson said before he suddenly noticed the other children bounding down the stairs.

Rodney reached the bottom first. Elated to see her, he ran to his sister. Then suddenly he stopped. "Camille, you stink," he said. He held his nose with his fingers.

"Rodney, you're funny looking," Camille slurred. Then she began laughing hysterically.

"Jackson, take her up to her room," Leon ordered.

Holding on to her arm, Jackson obeyed. The other children stared at her as she stumbled up the stairs, giggling. They turned their stares to Leon, waiting for an explanation.

"Camille needs to rest," he said.

"But, Dad . . ." Jeanna began.

"Consuela is waiting for you both in the car. Hurry up so you aren't late for school." He reached down and hugged them both, holding on just a little bit longer than normal.

Leon was still standing by the front door in a slight state of shock when Jackson came down the stairs. He looked up at his brother. Taking him by the arm, Jackson led him into the den. "Sit down, baby brother. I know this is rough," he said.

"Where did you find her?" Leon asked.

"I was on my way here and I saw her getting out of a blue Jeep parked on the corner."

Leon couldn't remember any of Camille's friends who owned a blue Jeep. "Did you see who was driving?"

"Some thug with a bald head. I really didn't get a good look at him, though."

Leon slowly shook his head. "This situation is getting out of hand, Jack. I don't know what I'm going to do."

"Well, first of all you need to ground her until she's twenty-one. Then we need to go upstairs and take her cell phone, laptop, and any other communication device. I say we strip the room and just leave her a bed to sleep in. You've got to lay the smack-down of punishment on her."

"She was already grounded. What difference does it make if I ground her and she sneaks out?"

"Leon, you can't just let this slide. I know you're upset, but she has got to be punished. You've got to let her know that you will not tolerate drug use in your house."

Leon sighed loudly. "Jackson, you don't understand. I know that Camille should be punished for sneaking out and for smoking pot, but that's not the whole issue here."

Jackson stared at him puzzled. "Then what is?"

"I need to find out why my daughter is using drugs. This is not like Camille. Ever since this whole situation with Sharmaine happened, she's becoming a different person. I don't even recognize her anymore."

"When kids become teenagers they change, baby brother. I mean, do you really think this is all about Sharmaine?"

"I know it is. She says she hates her mother, and I know that's not true. The lying, the sneaking out, and the drugs; it all began when her mother left. I know I should punish her, but all I want to do is get her some help."

Suddenly they heard noises coming from the kitchen. Rushing in, they found Camille seated on the floor with her hand jammed inside a cereal box. The kitchen was in disarray, with all of the cabinets standing open. Various items were scattered all over the counter. She squinted at them as they walked over to her.

"I got hungry. Leave me alone," she slurred. Camille tossed a handful of cereal into her mouth and dug in for more.

Leon snatched the box of cereal from her hands and laid it on the counter. Then he reached under Camille's arms and pulled her to her feet.

"That's it, Camille. I will not have you disrupting this house any further. Get upstairs to your room and take a shower. Now!" he screamed.

The boom of his voice seemed to shock her sober. Her lip began quivering and she started to cry.

"Get upstairs!" Leon yelled directly into her face.

Camille sprinted out of the kitchen and up the staircase. They heard her bedroom door slam.

Jackson slowly began closing cabinets and putting items away.

"Leave it for Consuela," Leon said. "I need you to come upstairs with me."

With Jackson close on his heels, he ran up the stairs, taking them two at a time. They entered Camille's room without knocking. Her shower was running, so he knew she was in the bathroom.

"Search every inch of this room, Jackson. I want to make sure she didn't bring any drugs into my house."

They searched through the dresser, the desk drawers, and the shelves of Camille's closet. Leon knelt down and searched under her bed. He stood up, and with Jackson's help, he flipped the mattress. When they found nothing, they dumped out her clothes hamper and searched the pockets of all of her jeans. Satisfied, they sat down on the bed.

Camille emerged from the bathroom a few moments later wrapped in her bathrobe. "What did you do to my room?" she demanded.

"Camille, where were you last night? Who was that guy you were with, and where did you get drugs?" Leon asked.

"I was in the SWAT," she said. Camille began picking up her clothes that were scattered all over the floor.

Leon looked to Jackson for help. He mouthed the word Camille had used.

"The SWAT is southwest Atlanta," Jackson answered.

"Is that a bad neighborhood?" Leon asked.

"It depends on where you live. Some is really hood. Some is middle class. And then there is some that is very affluent. It just depends on the street you live on. I'm guessing she was in the roughest part."

Leon turned his attention back to his daughter. "Is that why you asked me for money? Did you spend the fifty I gave you on drugs?"

Camille ignored him and continued picking up her clothes.

Fuming, Leon stood up. "Give me your cell phone. You're grounded for the next month. If this continues, it will stretch into the entire summer."

Still not speaking to him, Camille pointed toward her dresser where the phone sat.

Leon grabbed it and shoved it into his pocket. He then walked over to her desk and picked up her laptop computer. He handed it to Jackson. Then he went to her entertainment center and disconnected the TV, stereo, and DVD player. He snatched the cords loose and handed them to Jackson as well. Finally, he grabbed her MP3 player, and the two men left the room.

In the hallway, Jackson slowly shook his head. "I see what you mean, man. There's a lot of anger bottled up inside her."

"Doesn't the church have a drug counseling program?" Leon asked.

Jackson nodded. "I think so. Put this stuff in your bedroom. I'll go call Bishop Snow."

Camille locked her bedroom door behind Jackson and Leon. Then she went into the bathroom and pulled off the top of the toilet tank. She stuck her arm through the water to the bottom and retrieved the bag of weed Danté had helped her purchase. Glad they were done searching her room, she left the bathroom and hid it in the back of her closet.

Chapter Twelve

Sharmaine walked into her dining room and sat down at the table to begin her morning devotion. Although she took time every morning to talk with God, this particular morning she had a specific purpose in mind. Her attorney, Victor, had called the previous evening to let her know that he was unsuccessful in getting her trial date moved back. That meant Sharmaine would go on trial for the attempted murder of Leon in one week.

Opening her Bible, she asked God for strength and guidance. The Spirit led her to the book of Isaiah, 54:7 . She read it silently:

No weapon that is formed against thee shall prosper; and every tongue that shall rise against thee in judgment thou shalt condemn. This is the heritage of the servants of the Lord, and their righteousness is of me, saith the Lord.

Sharmaine closed her eyes and recited the scripture over and over. She knew that the power of God was her only defense at the upcoming trial. When she was done meditating over the words, her mind wandered back to her last meeting with Victor.

"Sharmaine, the district attorney's office has offered a plea bargain. I strongly suggest you take it," he had said.

"What is it?"

"If you plead guilty to attempted second degree murder, you will be sentenced to ten years in prison. I'm sure with good behavior you could be out in between five to seven years tops. This is your first offense."

Sharmaine looked at him in disbelief. "I can't go to jail for five to seven years. My son would be almost grown when I got out."

"If you are convicted, Sharmaine, you could go to jail for twenty years. Your son would be grown, and you'd be an old woman when you got out."

"No. Tell them no." She shook her head.

Victor slowly closed his folder and stared at Sharmaine across his desk. "Do you understand that you have no defense, Sharmaine? I'm going to walk into that courtroom and tell them that you didn't do it, because you say so. You don't even have an alibi other than you were asleep. I'm trying here, Sharmaine, but I've got nothing."

"I know, Victor. I just don't know how you expect me to willingly go to jail for five years without a fight."

Victor sighed. "Fine. Were you able to get me that list of character witnesses I asked for? I need to subpoena those people to speak on your behalf."

Sharmaine reached into her purse and pulled out a small piece of paper with two names written on it. She handed it to Victor.

"Bishop Jimmy Snow and Keisha Williams? Your minister and your assistant are the only two people you have on here."

"I tried to get Shawn Reeves also. He agreed at first, but then he called and recanted. I'm sure Brenetta had a lot to do with it."

Victor picked up his pen and added Shawn's name to the

list. "We can subpoena him anyway. His wife's opinion of you won't matter once he's on the stand. I'm sure he'll be truthful."

"What about Leon? Is he going to testify?"

Victor nodded. "The prosecution has him on their list. The good thing is his testimony does not directly implicate you. It's circumstantial. The bad part is the gun is registered to you, and your prints were all over it."

"I just don't understand. How did a gun get registered in my name if I didn't apply for it?"

"I'm still working on that. The paperwork has your signature on it. I plan to call a handwriting expert to the stand to dispute it. Also, I have the gun shop checking their records to see if they have a photo of the person who picked up the gun."

The meeting continued for more than an hour, with Victor giving Sharmaine details of what to expect when they went to court. With no other choice, his outline of defense was that Sharmaine had been framed. He intended to use the handwriting expert to cast doubt that she purchased the gun. He also had the forensics report. There was no evidence that Sharmaine had fired a gun, as no powder residue was found on her hands. The prosecution would simply say she washed it off, but he intended to bring it up anyway.

She listened intently, until he said something that stunned her.

"The judge made a ruling, and they are going to allow the sex tape as evidence. Clips will be shown to the jury," he said.

Gasping, Sharmaine covered her mouth with her hand. "You have got to be kidding."

"I'm afraid I'm not. I fought it as hard as I could. I argued that it had nothing to do with this case. The prosecution says it's relevant to your motive. They state you shot Leon after he confronted you about the tape. It also serves to strip your credibility as a loving and devoted wife."

"This is horrible. That means any bystander in the courtroom will be able to see it."

"Well, no. The good news is that the courtroom will be invitation only. Because of your celebrity status, I was able to get the media banned. No one will be allowed inside unless they have a court-ordered reason to be there. Also, there is no proof that it's even you in those tapes, and I will make a point of that."

"Thank you, Victor. I know that things don't look good right now, but I really do appreciate everything you're doing to help me."

As she sat at her dining room table praying, Sharmaine called on a higher power to assist Victor with her defense.

Her prayers were suddenly interrupted when she heard keys unlocking her front door and someone walking in. "Is that you, Keisha?" she called out.

A short and stocky man with greasy black hair and hairy arms entered her dining room. "No, it's not," he answered.

Frightened, Sharmaine stood up from the table and backed up near the wall. "Who are you, and what are you doing in my house?"

"This isn't your house anymore. Hey, are you that actress?" he asked, suddenly recognizing her.

"Yes. Who are you?" she demanded.

The man extended his tanned hand for her to shake. "The name's Lou Giordano," he answered. He pulled his hand back when he realized she wasn't going to take it.

"Okay, Mr. Giordano—"

"Call me Lou," he said, interrupting her.

"All right then, Lou. What are you doing in my house?"

"I thought you'd be gone by now. I bought this place at auction a week ago."

Sharmaine's brow wrinkled in confusion. "What do you mean you bought it at auction? I never authorized anyone to sell this condo."

Lou looked at her strangely. "This property went up for auction for delinquent property taxes. Maybe you didn't authorize the sale, but DeKalb County certainly did. I own it." He reached into his back pocket and pulled out a deed of sale. He handed it to Sharmaine.

Sharmaine skimmed the paper with her address written at the top. When she was done, she handed it back to Lou. "There must be some mistake. I'm sure my accountant has kept up with the tax payments."

"I don't know about all that. All I know is that you're in my place. I came over to see what kind of shape it was in. You've taken good care of it. I appreciate that. Most of the times when I buy these places, even in a good neighborhood like this, it's a mess. I'm sure you understand." He looked around the dining room, then pulled a tape measure from his pocket and began measuring the length of the room.

Sharmaine understood perfectly. Leon's business purchased several foreclosed or tax delinquent properties, and he spent thousands repairing them. "I do understand, Lou, but this condo is not one of those properties."

Lou put his tape measure back into his pocket. "Look, lady, it's obvious there is some kind of confusion. Tell ya what. I'll give you a few days to vacate the place. I paid my money, so I know this is my property, but I won't throw you out on the street." He reached into his burgeoning back pocket and pulled out his wallet. He reached inside it for a business card then handed it to Sharmaine. "You can reach me at this number once you have your affairs squared away."

He turned to walk out of the dining room then stopped. "I'll be back on Friday, whether I hear from you or not. I'd suggest you have all of your things out."

As soon as he was gone, Sharmaine locked the door, turned the deadbolt, and latched the chain. She went to the phone to call Keisha.

"Hey, Sharmaine, what's up?" she asked.

"Some weird Italian guy was just here and he says he owns my condo."

"What are you talking about? You own your condo."

"He says that the taxes were not paid and he bought it at an auction. Do you know anything about delinquent tax notices?"

Keisha shifted the phone from her right to her left ear. "Sharmaine, I never handled any of that stuff. Have you called your accountant?"

"Will you call him for me?" she whined. "I just can't deal with any more bad news right now. See if you can find out what's going on and get back to me."

"Sure," Keisha answered. "Just relax. I left you some home-made smoothies in the refrigerator. Why don't you drink one for breakfast, and I'll be over this afternoon. It's probably some stupid clerk's error."

"That's a good idea, Keisha. I'll see you when you get here."

***

Three hours later, Keisha arrived at Sharmaine's condo. She tried using her key to get in the front door, but was blocked by the deadbolt and the chain. She knocked loudly on the door. "Sharmaine, it's me, Keisha. Let me in."

When there was no answer, Keisha went around the yard to the back door. She let herself into Sharmaine's kitchen. Leisurely, she walked around the condo, leaving items. Finally, she went into the master bedroom, where she found Sharmaine face down on the floor. Keisha walked over and knelt beside her. She lifted her wrist to check for a pulse. It was faint, but steady.

Casually, she walked into the living room and dialed 911. When she was through speaking with the dispatcher, she sat down on the couch and flipped on the television. Scanning channels, she stopped at a rerun of *Sanford and Son* and began laughing hysterically.

Sharmaine blinked at the blaring white light shining in her face. Momentarily, she wondered if this was the end. She'd heard stories of people dying and seeing a calming bright light that beckoned them forward. But this light was different. It moved and flashed back and forth, almost blinding her. She didn't feel calm or want to go toward it. It frightened her. She blinked again, trying to make it go away.

"Mrs. Cleveland, can you hear me?"

Suddenly, Sharmaine opened her eyes. She stared into the young Caucasian doctor's face as he flashed his pen light from one pupil to the other. Confused, Sharmaine looked around the white room.

"Where am I?" she asked

"You're in the hospital, Mrs. Cleveland," the doctor answered.

"What . . . what happened to me?" she asked.

"I was hoping you would tell me that."

Sharmaine just stared at him, confused. The doctor put his pen light into his jacket pocket; then he put the end of his stethoscope into his ears. Holding it to Sharmaine's chest, he listened intently for a few moments.

"Your heart rate is almost back to normal. I'll be back to check on you again later," he stated. After scribbling notes on her chart, he walked out.

Looking around the room Sharmaine was scared and confused. *Did I have another blackout?* she wondered. After the last incident, she'd finally gone to see a doctor. He ran a myriad of tests, but said he couldn't find anything physically wrong with her. He'd suggested the blackouts were mental. Sharmaine was under a lot of stress with the sex tape and upcoming trial, he had told her. They were probably the reason she was forgetful.

Sharmaine had left his office in a huff. Her condition was much more than being forgetful. Keisha told her she'd find another doctor for a second opinion, but it did little to ease her mind.

Now, lying in a hospital bed, Sharmaine feared the worst. She held up her arms and turned them, searching her arms and hands for wounds. She pulled up the blanket and looked over her body, but saw nothing out of the ordinary. Pushing the button on the bed, she raised her head and sat up. She was slightly dizzy, but otherwise she felt fine. Still confused, she tried to remember where she'd been before she woke up.

The hospital room door creaked open and someone walked in. Sharmaine felt relieved to see a familiar face.

"Keisha, what happened? How did I get here?" she asked.

"I found you in your bedroom on the floor. Sharmaine, why did you do it? I told you everything would be okay." Keisha's voice was high and frantic.

"Do what? I don't understand."

Keisha sat down on the bed and hugged Sharmaine tightly. "I'm just so glad that you're okay. Please, don't try to hurt yourself again."

Sharmaine suddenly pulled away from her. "Keisha, what are you talking about? Tell me what happened."

"You . . . you tried to kill yourself," Keisha said softly.

"No, I didn't." Sharmaine rapidly shook her head. "I wouldn't do that. There has to be some kind of mistake."

"Calm down, honey. Just calm down. It's okay now. The doctor says you are going to be just fine. They pumped your stomach just in time."

"No, I didn't do it. No." Sharmaine began weeping. Keisha held her gently in her arms.

"I found the empty pill bottles when I arrived. You had the door bolted and chained." She rubbed her hand up and down Sharmaine's back to soothe her.

"No, I did that to keep Lou out. He had a key."

"Who is Lou?"

"The man who said he bought the condo. I deadbolted the door after he left. But I didn't try to kill myself. I was waiting for you. That's the last thing that I remember."

Keisha held her tighter and patted her back. "You probably had another blackout, honey. I just thank God I arrived in time to call the paramedics."

Sharmaine held tightly to Keisha and sniffed loudly, believing she was telling the truth. There couldn't be any other explanation, she reasoned. This was more frightening than forgetting she went shopping, or even appearing drunk to her children. She'd almost taken her own life, and she had no memory of it.

"Dear God, please help me," she cried.

As if on cue, Bishop Snow walked into the room. "Hello, Sister Williams." He extended his hand to Keisha.

"Bishop Snow, what are you doing here?" Keisha asked.

"I came to see Sister Cleveland."

Keisha stood up from the bed and shook his hand then walked away from the bed to the other side of the room.

Bishop Snow stepped closer to the bed to greet Sharmaine. "How are you feeling, Sister?" he asked.

"Bishop, I . . . I . . ." Sharmaine tried to speak, but her tears washed away the words.

Taking a seat in the chair next to the bed, Bishop Snow reached out and took her hand. "You don't have to speak, Sister. God knows what's on your heart."

Sharmaine nodded and held his hands tightly. Bishop Snow closed his eyes and began to pray reverently.

"Dear God, I come to you on behalf of your daughter, Sharmaine. Her heart is heavy with fear and confusion. We plead the blood into Sister Cleveland's life, and ask for your covering."

"Yes, Father. Oh, please, Father," Sharmaine chanted with her eyes tightly closed.

"We thank you for your grace and mercy. Father in heaven, we bind this evil that has come into her life. We bind it in the

name of your son, Jesus Christ. You said in your words whatever is bound on earth shall be bound in heaven, Father."

Bishop Snow suddenly opened his eyes and stared directly
at Keisha. Staring deep into her eyes, he continued to pray.
"Satan has no power over your daughter. No matter what, I
know you will not allow him to harm one hair on her head.
All power is in your hands, oh Heavenly Father. We love you
and we praise you."

"Thank you, Father. I praise you, dear Father," Sharmaine
whispered.

"I submit to you our prayer in the name of Jesus Christ.
Amen." Bishop Snow turned back to Sharmaine and patted
her hand with reassurance.

Keisha stood in the corner of the room, shaking with fear
as she watched Bishop Snow walk out.

Three days later, Sharmaine was released from the hospital.
She felt happy to finally be able to leave, but that was the only
joy she felt. While she was recuperating, Keisha had told her
that Lou Giordano really did own her condo. When she was
released on bail, the judge had ordered a freeze placed on
her personal bank accounts. Keisha explained that this was
done to prevent her from leaving the country. The judge felt
that with her wealth and celebrity status, she was a flight risk.
Because of the freeze on the accounts, the tax bill, which was
placed on auto-draft from Sharmaine's account, went unpaid
for several months before being placed up for auction. A notice had been placed in the newspaper regarding the sale, but
went unanswered.

Keisha arranged for all of Sharmaine's furniture to be

placed in storage. She also informed her that with the freeze on her accounts, she was running very low on money. There wasn't enough to move into a hotel. Instead, Sharmaine was moving in with Keisha at her apartment. It wasn't as luxurious as she'd been used to, but Sharmaine paid Keisha well. She had a nice apartment located in downtown Atlanta. Sharmaine would be moving into her guest bedroom, at least until after the trial.

Sharmaine sat on the edge of her hospital bed and signed the paperwork the nurse put in front of her. When she was done, she waited for Keisha to arrive to pick her up.

"Hey, girl," Keisha said, smiling. She walked in carrying a small bouquet of flowers. "I picked these up in the gift shop for you."

"Thank you, Keisha. I've signed everything and I'm ready to go."

"Great. I packed your clothes and moved them to my place. I also sent your keys to Lou. He said he's probably changing the locks anyway."

"I still can't believe I lost my condo. Leon and I originally bought it as investment property, but over the past few months it's become like home. I'm going to miss it."

Keisha nodded. "I understand. Oh, but I do have some good news for you."

"What is it? I need to hear something good."

"Victor called and told me that he was able to get your trial date moved back due to your hospital stay. It's been pushed back another month, so you don't have to show up in court on Monday."

Sharmaine smiled weakly then followed Keisha out of the room. The hospital security guard that was waiting in the hallway led them downstairs and out of the private entrance to avoid the paparazzi that had been camped outside during her visit.

When they arrived at her apartment, Keisha unlocked the door. "Home, sweet home," she sang. She pushed the door open and held out her arm, inviting Sharmaine to go in first.

The apartment was modestly furnished, with minimal decorations. There was a small couch and love seat in the living room, and a throw rug under the coffee table.

"Where's my room?" Sharmaine asked as soon as she was inside.

"It's the last door on the left. All of your things are already in there. Why don't you lie down for a while?"

Sharmaine nodded and walked down the hallway to her room.

Keisha closed the front door and leaned on it. "Things are working out way better than I imagined." She smiled contently to herself.

Chapter Thirteen

Camille ran to Danté as soon as she saw him and hugged him tightly. "I missed you so much," she said.

Danté smiled as he leaned down and kissed her lips. "Me too, baby. How'd you get away from the warden?"

"I asked to take my little brother and sister to visit my mom. He's been bugging me to visit her for a while, so I knew it was a surefire way to get out of the house."

Danté looked behind Camille and suddenly noticed Jeanna and Rodney. He cocked his head back and nodded at them. "What up?" he said.

"Weren't you at the pool party at our house last summer?" Jeanna asked.

"Yeah, that was me." Dante turned back to Camille. "Are they cool?" He motioned toward Rodney and Jeanna.

Camille turned and glared at them. "They had better be," she answered.

It had been an uphill battle getting Leon to agree to another visit after the last had gone so horribly wrong. Rodney and Jeanna believed their mother had gotten sick, so they could not understand why Leon wouldn't let them visit her again.

One night, while they were all watching television, there was a news report that Sharmaine was in the hospital. The report said Sharmaine had attempted suicide. Rodney and

Jeanna begged to be allowed to visit her at the hospital, but Leon said no; however, he had called and spoken to Keisha in order to ease their worry.

After Sharmaine moved into Keisha's apartment, Jeanna restarted her campaign to visit her mother. They would not be alone, as Keisha would be there, she reasoned. They wouldn't stay long, because Keisha's apartment wasn't very big. Rodney argued that their mother was depressed and needed to be cheered up. Leon wouldn't budge.

During this time, Camille was busy trying her best to fly under the radar, as she knew Leon was watching her every move. She still sneaked outside to the playhouse regularly in order to smoke weed, but she decided to be more discreet. Instead of sneaking out late at night, as she felt Leon expected, she switched to sneaking out in the early morning hours before dawn. By getting up at 4:30 A.M. she was able to sneak outside, leisurely smoke a joint, then come back inside and shower and brush her teeth before he and the rest of the family were awake.

That had worked successfully for a few weeks, but she'd smoked the last of her stash and needed more. Leon still had possession of her cell phone, so she realized she had to find another way to get in touch with Danté.

With that in mind, she had barged into Jeanna's bedroom without knocking. "I need to use your cell phone," she said.

Jeanna was lying in the middle of the floor on her stomach. She looked up from the novel she was reading. "Where's your new phone?"

"Dad took it when he grounded me. I just need to make one quick phone call. Come on, give it to me."

Jeanna stared at her sister, noticing she was jumpy and

fidgeting. She couldn't stand still, and she kept shifting her weight back and forth on her feet.

"I will if you tell me something."

"What?" Camille said. Her voice was agitated.

"Where were you that night you disappeared? Everybody was worried about you, Camille."

"It's none of your business where I was," she snapped.

Jeanna rolled her eyes and went back to reading her book.

Trying to stop fidgeting, Camille sat down on Jeanna's bed. "Okay, I was with a boy. We didn't do anything. We were just hanging out, and I lost track of time."

Jeanna put down her book and looked at Camille. "Why were you acting so funny when you came home?"

"I don't know. I guess I was just tired. Uncle Jack was trippin'. It was just a crazy morning." Camille paused. "I told you. Can I use the phone?"

Jeanna got up from the floor and retrieved the phone from her purse. She handed it to Camille.

Danté was glad to hear from her. He had wondered where she was. He had called her phone once, but when her dad answered, he hung up. Camille filled him in on her punishment. Then Danté asked if he could see her again and she happily agreed, until she realized that once again she needed a plan to get out of the house. This time, she didn't intend to end up grounded for two more weeks.

The next morning, she walked into the kitchen as Rodney and Jeanna were in the midst of begging to see Sharmaine again, and a light bulb seemed to appear over her head. Casually, she sat down at the table and took a bite out of her bacon. "I'll take them," she said, surprising everyone.

"What did you say?" Leon asked.

"I said I'll take them. If you let me drive my own car, I'll take them to see Mom." Camille took another bite of bacon and sipped her juice.

"What's this all about? I thought you didn't want to see your mother."

"Being grounded gives a person a lot of time to think, Dad. Besides, I saw the news report. Mom had to be really depressed to attempt suicide. We should go see her."

Leon sat back in his chair, amazed. Over the past few weeks, he'd stayed up past one A.M., sometimes even two A.M., each night waiting to catch Camille sneaking out, but he never had. When he peeked into her room each night, she was sound asleep. Each morning, she'd been up and dressed for school with the other children with no problem. She still spent most of her time in her room, sulking and brooding, but he had to admit there had been no new incidents. He also felt that having Camille with them would make him feel more at ease. If Sharmaine was drinking or got drunk, Camille would bring the kids right home.

"I'll think about it," he answered. "Finish your breakfast."

When the kids returned from school that afternoon, Leon had given his answer. They were all in the family room watching television when he walked in.

"I've decided to let Camille drive you guys to visit your mother."

Jeanna and Rodney jumped up and squealed.

"Wait. There are some rules." Leon turned to Camille. "I'm putting my trust in you, Camille. Please don't let me down again. I've spoken to Keisha, and she and your mother are expecting you tomorrow at six. Since Keisha's apartment is so small, your mother wants to take you to dinner. I expect you to be there on time, and back here before eleven o'clock."

Camille grinned. "I promise, Dad." She reached out and hugged him tightly.

Later that evening, she'd borrowed Jeanna's phone and called Danté again to make plans. He told her he was no longer living at the shelter, and gave her directions to his apartment in Bankhead. She wrote it all down, and hid it in her jeans pocket.

On the drive over, Camille had told Rodney and Jeanna that she had to make a quick stop and pick up a package. She had promised that when she was done, they'd go over to Keisha's and visit Sharmaine. Then she warned them if they breathed a word of where they'd been to their dad or anyone else, she'd never take them to see Sharmaine again.

They drove for more than a half hour to northwest Atlanta. The closer they got to Danté's apartment, the worse the neighborhoods became. They passed dilapidated buildings, liquor stores, and an assortment of unsavory-looking individuals. Finally, they pulled into the apartment complex where he lived. It was a collection of two-story brick buildings with four apartments on each level. Camille felt a slight twinge of apprehension as she'd never been that far into the ghetto before. She quickly checked to be sure all of the car doors were locked.

As soon as she parked in front of Danté's building, she borrowed Jeanna's phone and called Keisha. "There's a bad traffic accident. We are running late. I called so you guys wouldn't be worried," she lied.

Then, just to cover her tracks, she called Leon and told him the same thing. She'd just hung up the phone when Danté strolled into the breezeway. She jumped out and ran to him.

"So, you say you missed me, huh?" he asked.

Camille nodded. "But I can't stay long. I told them we were delayed by a traffic accident."

"Come on, let's go upstairs," he said.

Camille turned to Rodney and Jeanna. "You guys stay right here by the car. Don't move, and don't talk to anybody. Do you understand?"

Nodding their heads in unison, Rodney and Jeanna huddled closer together. Camille turned around to join Danté without noticing how frightened they looked. Their eyes darted around the parking lot. A group of teenagers was loitering on the sidewalk, staring at them. In the opposite direction they saw an old man sitting on the ground with a flattened cardboard box under him. His clothes were filthy and his hair was uncombed. They saw him scratch himself in private places while being thoroughly engrossed in an in-depth conversation with himself.

"Hold up, Camille," Danté said. He turned to the children. "Come on, shorties. It's not safe to stand around out here."

Rodney and Jeanna quickly obeyed, and the four of them climbed the steel stairs to Danté's tiny apartment. He opened the door and walked in with them close on his heels. Camille looked around the front room that appeared to be both a living room and a dining room. There was a table in the corner near the kitchen with four mismatched chairs. On the other side of the room appeared to be the living room area. It had a table with a television on it, and two end tables each with a lamp. One of the lamp shades was blue, and the other was green. Near the tables there was a rust-colored couch that appeared to have no legs because it sat extremely close to the floor.

Seated on the couch watching television was a visibly pregnant teenager. She looked to be at least seven months along. She looked up and smiled as they walked in.

"This is my sister, Nichole," Danté said. "Nichole, this is my girl, Camille. The little ones are her brother and sister." He closed the door behind them.

"Hey, y'all," Nichole answered. She leaned over and moved a pillow and some newspapers from the couch. "Have a seat."

Rodney and Jeanna cautiously sat down next to her.

"You like Tyler Perry?" she asked.

They both nodded their heads.

"I was just about to watch his latest movie on DVD. Y'all can watch with me if you want." She pressed the play button to start the movie on the old nineteen-inch television.

Danté took Camille by the hand and led her down the short hallway into the back of the apartment to his bedroom. Inside he had a twin bed, and a chest of drawers with the top drawer missing. He closed the door then he pulled her close and kissed her. The two of them stood by the door necking for several minutes, until Camille broke the kiss.

"I gotta hurry up and go. My mom is waiting on us. You got what I asked for?"

"A'ight, baby, I'll get it." Danté kissed her once more then walked to his chest and opened the second drawer. He reached inside and pulled out a large Ziploc bag of weed. He handed it to Camille.

"I sneaked a hundred dollars out of my dad's wallet." She reached into her pocket to get the money.

Danté frowned. "You stole from your dad?"

"He wouldn't give me any money after the last time." She held the bills out to him.

Danté sat down on the bed and looked at her. "Camille, I don't want you stealing, especially not from your parents. Maybe I shouldn't give you this."

"What's the big deal? My dad is rich. He won't miss it."

Danté sighed. Although he had not told Camille, he had quit smoking weed. He no longer found pleasure in it, and his new job at a plastics factory required random drug tests. He was not taking any chances on getting fired by doing something stupid.

Hearing her brag about stealing, he feared Camille was smoking way too much. He was surprised when she told him she'd smoked the whole bag he'd given her before so quickly. A bag that large would have lasted him several months if he still indulged. The fact that she had smoked it in two weeks really bothered him. Now he was worried that she was getting in too deep. He felt guilty, and regretted getting her started.

"Look, stealing is wrong. It doesn't matter if your dad can afford it or not. When you get home, put that money back in your dad's wallet. I'll give you this, my treat. Just promise me you won't steal anymore."

Camille grinned. "I promise, baby."

They heard a knock at Danté's door. Camille quickly stuffed the bag into her pocket while Danté walked over and opened it. Jeanna stood there holding out her cell phone.

"Camille, it's Ms. Keisha," she said.

Nervously, Camille took the phone. "Um . . . hello," she said.

"Are you guys still stuck on Eighty-five?" Keisha asked.

"Yeah, we've only inched up a little bit."

"Take the next exit you get to, then turn around and head

back home. I saw the accident on the news. The highway is going to be tied up for a while."

Camille was shocked. "Um, the accident is on the news?"

"Yes, it looks like an overturned tanker. It will probably not be cleared for several hours." Keisha paused. "Your mom wants to speak to you for a moment."

Camille tensed up. She had not spoken to her mother at all since she'd moved out. Planning to sneak away and see Danté had occupied her thoughts so much that she'd completely forgotten how she'd react when she actually had to see her face to face. She definitely was not prepared to talk to her. She quickly handed the phone to Jeanna as soon as she heard her voice. "It's Mom," she said.

Camille sat down on the bed next to Danté and laid her head on his shoulder.

When she was done speaking to Sharmaine, Jeanna closed her cell phone and explained the conversation to them. "Mom says for us to ask Dad if we can meet her for dinner next Friday. She said she'd make it easier and meet us at the restaurant."

Camille nodded. "I guess we'd better head home then before she calls Dad."

"I told her not to bother because I'd tell him what happened and get his permission for next week. Can we stay and finish the movie?" Jeanna asked.

"Are you trying to get me grounded again?" Camille looked at her as if she had antennas growing from her head.

"No, I just really want to see this movie. As long as we're home by eleven, Dad doesn't have to know where we were."

Camille laid her head back on Danté s shoulder "Okay by me," she answered.

Jeanna closed the door and went back to the living room.

"Your little sister is mad cool," Dante said.

"Yeah, who knew?" Camille laughed. "Hey, you never told me you had a sister."

Danté chuckled. "You never asked."

He lay back on the bed, pulling Camille down next to him. He kissed her forehead and snuggled up closer to her.

"How come she wasn't with you at the pool party?" Camille asked.

"She was still at the foster home last year. As soon as I turned eighteen and found a job, I rented this place for the two of us. It's not much, but it's clean and it's ours. Nobody can make us leave."

"How old is she?"

"She just turned fifteen."

"Wow, that's awfully young. I mean, I don't know what I'd do if I'd gotten pregnant that young."

Danté suddenly sat up on the bed. "Don't judge her. It's not her fault. It's mine."

Surprised, Camille sat up beside him. "What do you mean it's your fault?"

Danté looked over at her. "I never should've left her alone there. I knew our foster dad was a jerk. His wife was cool, but he seemed to be jealous that she took an interest in us. Miss Donna took me and Nichole to church on Sundays. She helped us with our homework. That lady even baked home-made cookies. For a while it was a decent place to live."

Camille scooted closer to Danté. "So what happened? Why'd you leave?"

"Neville, that was his name, he had a poker game while Miss Donna was at choir rehearsal, and he lost a lot of money. That fool was always gambling and losing money. Anyway, when Miss Donna asked him about it, he lied and said that I stole the money. As if it wasn't bad enough that he lied on me, he told Miss Donna I had to be punished." Danté stopped talking and raised his shirt, then turned around so Camille could see his back. "He tied me to the bed and beat me with a thick strap until I was bloody. You can still see the scars."

Camille stared at the lines on his back. Gently, she touched them with her fingers. "Wow," she whispered.

Danté lowered his shirt and turned around. "That's why I didn't get in the pool at your party. My back wasn't completely healed. After he went to sleep that night, I climbed out of the window and I left. I couldn't deal with it anymore. But I should've taken Nichole with me, or I should have stayed, but I never should've left her there alone with that monster." His voice cracked with emotion. "She was just a kid. She trusted him and he took advantage. He raped her. He waited until his wife was gone to work, and he raped my little sister. The baby is his."

Camille put her arm around him. "I'm so sorry," she said.

Danté struggled to keep from falling apart in front of Camille while he continued telling her the story. "She ran away, too, after that, and we stayed at the shelter for a few months. But when she discovered she was pregnant, they said she had to leave. They didn't even let her tell them the situation. They just said pregnancy was unacceptable for any teen at that shelter. They offered to transfer her to a home for unwed mothers, but it was in South Carolina. I wasn't about to let them split us up again. I'm just glad that we found this place."

Camille could not find any words to say after his story. She just held him as close as she could. They sat in silence for several minutes.

"Hey, you wanna help me smoke this?" Camille said. She reached into her pocket.

"Um . . . I don't smoke in the apartment. It's not good for my sister."

"Then let's go outside," she suggested.

Danté looked at her oddly. "I don't wanna smoke any weed. Can't we just sit here and chill for a while?"

"We can chill while we get high." She stood up and grabbed his arm, trying to pull him off the bed.

"Camille, I said no." He pulled his arm away from her.

Camille suddenly blew up. "What is wrong with you?" she screamed. "I spent all week planning to come over here, and now you're acting all stupid."

Danté stared at Camille, wondering not what was wrong with him, but what was wrong with her. "I don't wanna get high, and I don't think you should either. I made a mistake. Gimme the weed back." He held out his hand.

"No! It's mine," she screamed.

He stood up. "Come on, Camille. Give it to me."

She stuffed the bag into her pocket. "No. You said I could have it. We don't have to smoke it now. I can wait until I get home." Tears welled up in her eyes. "Don't take it away from me," she pleaded.

His heart crumbled as she started to cry. He reached out to hug her and she backed away. "I'm not gonna take it from you." He held his arms open for her and she slowly walked in. He held her tightly. "Don't cry, baby."

Danté held her closely, feeling guilt and shame. He realized he'd made a huge mistake giving her weed, and now she was hooked. He knew it was only a matter of time before she'd need a bigger high and turn to stronger drugs. "Come on, let's just chill and listen to some music," he said.

She nodded her head and they lay back on the bed in each other's arms.

When the movie they had been watching was over, Jeanna came back to Danté's room and knocked on the door. He got up off the bed and opened it.

"I think we'd better go. It's almost ten," Jeanna said.

They all said good-bye to Nichole, then Danté walked them outside to Camille's car. He opened Camille's door and closed it for her after she was inside. He leaned down into the window. "See ya later, shorties" he said to Rodney and Jeanna. They smiled and waved at him. He leaned in and kissed Camille lightly on the lips.

Danté stood outside and watched them drive away. He made a mental note that he would not give Camille weed again. He knew she'd be upset, but he had to help her quit since he felt responsible for getting her started. After the car lights disappeared, he trotted back up the stairs to his apartment.

Camille pulled into the gate of their home at 10:45. "We're on time with a few minutes to spare," she said. "Now, do we all have our stories straight for Dad?"

"Yeah," Rodney answered. "We were delayed by the accident on the highway, so we got to Mom's late and decided not to go out to dinner. She made us sandwiches and we talked."

"Okay, that's good. That way if Dad saw the accident on the news too, our story makes sense. Are you guys hungry? I forgot we didn't eat."

"Nichole gave us spaghetti. She's a great cook," Jeanna answered.

"Well, I guess I'm the only one who didn't eat. I'll grab a snack before I go to bed." Camille pulled her car into the garage and parked it.

The three of them walked into the house through the back door into the kitchen. They were surprised to see Leon sitting at the table waiting for them.

"Hey, Dad," Camille said. She walked over and hung her car keys on the hook by the stove.

"Where have you been?" he asked.

"We were at Mom's. We got there late because of the accident on the highway," Rodney answered.

"We had a good time," Jeanna chimed in.

Leon slowly stood up from the table. "Keisha called me hours ago. She said that she told you to turn around and come home because of the accident." He turned to Camille. "Now you've got your brother and sister lying for you too?"

Camille's eyes grew big and she stared at him in disbelief. "Dad . . . we, um . . ." she stammered.

"Please don't tell me another lie, Camille."

"Dad, I'm sorry. Please don't punish Rodney and Jeanna. It was my fault. I wanted to see Danté, so I asked them to cover for me. We were going to go see Mom too, but Ms. Keisha told us not to come. I know we should have come straight back. I'm sorry, Dad."

"Who is Danté?" he asked.

Camille stared at the floor. "He's the boy I met at the pool party last summer."

Leon searched his memory banks until it registered on the bald-headed kid Camille had spent most of the party with. He realized that must also be who Jackson had seen her with the night she disappeared. "Is that who you spent the night with? Are you having sex with this boy?"

"No, Dad. I swear it. Rodney and Jeanna were there the whole time. Nothing happened." She looked over at her siblings for help.

"He's a nice guy, and his sister cooked us dinner," Rodney said.

"Yeah, Nichole is really sweet. We watched a movie together. She said if I wanted, I could babysit for her," Jeanna said.

Leon stared at his three children with a bewildered look. Then he turned to Camille. "You took your brother and sister to the shelter to visit a boy, and he had a sister with a child?"

"No, Dad, he doesn't live at the shelter anymore. They have their own apartment out in Bankhead. Nichole doesn't have a child, but she's pregnant."

"I've heard enough. I can't believe you three were hanging out in the ghetto with some thug and his pregnant sister. I want you all upstairs in your rooms. I can't stand to hear any more of this. Camille, I don't want you sneaking out to see Danté anymore. Now, all of you need to go to bed."

"But, Dad, you don't understand," Camille whined.

"Go upstairs now!" he yelled.

Rodney and Jeanna quickly obeyed, but Camille stood defiantly staring at her father. "You don't know anything about them, and you stand here and pass judgments. How dare you?"

Leon pointed his finger. "Camille, I'm warning you," he said.

"I don't care, Dad! You can ground me forever. It won't matter. You can't lock me in my room. You have no right to stand here all high and mighty calling them names. Your wife is an adulterer and an attempted murderer. If you want to keep me away from somebody, why don't you start with her?"

Camille ran from the kitchen and up to her room.

Chapter Fourteen

Leon lay awake in the darkness for hours, unable to sleep. He finally grew weary of tossing and turning, so he got up and sat on the edge of his bed. Turning on the light by his bedside, he noticed his Bible was lying on the nightstand and he picked it up. Flipping through the pages, he searched for answers.

Although he'd repeatedly told himself that it was important, he still had not set up a drug counseling session for Camille. He'd allowed himself to be lulled into a false sense of accomplishment since there had been no new problems. He also was reluctant because he'd realized that being focused on Camille's issue allowed him the freedom to hide from his own feelings. Leon knew that if he took Camille to counseling to discuss her feelings for Sharmaine, then inevitably he'd be asked to discuss his own. He wasn't ready to do that.

In the past months, he'd averted his feelings by first focusing on his health. It wasn't easy to recover from four bullet wounds, he'd told himself. That's the excuse he'd given his board of directors to justify the leave of absence he had taken from his company. While they thought he spent his days growing healthier and stronger, the truth was he spent most days daydreaming of Sharmaine and better times.

When the problems began with Camille, he threw himself

head first into the role of Super Dad. He loved her and was genuinely worried, but he was also using it as a way to hide. Leon felt he had to hide in order to cope. Although he'd begun to believe the woman in the video was Sharmaine, he still could not wrap his mind around the thought that she'd actually shot him. He was sure there was some other explanation; that is, until Jackson told him she'd gotten drunk while visiting with the kids. That revelation caused him to question everything he'd ever believed to be true about the woman he'd married.

Just when Leon began to believe he was dealing with his emotions and beginning to put his relationship with Sharmaine out of his mind, he'd seen the news report of her attempted suicide. Without thinking, he'd gotten in his car and driven to the hospital. He had to see her. He couldn't let her die without him by her side. When he arrived, he found that he didn't have the nerve to get out of the car. Instead, he'd called Bishop Snow and asked him to check on Sharmaine for him. When he found out she'd be okay, he sat in the hospital parking lot and wept with relief.

Leon stopped flipping through his Bible and checked the bedside clock. It was almost four A.M. and he had not had a wink of sleep. Kneeling beside the bed, he began to pray. As he prayed, he heard a clear, still, small voice speaking. The Spirit let him know that he could not help Camille until he took the necessary steps to help himself.

Leon put on his robe and slippers and left his bedroom. Without bothering to turn on any lights, he went downstairs to Sharmaine's office. He had not entered the room even once since he returned home after being shot. In Leon's mind, that room was Sharmaine. It contained her awards, her accomplishments, her photographs, and her essence. Everything anyone would ever want to know about Sharmaine Cleveland was contained in that room. Somehow, Leon felt there had to be something that would lead him to some answers to the questions dancing around in his head. There had to be a reasonable explanation for the video, the shooting, and the drinking. He just had to find it; and he reasoned that her office was the best place to start.

When he arrived downstairs, he walked over to the office. The mahogany door stood staring him down like a worthy opponent as Leon wrestled with the courage to push it open and walk in. He stood in the doorway for several moments before reaching for the light and turning it on. Once inside, he closed the door behind him.

For several moments, he stood in the middle of the floor just looking around. The cover photo of Sharmaine's first CD release hanging on the wall caught his eye, and he stared at it for several moments. In the photo, her hair was long and wavy, and she seemed to be floating in a sea of clouds. They swirled around her head and body, causing her to appear almost angelic.

Next he turned toward the wall that contained her Grammy and American Music Awards. They were dusty, as he'd kept the room closed since Sharmaine's departure. Consuela had opened it once, intending to clean, but he'd quickly stopped her. Walking over, he picked each award up, studied it, and then returned it to its place.

Leon walked over to Sharmaine's desk and sat down. He opened her drawers and rifled through the papers contained inside. He picked up each one and glanced over it before putting it back.

There's nothing here I haven't seen before, he thought.

Finally, his attention turned to her laptop computer sitting on the desk. It was the first time he'd realized that she didn't take it with her. Momentarily, he wondered why; then he assumed that it was because neither expected she'd be gone for five months.

Leon opened the computer and put in Sharmaine's password. The computer booted up, and to his surprise, he was greeted by several hundred unread emails. *Keisha usually reads all of this stuff. I wonder why she's not checking it anymore.*

Still hoping for answers, he randomly clicked on e-mails, reading them until he came to one from Chase Vinton that held his interest.

> Sharmaine,
> I'm livid that this video is still floating around the Internet. You and your people need to get busy doing something about this. I'm sure with your upcoming trial the chance of a movie release is unlikely; however, I'd like to try to have a career after this fiasco. Do something about this!
> Chase

The email had a video attached. Leon sat staring at the link, wondering if he should click on it. Other than the few moments in the detective's office, Leon had not seen the now infamous video. At first he'd wanted to obtain a copy, but Jackson convinced him it was a bad idea. Now with it sitting in front him, Leon wasn't sure why, but he felt compelled to watch it. With his hands shaking, he pressed the computer mouse and clicked on the video. Silently, he sat watching his wife perform acts that were supposed to be reserved only for him. His heart ached and tears were streaming down his face, but he vowed not to turn away.

The camera zoomed in, and Leon's eyes grew wide with surprise. All of a sudden, he noticed something vaguely familiar about the room that Sharmaine and the mystery man were in. Leon put the video on pause and took a closer look. When he did, he noticed something else that caught his eye. He was still staring at it when he heard a thump. He quickly shut down the computer to investigate.

Leon opened the office door and looked out into the hallway from right to left. He saw nothing, but he heard another thump and realized it was coming from the kitchen. Slowly, he tiptoed toward the sound. He arrived in the kitchen just as Camille was disarming the alarm. Without a word, he watched her punch in the numbers; then she reached for the back door. She turned the knob slowly, trying not to make a sound.

"Camille Amanda Cleveland, what are you doing?"

Startled, Camille almost jumped out of her skin. "Dad, what are you doing up?" she stammered.

"I think you need to answer that question for me."

"Oh, I was hungry. I came down for a snack. I'm sorry if I woke you."

He shook his head at her latest lie. "I stood here and watched you turn off the alarm and try to go out the back door. Where were you going?"

"Nowhere. I just wanted to take a walk."

Leon stepped closer to Camille and she backed up. He took another step and she backed up even farther. Camille kept backing away from him until she found herself trapped like a rat with her back against the counter.

"Give it to me," Leon said.

"I . . . I don't know what you're talking about."

"The weed, Camille. Give it to me now." Leon held out his hand and stared directly at her.

"Why are you always accusing me of things? All I did was come to the kitchen for a snack and then try to take a walk," she whined.

Leon stood very still, not moving a muscle. Inside, he was struggling with his anger and emotions. In his entire life, he'd never put his hands on Camille except in a loving manner. Even when she was younger and received spankings, it was always Sharmaine who'd administered them. They agreed that he was too big and too strong to ever lay his hands on the children. It had never been a problem for Leon, as he felt capital punishment should only be used sparingly. Camille had long ago outgrown being spanked by either of her parents; however, as he stood there staring at her, lying and rebellious, it took all of his inner strength not to draw back and knock her out.

Taking a deep breath, he asked her once more. "Camille, I know that you have weed on you and that you were sneaking out to smoke it. Now, you can either give it to me willingly, or I'm going to pin you down and take it. It's your choice."

Camille looked around the kitchen, trying to determine if she had enough room to run. If she went to her left, she thought she could make it outside; but she realized that even if she did, he'd catch up to her within seconds. Looking into her father's face, she saw an urgency she'd never seen before, and it frightened her. Feeling defeated, she reached into her pocket and pulled out the Ziploc bag of weed. Slowly, she handed it to Leon.

When he returned to the kitchen a few moments later after flushing it down the toilet, Camille was sitting at the table with her head lying on her arms. Leon walked closer to her and noticed her shoulders shaking as she sobbed. Quietly, he sat down beside her and rubbed her back for comfort.

"Camille, I don't understand. We've talked about drugs and how they can hurt you. You've seen the videos at school and church. Please, tell me why." Leon handed her a napkin from the table to dry her tears as she slowly sat up.

"Everything is all messed up. Nothing makes sense anymore."

"Do you mean the situation with your mother and the trial?"

"I mean everything. This house doesn't feel like home anymore; it feels like a prison. We never do fun things. We hardly ever go anywhere. The kids at school call us ugly names, but you make us go every day."

Leon sighed. "I know it's hard, honey."

"No, you don't. If you did, you'd do something about it. Instead, all you do is feel sorry for yourself and mope around this house." Camille stood up from the table. "I'm going back to bed."

Stunned, all he could manage to mumble was a weak, "Good night, honey."

Sitting alone in his kitchen, Leon stared outside the window until the sun began to rise. For months, he'd told himself that the problems with his family, his children, and his life were all due to the incidents with Sharmaine. He'd barely taken the time to notice that his actions were also negatively affecting his children. As difficult as it was to admit, Camille was absolutely correct.

When he had returned home from the hospital, he immediately demanded that they return also. His mother and father had pleaded with him to allow the children to remain with them. They told him that they could finish out the school year there, but he refused. He'd told them and himself that it was to put his family back together; but other than living under the same roof, they had never done that. The children went to school, and while they were gone, he sulked. They returned home and tried to talk to him during meals, and he sulked. He had to admit that it was his sulking that caused him to take them from church the one time he'd attended. Since that Sunday, they had not returned.

Jeanna spent most of her time watching one movie after the other. It seemed as if she was always staring at the television or her head was buried inside a book. He realized that she rarely talked, laughed, or smiled.

His mind wandered to Rodney and his behavior the past few months. His son had almost disappeared. Without Leon or anyone stopping him, Rodney, who was once a loud and rambunctious kid, had become as quiet and obscure as a piece of the furniture. The only time either of them spoke or showed any emotions was when they were begging Leon to allow them to visit their mother, and he'd repeatedly shut them down. Leon felt shame that he'd selfishly cut off their visits.

Believing it was for their own good, he'd avoided discussing Sharmaine or anything about her until the fight happened between Jeanna and Camille. He'd promised them at that time that he would be honest and open, but since then, he'd clammed up again on the subject of their mother. Without his guidance to help them understand, his children had been forced to rely on the things they saw on television, read on gossip blogs online, or the horrible words spoken to them by their peers.

"How could I have been so stupid?" he wondered aloud.

Consuela suddenly entered the back door and interrupted his thoughts. "Good morning, Mr. Leon," she said.

Having been awake all night, Leon abruptly realized that it was a new day and his children would be coming downstairs for breakfast soon. "Good morning, Consuela," he replied politely.

"Do you and the children have any special plans today? It's a beautiful Saturday morning."

An idea struck him out of nowhere. "Yes. I'm going to take them to visit their mother."

Chapter Fifteen

Keisha knocked lightly on the door to her guest bedroom, where Sharmaine was staying. "Are you awake?" She poked her head in to the bedroom.

"Yeah, what is it, Keisha?"

"Um . . . you have a phone call."

"Can you take a message? I don't feel like talking to anyone right now." Sharmaine rolled over in bed, turning her back.

Keisha shrugged her shoulders and began backing out of the room, then changed her mind. "I think you want to take this call." She laid the phone on the bed and walked out.

Sharmaine sat up in bed and grabbed the phone. "Hello," she said tentatively. All she heard was breathing on the other end. "Who is this?" The breathing continued. "Look, I don't have time for games. Stop playing on my phone." She pressed the end button and hung up, then tunneled back up under the covers. *I can't believe Keisha is not screening my calls.*

The phone rang again, almost immediately. Sharmaine snatched it up without checking the caller ID. "Hello!" she yelled.

"Don't hang up, Sharmaine. It's me, Leon."

Now it was Sharmaine's turn to just sit and breathe, as she searched for the words to say in response to him. Although she'd fantasized about it a million times, lately she'd come to believe she'd never speak to him again. At first she felt he believed in her innocence, but in the months that had passed, with no words exchanged, she'd given up that hope. Yet, from time to time she had fantasized that he would call. In her fantasy, he would suddenly remember the identity of the shooter, clearing her name. He would tell her that he still loved her. They would both feel relieved, and things would miraculously go back to the way they were. But this was no fantasy. He was really on the line, waiting for her to speak. "Hi," she said.

"Um . . . I'll make this quick. If you aren't busy, I wanted to bring the children over to spend the day with you. I'm sorry they couldn't make it last night."

"It's not your fault. Atlanta is notorious for bad accidents. I told Jeanna that we could meet for dinner next Friday. I'm sorry. I just assumed the children would have plans today."

"No, they are not doing anything important. I can drive them over around noon." Leon paused. "I won't stay," he said finally.

Sharmaine's excitement faded slightly. "Um . . . sure, that's okay. I'll let Keisha know that they are coming."

"Okay." Leon paused, and Sharmaine held her breath, hoping he had something else to say. After several seconds, he did. "Good-bye, Sharmaine."

Sharmaine threw back her covers, hopping out of bed. She quickly ran to the kitchen. "Keisha, that was Leon on the phone. He's bringing the children over to see me this afternoon." Sharmaine beamed.

"He's doing what?" Keisha looked up from her bowl of Frosted Flakes, her spoon suspended in midair.

"He's bringing the children over this afternoon. Can you

believe it? He called me. I actually spoke to Leon. Oh, Keisha, he sounded so wonderful."

Keisha put the spoon down in her bowl. "Did you think about asking me first? You are living in my home now."

The smile slowly faded from Sharmaine's face. "Oh, I'm sorry. You're right. I should have asked first. I was just so excited to be talking to Leon. I guess I forgot."

"I have plans this afternoon." Keisha stood and took her bowl to the sink. She rinsed it out then placed it in the dishwasher.

"Um, well, you go ahead with your plans. The kids and I will just hang out here. I think they opened the pool earlier this week. We could go down there."

Keisha gave her a side-eyed look. "You must be trying to make my neighbors rich by selling the photos to the *National Enquirer*. Sharmaine, you can't take your children to a public swimming pool."

"Then we can just stay here in the apartment. We could watch a movie on TV, or play games."

"What if you have another, um, episode?" Keisha eyed her closely.

Sharmaine stared at her feet. Since she'd moved in with Keisha, her health had continued to decline. She experienced headaches, blackouts, confusion, and memory loss. One morning, she'd awakened with a ringing in her ears and heart palpitations. Frantic, she had run to Keisha's room and begged to be taken to a doctor. Instead, Keisha had slowly led her back to her room.

"You forgot to take your medicine again," she had told her.

Sharmaine just stared while Keisha reminded her that she'd visited the doctor just a few days before and he'd prescribed medication for her. As hard as she tried, Sharmaine had no recollection of seeing a doctor. Keisha calmly showed her the bottle and read her name to her. Then Keisha helped her swallow her pills, and promised to remind her every day from that point on.

So far, she had kept that promise, but Sharmaine felt it didn't matter, as she increasingly felt worse. Her body ached from head to toe, and it was a struggle to even get out of bed each day. She frequently had dizzy spells and had fainted several times, prompting Keisha to advise her that she could no longer drive around on her own. Her weight was down at least twenty pounds, as she alternated between vomiting and diarrhea. Worst of all, as she'd stood in front of the bathroom mirror that previous Monday morning, Sharmaine suddenly realized her hair was falling out in big clumps. She ran her fingers across her scalp, and the pieces fell out in her hands. Once again, she'd run to Keisha for help.

"Extreme stress can cause hair loss," Keisha had calmly told her; however, to please Sharmaine, she made her an appointment to see a dermatologist. He prescribed a special shampoo that she'd used daily, but it didn't seem to be helping. With Keisha's help, she'd brushed her short hair down, covering the bald patches.

"I should be okay, Keisha. I'm going to take my medicine as soon as I go back to my room. It will only be for a few hours. I just need to see my children so badly."

Keisha sighed loudly. "I'll change my plans and stay here with you."

"Please don't do that. Go ahead with your plans. I promise the kids and I will be just fine here alone."

"It's okay, Sharmaine. I would never forgive myself if something happened to you like last time. No, I think it's best if I just stay here with you."

Sharmaine hugged her tightly. "Thank you so much. You are too good to me, Keisha."

At their Buckhead estate, Camille, Rodney, and Jeanna looked up from their breakfasts and stared at their dad in disbelief.

"You are going to take us where?" Camille asked.

"I've decided to take you to visit your mother. It's not your fault there was an accident last night. So, you can go today," Leon answered.

"Why don't I just drive us over there, Dad? We can go in my car, and you can stay here," Camille suggested.

"I'm sorry, honey, but after what happened last night, I think it's best that I drive you myself." Leon was fine with the three of them visiting their mother, but he still did not want Camille sneaking off to visit Danté.

Rodney and Jeanna were excited. Their faces lit up, and they began to chatter on and on about what they were going to do as soon as they saw their mother.

Leon listened to them for a few moments before noticing a change in Camille's demeanor. He put down his cup of coffee and turned to her. "Camille, are you okay?"

"I'm fine," she answered. Her eggs were half eaten and she had not touched her bacon, but Camille got up and left the kitchen without another word.

***

The four of them arrived at Keisha's apartment shortly after noon. Leon pulled into the parking garage and paid the attendant ten dollars to park his car. Then he and the children boarded the elevator and went up to Keisha's apartment.

Sharmaine rushed to the door as soon as she heard the doorbell. Flinging it open, her heart skipped a beat as she laid eyes on Leon for the first time since he'd been shot. He was even more handsome than she'd remembered, and she had to fight the urge to attack him with hugs and kisses.

"Hey, Mommy," Rodney said. His voice was filled with excitement and joy.

Sharmaine bent down and hugged him tightly. He went inside as she greeted Jeanna with a warm hug also. Jeanna kissed her mother's cheek then went inside the apartment.

Then there was Camille. Sharmaine put her arms around her, and Camille immediately tensed up. She stood there with her arms hanging to her side, until Sharmaine accepted the fact that she wasn't going to hug her back. Releasing her, she stepped away from the door so that Camille could enter and join the other children inside.

Sharmaine looked up at Leon still standing in the doorway. She tried to think of something clever or witty to say, but nothing came out. The two of them just stood staring at each other. Neither of them said a word.

After becoming lost in her eyes, his feet would not move Leon from the spot they were in. He wanted to hug her and kiss her and love her as if nothing had ever happened between them. Instead, he stood frozen like an iceberg, unable to budge.

Irritated by the obviously intimate moment they were sharing, Keisha stepped to the doorway and gently pushed Sharmaine aside. "I think you'd better go now, Leon. It's not good for Sharmaine's case for you to be here. I can bring the children home later."

"No, that's not necessary. But you are right. I'll send my security officer, Otis, to pick them up. He'll be here at six sharp." Without another word, Leon turned and walked down the hallway.

As Keisha returned back inside her apartment, Jeanna was excitedly telling Sharmaine about the movie she'd brought with her.

"It's about these genetically altered rabbits who take over the world. The scientist who bred them has to work with the government to stop them," she said.

"Wow, that sounds exciting," Sharmaine answered.

"Not to me it doesn't. Can we play a game instead?" Rodney asked.

"I'm sorry, honey. I don't have the Wii game here," Sharmaine answered. "But I have a bunch of other games. I have Operation, Monopoly, Connect Four and Scrabble. I bet I could beat you," Sharmaine teased.

Rodney, Jeanna, and Sharmaine all agreed to play Monopoly. While Sharmaine went to the bedroom to retrieve the games, Jeanna turned to her sister. "What's the matter with you, Camille? Come on and play the game with us. It will be fun."

"Look, I'm here. That should be enough." Camille rolled her eyes.

"Well, it's not enough. You heard what Dad said in the car. We need Mom, but most of all she needs us. You can't just sit here ignoring her all day."

"I can and I will."

"No, you won't," Rodney said. He wagged his finger at Camille. "We lied for you so that you could see Danté. Now you owe us."

Camille was surprised. Her little brother had never stood up to her before. "We got caught, so it doesn't matter," she answered. "So? We did what you asked, Camille. It's only fair that you do this for us," Rodney shot back.

Jeanna nodded her head in agreement.

"Fine. I'll play one game; then my debt is paid. You li'l rug rats will not blackmail me anymore," Camille huffed.

"Would you like to play too, Ms. Keisha?" Jeanna asked.

Keisha was sitting in the chair by the window, ignoring them as she gazed outside, appearing to be in a daze. She looked startled as she heard her name. "What did you say, sweetie?"

"We're all going to play Monopoly. Do you want to join us?"

Unable to think up a good excuse fast enough, Keisha nodded her head in agreement. She followed the children into the dining room, where Sharmaine was setting up the board game.

"I want to be the shoe," Rodney squealed. He sat down next to Sharmaine.

"You are always the shoe," Jeanna replied. "I want to be the race car."

"Give me the thimble," Keisha said. She'd suddenly decided playing games with Sharmaine's kids might be fun. "I'm the Monopoly champ. You all are going down."

Sharmaine looked over at Camille, who'd taken a seat, but was still obviously unhappy. "Here you are, Camille. I saved the top hat for you," she said and smiled at her.

Camille took her board piece without a word.

The five of them began playing, and before long, Camille was enthused and actually enjoying the game. They laughed when Keisha ended up in jail for three rounds. Then they were in hysterics when Rodney made Sharmaine pay out almost all of her money to him for his hotel on Boardwalk.

Jeanna picked up the dice for her next turn just as the front doorbell rang.

"I wonder who that is," Keisha said. She left the dining room and went to the front door.

"I'm thirsty. May I have something to drink?" Rodney asked.

"Sure. Go to the kitchen and help yourself," Sharmaine said. "We'll take a break until you and Keisha get back."

Rodney sauntered into the kitchen and opened the refrigerator. He was just about to take out a soda when he noticed a pitcher of thick pink stuff sitting on the shelf. He stuck his finger in and tasted it. Excited, he realized it was a strawberry banana smoothie, his favorite. Momentarily closing the refrigerator door, he went to the cabinet and took out a tall glass. Then he returned to the refrigerator and poured the smoothie into it. He took a long sip, drinking half of it. Rodney licked his lips, and then poured more. Rodney stood in the kitchen and drank another full glass of smoothie. When he was satisfied, he placed the pitcher back in the refrigerator and returned to the game.

Camille, Sharmaine, and Jeanna were talking idly as they waited for Keisha to return. Rodney joined them at the table.

"Who was at the door?" Sharmaine asked when Keisha returned almost twenty minutes later.

"A delivery guy, but he had the wrong address. I walked him

down the hallway to Mrs. Forrester's apartment. You know that woman loves to talk. Whose turn is it?" Keisha asked.

"Mommy, I don't feel so good," Rodney said.

Back home at his estate, Leon went to the phone to call Jackson.

"Hello."

"Jack, I need your help," Leon said.

"What's going on?" Jackson asked.

"I need you to help me find a high resolution copy of . . . of the video with Sharmaine in it."

Jackson sighed. "Not that again. I told you that you don't need to torture yourself with that video. You know it's her; now let it go."

"You don't understand, Jack. I know it's Sharmaine in the video, but, um, I think I recognize the man she's with. There's something familiar about the whole thing, but the copy I have is too distorted."

"Leon, let it go! Why does it matter who the man was?" he yelled.

"Never mind, Jackson. If you won't help me, I'll find someone else who will." Leon hung up the phone and immediately dialed another number.

"Shawn Reeves," he said when he answered.

"Hello, Shawn, it's Leon Cleveland. I need your help."

Shawn glanced over at Brenetta sitting a few feet away from him on the sofa with their pet Pekingese resting comfortably in her lap. The two of them were wearing matching leopard print jackets. Brenetta gently stroked the dog's head and made funny faces at her.

"This is a business call, baby. I'm going to take it in my office."

"Sure, baby," she answered without turning her attention from the dog.

Shawn walked out of the den and up the huge winding staircase to his home office on the second floor of their home. He took a seat behind his desk then put the phone back up to his ear. "Leon, are you still there?"

"Yes. Thank you for speaking to me in private."

"No problem. What's up?"

Leon sat down on a bar stool in his kitchen while he gathered the nerve to speak. "I was wondering if you could help me get a high resolution copy of the video featuring Sharmaine."

Shawn was taken aback. "What makes you think I have access to anything like that?"

"I was going through some paperwork in Sharmaine's office and I found the offer you made her for distribution of the videos."

"Yeah, the offer she turned down flat. That deal could have made us all a lot of money, but I've since come to realize why she said no."

"Can you get me a copy, Shawn? It's imperative that I get it as soon as possible. I can't explain it all now, but I promise if you help me, I will tell you everything."

Shawn thought for a moment. He still had the videos locked in the vault at his downtown office. After Sharmaine turned him down, he'd had several offers to sell them, but he'd declined. They continued to sit gathering dust, and he'd seriously considered destroying them. Now her husband was asking for access. Momentarily, he wondered if Leon had a sales offer, but he quickly dismissed it. He'd known Leon a long time. If he needed the video, there was a logical reason for it.

After several moments of silence, he finally answered. "Sure. I'll get back to you in a couple of days."

Leon hung up the phone feeling a slight tinge of relief. His cell phone rang again, and he casually picked it up.

"Dad, Rodney's sick. We're on our way to the hospital," Camille said.

"What happened?" he frantically asked.

"I don't know. He just suddenly started vomiting, and then his eyes rolled back in his head and he passed out." Camille began sobbing. "It looked like he wasn't breathing, Dad. Mom called nine-one-one and they just took him away in the ambulance."

"I'll be right there."

When he arrived at the hospital, Leon rushed into the emergency entrance, anxiously searching for anyone he recognized. Jeanna ran to him as he rushed down the corridor.

"Dad!" she yelled.

"Where's Rodney? How is he?"

"The doctors took him in the back. Mom and Camille are over there."

Leon ran over and embraced the two of them. He held Sharmaine tightly as they all forgot everything else that had transpired. The only thing that mattered at that moment was the health of their son.

When they finally broke the embrace, Leon began asking

questions. "He seemed fine when we left home today. Did he eat anything at your house, Sharmaine?" he asked.

"No. None of us had eaten anything. We were all sitting in the dining room playing Monopoly," she answered.

"Rodney had something to drink," Jeanna suddenly remembered.

Camille nodded her head. "That's right. He went into the kitchen for a soda right before he got sick."

The family sat for several hours, waiting for news on Rodney's condition. Leon alternated between pacing back and forth in the hallway and talking on the phone. He'd called Jackson and advised him to alert the rest of their family. As his parents and each of his brothers learned the news, they called. Leon felt helpless, as he was unable to give them any updates on Rodney's condition.

On the other end of the hallway, Sharmaine stood praying and crying. It seemed that something terrible happened whenever she was with her children, and it was tearing her apart inside. She pleaded with God to heal Rodney. As she waited and prayed, she also struggled with her own health. Her head was aching, and she'd gone to the bathroom as least three times with diarrhea.

Please, God, don't let me black out now, she prayed.

Jeanna found a television and retreated into her usual escape of watching movies, while Camille sat in a corner emotionless.

Finally, when they all felt they could not wait any longer, a young black doctor approached Leon as he was pacing up and down the corridor. Jeanna, Camille, and Sharmaine ran to his side as soon as they saw the doctor.

"Mr. Cleveland," he said as he extended his hand to Leon. Suddenly, he recognized Sharmaine. "Um, wow . . . I didn't realize I was treating your son. I'm a fan of your work," he said.

"Thank you. I appreciate that, but can you please just tell us how he is?" she asked

"Of course," he said and opened his chart. "We were finally able to stabilize him. The next few hours are going to be very critical for him. We will have to watch him closely to make sure that no significant damage has been done to any of his internal organs."

"I don't understand. He was fine one minute and the next he was violently vomiting. What happened to him?" Sharmaine asked.

The doctor looked at them all solemnly before responding. "Your son has been poisoned," he said.

Chapter Sixteen

Keisha sat in complete darkness in her apartment, trying desperately to think of her next move. As she sat moping, she deeply regretted the decision to allow Sharmaine's children into her apartment. *I knew I should never have let them come over.*

The moment Rodney began vomiting, Keisha realized that she had missed something important when she left to deal with the delivery man. While Sharmaine was dialing 911, Keisha had run into the kitchen. Just as she suspected, Rodney had gulped down half a pitcher of the special smoothies she'd been serving Sharmaine. Prior to this glitch, Keisha believed her plan was foolproof, and the smoothies were the last nail in Sharmaine's proverbial coffin. She was certain it would have worked—if Rodney had not drunk it instead.

A smile spread across Keisha's face as she thought about how easy it had been to bring down the great Sharmaine Cleveland. In Keisha's opinion, Sharmaine was lazy and stupid. From the moment she took over managing Sharmaine's career, Keisha discovered that if left to her own devices, Sharmaine would fail miserably.

At first she'd taken the job out of loyalty and friendship. For more than ten years, she'd worked diligently for Sharmaine out of sheer love, and sincerely considered her to be family. She reveled in her best friend's happiness and success. But then, Sharmaine betrayed her.

After that, Keisha's whole outlook changed. As hard as she tried, she could not get over it, and eventually, she vowed that she would do whatever it took in order to put Sharmaine in her place. It's true what they say: There's a thin line between love and hate. The depths of Keisha's hatred for Sharmaine were as deep as the love she'd once felt for her. For all of the things she'd done to help Sharmaine's career succeed, she vowed to do equal amounts to ensure that it failed.

The fact that Sharmaine had put her absolute trust in Keisha acted as gasoline for the fire she was building. It was all very comical to Keisha as she made up stories to feed Sharmaine that she swallowed hook, line, and sinker. Keisha felt it was much easier than fishing in a barrel. Keisha giggled when she'd tell Sharmaine she'd signed papers that didn't exist. The fact that it never occurred to her that Keisha had been signing her name for several years was hysterical.

It took all of her restraint not to guffaw like a donkey right in her face each time she handed her a pill and Sharmaine popped it into her mouth without a second glance. Even with it sitting on her nightstand, Keisha believed Sharmaine was too lazy and incompetent to take the time to read the label. Accepting every word that Keisha said to her, Sharmaine believed she'd been places she had never been, and done things she'd never done. *What a freaking idiot.*

Keisha's cell phone rang loudly, disturbing her thoughts. Annoyed, she flipped on the lamp and answered. A sobbing Sharmaine was on the other end.

"Is Rodney okay?" Keisha asked.

"The doctors have him stabilized, but he's still unconscious. Oh, Keisha, I don't know what I'll do if I lose my baby."

"You won't lose him, Sharmaine. I'm sure he's going to be fine."

Keisha held the line as Sharmaine cried in her ear for several minutes. Unable to stand it any longer, she spoke. "Listen. Do you want me to come to the hospital? Is there anything I can do?"

Of course there is. I do everything for your precious family, Keisha thought after asking the question.

"No, it's late. You go ahead and get some rest. Leon called Jackson to pick up Jeanna and Camille. He's going to take them home and stay with them. I'm going to spend the night here with Leon. I just called to give you an update."

"Is that a good idea? What about your case, and the stipulations of your bail?"

"That is the last thing on my mind right now, Keisha. If they want to arrest me for being near Leon, then they can just come up here and do it, but I am not leaving this hospital."

"Okay, if that's what you want. I'll bring you some fresh clothes in the morning." Keisha waited for Sharmaine to continue, but all she heard was the sound of her sniffling and blowing her nose.

She was positive of the answer, but she had to ask. "Um, did the doctor say what's wrong with him? I mean, he just got sick so fast."

"Keisha, you won't believe this. They say that he's been poisoned." Sharmaine cried harder and louder.

The phone hit the floor as Keisha could no longer hold it in her hand. She'd hoped it would take the doctors much longer to figure it out. She stared at her phone lying on the floor for several seconds before picking it up again. Grateful that Sharmaine was too consumed in tears to have noticed, she gathered her composure. "Do they know how?"

"No . . . They are still running tests."

"I'll see you in the morning," Keisha said.

Quickly, she hung up the phone and rushed to her kitchen. She had poured the remainder of the smoothie down the garbage disposal as soon as everyone left for the hospital. Now she realized she had to be sure to cover her tracks. Under the sink, she found some bleach and poured it down the drain, then mixed in hot water. That would get rid of any smoothie residue, she reasoned. Next, she went out the back door to her storage closet to get rid of the boxes of rat poison she'd been storing.

Each day since Sharmaine had moved in, Keisha had ground up a few pellets of poison in her blender along with a strawberry banana smoothie for Sharmaine. The small doses made Sharmaine sick, but Keisha knew they would not kill her. It had never occurred to her that Rodney would get his hands on it. His small size, combined with the amount he drank, was potentially deadly.

Standing in the closet, Keisha stared up at the mountain of boxes, realizing there was no way she could carry them all at once. It had taken her six months of shopping to accumulate so much. Each time she went to the store, she'd pick up one or two boxes. There was no way she'd buy enough at one time to arouse suspicion. Now she had to get rid of it all in just a few hours. She rushed to the kitchen for garbage bags.

The bags were stuffed when Keisha suddenly realized the police would search her dumpster as well as her apartment. Sitting on the floor, she began to cry. Her plan was falling apart right before her eyes, and she was at a loss for how to stop it. She sat bawling for a half hour, going over and over in her head each detail that she'd meticulously planned. Then it suddenly dawned on her. Standing up, she began unpacking the bags and placing the boxes back on the shelves. The answer was simple. She just wished she'd thought of it sooner.

I'll just frame Sharmaine for poisoning Rodney, just like I did when I shot Leon.

Cackling like an old witch, Keisha left the storage closet.

When they arrived at their home, Camille and Jeanna slowly climbed the stairs to their rooms. Just as they neared the top, Jackson called out to them. "Are you girls hungry? I can ask Consuela to fix us something."

"No thanks, Uncle Jack. I'm going to my room and watch a movie," Jeanna answered.

"What about you, Camille?"

"No. I can't eat," she answered. Camille went into her room and lay down on her bed. Tears welled up in her eyes, but she brushed them away, reluctant to cry. Instead, she got up and went to Jeanna's room. She knocked on the door then waited for her sister to answer.

"Come in."

"Can I use your phone? I want to call Danté."

Jeanna pressed pause on the movie she was watching. She turned around and looked at Camille. Her face was scrunched up, as if she were trying to remember something. "In all the excitement, I think I left my purse at Mom's. I don't have it," she said.

Camille plopped down on Jeanna's bed. "Dad still has mine."

"Why don't you just use the house phone?"

"Uncle Jack is downstairs. He's worse than Dad. I don't want to hear his mouth." Camille sighed loudly.

Ignoring her, Jeanna pressed play and went back to her movie. Camille pushed some clothes aside and lay down on her sister's bed to watch with her. When the movie was over, she reluctantly went back to her room. After a long, hot shower she put on her pajamas and climbed into bed, but as hard as she tried, Camille could not fall asleep. She got out of her bed then went to her dresser and opened the drawer. Digging through her underwear and bras, she searched, hoping she'd find a joint she'd forgotten about. But there was no use; it was all gone.

Camille went to her closet and pulled out a pair of jeans and a T-shirt. She dressed quickly then checked the hallway. The upstairs was completely dark. She sneaked downstairs and froze when she heard noises. Peeking into the family room, she saw that Jackson had dozed off on the sofa with the television on. She tipped past the open door as he snored loudly.

As she reached the back door, she realized Jackson had not set the alarm. That meant she could easily get out of the house and get her car out of the garage. Still tiptoeing, she grabbed her keys from the hook and went out the back door.

Once outside, she saw the garage doors standing open. Quickly, she ran to her Honda Accord and hopped inside. As she started the engine, she thought up a quick lie. She pulled up to the gate and stopped.

Otis poked his head out. "What are you doing out so late, Miss Camille?"

"I'm taking my dad a change of clothes at the hospital. Uncle Jackson is staying here with Jeanna."

"I sure was upset to hear about your little brother." Otis sadly shook his head.

"Thanks, Otis. I won't be gone long. I'm just going to drop these clothes off and come right back."

Otis looked at her oddly for a few seconds, and Camille thought that surely she was busted. Then Otis pulled his head back inside and pressed the button, opening the gate. He waved to her as she drove away.

It didn't take her long, as she exceeded all of the speed limit laws, before Camille was pulling up to Danté's apartment building. She jumped out of the car and rushed up the steel stairs. Once she reached the door, she pounded loudly. After several moments passed, she heard Nichole's voice on the other side.

"Who is it?"

"It's me, Camille. I came to see Danté."

Camille stood fidgeting as she heard several locks click before Nichole finally cracked the door open. "Danté is working the late shift tonight, Camille. He's not here."

"Um . . . I'm sorry to come by so late. My little brother is in the hospital, and I just really needed to see Danté."

"Oh, yeah, I saw that on *Entertainment Tonight!* Is Rodney gonna be okay?"

Camille shrugged her shoulders. "We don't really know yet." She shifted her weight from one foot to the other.

"I'll tell Danté you came by." Nichole put her hands on the door to close it.

"Um, wait. Do you know where I can get some weed?"

Nichole frowned at her. "No," she said. Then she closed the door.

Camille walked slowly back down the stairs to her car. She got inside and sat for several minutes, trying to remember how to get back to where Danté had taken her the first time she'd bought weed. He had been driving, and the whole trip was a blur.

She was still sitting and thinking when she heard someone tapping at her car window. Looking over, she thought she recognized his face, so she rolled down the window.

"What up? Ain't you Danté's girl?"

Camille stared into the dark brown face of the young man leaning into her car. "How do you know who I am?" she asked.

"I know everything that happens around here. I seen you with Danté the other night."

"Well, he's not here right now. I was just about to leave." Camille began to roll up her window. The young man stuck his hand in to stop her.

"What's your hurry?" he asked.

"I told you. Danté's not home, so I'm just—" Camille stopped talking as she noticed something tucked behind the young man's ear.

He noticed her looking and pulled the joint out. "You wanna smoke?" he asked.

Camille stared at him, not answering for several seconds, trying to decide what to do. She'd already sneaked out of the house, and Danté wasn't home. Her last stash of weed had been flushed down the toilet, and she desperately needed more. Besides, by the time she got home, she figured she'd be in a world of trouble anyway. This might be her last chance for a while.

She nodded her head. "Yeah," she said.

The young man stepped back and motioned for Camille to get out of the car. Without budging, she just stared at him.

"Come on, girl. I ain't gonna smoke this out in the open."

Then he suddenly noticed how scared she looked. Like a wolf that had just spotted a limping rabbit, he grinned at her and stepped closer to the car. He leaned in the window again. "My name is Alfonso, but everybody around here calls me Blue. Come on, get out. My apartment is right across the hall from Danté. We can hit this up there."

Slowly, Camille opened the car door and got out. She followed Blue up the stairs and into his apartment. The stench in the room caused her stomach to turn as soon as she was inside. Camille thought it smelled like a combination of urine, feces, sex, and strawberries. She covered her mouth and nose with her hand to keep from inhaling. Then she looked around the dimly lit living room; at least she assumed it was the living room. It was the identical space that Danté and Nichole used as one, but this one had no real furniture. There was a lamp sitting on top of an old milk crate, an ugly black bean bag chair that had burst, scattering beans all over the floor, and a filthy mattress with a dingy blanket on top.

Suddenly regretting her decision, Camille turned toward the door. Quick as a flash, Blue stood in front of it, blocking her way.

"I . . . I changed my mind. I don't wanna smoke," she stammered.

"Cool. Let's do something else." Blue stared at her from

head to toe. Then he stuck out his tongue and licked his crusty lips.

"No. I want to go." Camille's whole body was shaking with fear.

Blue ignored her and grabbed both of her arms. He violently threw her onto the mattress. She screamed as she landed on the floor. Blue quickly jumped on top of her, pinning her down.

"No! Stop!" she screamed as he tugged at her clothes.

"Don't pretend you don't want it. I saw that video of your mom. Whores run in the family." Blue ripped open her T-shirt, exposing her bra.

Camille struggled and kicked, but he was much stronger.

"Let me go! Stop it!" she screamed even louder.

Danté sauntered across the courtyard of his apartment complex on his way to his building. He stopped suddenly when he noticed Camille's car parked out front. Anxious to see her, he bounded up the stairs. He'd just put his key in the door when he heard screaming. Standing still, he strained his ears to see where it was coming from.

Blue grinned perversely at Camille's exposed breasts inside her bra. Then he bent down to kiss her. Frantic, Camille spit in his eye. Blue cursed her then viciously slapped her face. She screamed in pain.

Suddenly, the front door came crashing open with the power of Danté's foot.

"Get off of her!" he screamed.

"Are you crazy? You just broke my door!" Blue screamed back.

With his attention diverted, Camille drew up her knees and hit him directly in the groin. Blue cursed in pain and rolled off of her. Danté rushed over and helped Camille to her feet. The two of them ran across the breezeway to Danté's apartment, leaving Blue on the floor, cursing and screaming at them.

Once they were safely inside, Danté locked and chained the front door. Then he helped Camille sit on the couch. He looked at her, confused. "What were you doing over there?"

Camille sat crying and still shaking, unable to answer him.

Danté went to the kitchen and came back carrying a small bag of ice. He handed it to Camille. "Put this on your face," he said.

When she reached out to take it, he noticed her ripped T-shirt and exposed bra. He quickly left the room.

Lightly, he knocked on his sister's bedroom door. "Nichole, you up?" He peeped in.

"Yeah," she answered.

"Um, can you come out here? I need your help."

Nichole waddled into the living room and saw Camille sitting on the couch. She sped up her waddle and sat down next to her, wrapping her arm around her shoulder. Realizing Camille was in no shape to answer, she looked at Danté. "What happened?"

"That crackhead Blue attacked her. Can you get her some more clothes?" Danté clenched his fists and paced around the room, trying to contain his anger.

A few moments later, the two of them returned to the living room. Nichole had given Camille a fresh T-shirt and helped her wash her tear-stained face. Before returning to her room, she gave Camille a warm hug. "It's over and you're fine," she said. Then she waddled back down the hallway to her room.

Danté sat down on the sofa and pulled Camille into his arms. He held her tightly.

"I'm sorry. It's all my fault. I never should have gone in there with him," Camille said softly.

"No, don't blame yourself. Blue is crazy. You're not the first girl around here he's attacked. I should have warned you to stay away from him."

Camille shook her head. "I went over there with him to . . . to smoke weed. I came to get you to buy some for me and he offered, and I . . . I'm just stupid," Camille cried.

Danté looked at her, surprised. "How could you have smoked that whole bag already?"

"I didn't. My dad flushed it down the toilet."

Danté sighed with relief. "I'm glad he did," he said. Then he paused and took a deep breath. "Camille, I think you are smoking too much. It's becoming a real problem for you. Please, don't do it anymore."

Shocked, she sat up and looked at him. "But you are the one who gave me the first joint."

"I know, and I'm sorry. I used to smoke back then, but I don't anymore. I quit, and I want you to quit too."

Camille folded her arms across her chest and slumped back into the couch. "You don't understand. My life is going crazy."

"Right. Poor little rich girl."

"Rich people have problems too. You have no idea what it feels like for people to call your mother a whore."

Dante turned to her slowly and looked her in the eye. "Did

you forget? My mother was a whore. I don't even know who mine or Nichole's father is because of what she did."

He was correct; Camille had momentarily forgotten.

"I'm sorry," she said. "But it's different. At least no one is trying to make you forgive your mom."

"You're right, but that's because they don't have to. I mean, I used to really hate her; then I realized that I was only hurting myself by holding in the hatred and anger, so I forgave her."

Camille was dumbfounded. "I don't understand. If you don't smoke anymore, why did you help me get weed?"

He turned away from her and blushed. "'Cause you're so beautiful. I wanted you to like me, and I was afraid to say no to you. Besides, I thought you could handle it. I was wrong."

Flattered by his admission, Camille snuggled up close to Danté and laid her head on his shoulder. "Can I chill here a little while before I go home?" she asked.

"You're staying here. It's too late for you to drive around Atlanta alone. I'll go with you in the morning. I can ride the bus back."

"My dad is gonna freak out again."

"I'm sure your parents have their hands full with Rodney. I'll explain it when we get there. How is he doing?"

She looked at him, confused.

"I saw it on the news," he explained.

"Oh . . . he's not doing good. I went home, but I couldn't sleep, so I came here."

"Getting high really doesn't make you feel better, Camille. It just helps you hide from your problems."

"Can you think of a better plan?"

Danté could, but he felt he'd said enough. Instead of answering, he got up and went to the closet. He came back carrying two pillows and two blankets. Placing a pillow on the edge of the couch, he invited Camille to lie down; then he covered her with one of the blankets.

"Don't leave me," she whispered.

"I'm not going anywhere."

He leaned down and kissed her forehead gently. He threw his pillow on the floor and lay down in front of the couch, then stretched out on the floor and covered himself with the other blanket.

Chapter Seventeen

When Jeanna awoke the next morning, she heard the buzzing of her television. She raised her head and looked around her room, realizing she'd fallen asleep with a movie still playing. She yawned and stretched then got out of bed. Her room was a complete mess, as she had not cleaned it since her mother left. As long as nobody bothered her, she watched movies all day and most of the night. Digging through the piles of clothes on her bedroom floor, she found a pair of shorts and a T-shirt. Holding them to her nose, she sniffed. *Clean enough,* she mused.

Without bothering to shower or even wash up, Jeanna peeled off the clothes she'd worn the day before and put on the shorts and T-shirt. She went to her dresser and grabbed a bottle. Holding it high, she spritzed herself all over with her favorite fragrance, Bath and Body Works' Sea Island Cotton. Then she left her room and headed downstairs.

Consuela was standing at the stove, scrambling eggs in a large cast iron skillet when Jeanna entered the kitchen. "Good morning, Miss Jeanna," she said.

Jeanna sat down at the kitchen table. "Morning. Where's Camille and Uncle Jack?"

"Your uncle went to the guest room to shower and get

dressed. I have not seen your sister this morning," she answered.

"I don't want any eggs today. I'll just have a glass of juice and take it to my room."

Consuela turned and looked at her. "Miss Jeanna, you need to eat something. Besides, I'm going to clean your room today."

"No! I mean, I told you I'd do it myself."

"You told me, but you did not do it. I peeked in there yesterday. As soon as I clear the breakfast dishes, I have to go in there and clean. You also have not been bringing your laundry down. Your room is full of dirty clothes."

"Just leave it alone. I'll do it!" Jeanna screamed, startling Consuela. She looked at her strangely then turned back to her pan of eggs.

"What's all the commotion about?" Jackson asked as he entered the kitchen.

Jeanna was surprised to see him dressed in a suit and tie. "Um, nothing. I just don't want Consuela cleaning my room," Jeanna answered.

Jackson straightened his tie then sat down at the table. "Just leave her room alone, Consuela. Leon and Sharmaine have spoiled these kids rotten. You have enough to do around this big house anyway. Let her live like a pig if she wants to."

"Yes, sir, Mr. Jack." Consuela fought the urge to say more. Maybe no one else noticed, but she knew that something was wrong with Jeanna.

Before Sharmaine left, Jeanna's room was always spotless. Consuela never had to clean it. The other children used to joke that Jeanna had OCD because she kept her room and herself immaculately clean. She wasn't sure, but Consuela also suspected that Jeanna was not bathing regularly either. Every morning, she knew Jeanna drowned herself in cologne, and that wasn't normal. Consuela realized, however, that she was only the maid, and it wasn't her place to interfere.

"Do you want bacon with your eggs, Mr. Jack?" Consuela asked.

"Give me beef bacon. I don't eat pork." He turned to Jeanna. "Why aren't you dressed?"

Jeanna looked down at herself. "I am dressed."

"Why aren't you dressed for church?"

"Um . . . we haven't been to church since, um, Dad made us leave 'cause Mom was there," she stammered.

"I know that, but you are going today. This family needs all the prayers it can get, especially with your brother in the hospital. Run upstairs and change." He smiled at Consuela as she placed a cup of coffee in front of him. "Thank you," he said.

Slowly sliding her chair back from the table, Jeanna obeyed. Just as she reached the kitchen door, Jackson called out to her. "Oh, be sure Camille is dressed for church also. We'll go visit your brother after service."

Jeanna nodded and left the kitchen. When she arrived upstairs, she went into her room and walked over to the closet. She stared inside at all of the dresses her mother had purchased for her. There had to be close to one hundred dresses neatly pressed and hanging on hangers, but Jeanna had no desire to wear any of them. Every time she chose one, she'd suddenly think of the day she and her Mom went shopping and bought it, or she'd suddenly remember a special occasion that they went to together, with Jeanna wearing one of the dresses. All of them held a special memory of Sharmaine, and Jeanna could not bear to look at them.

Instead, she left her room and went over to Camille's, hoping she had a dress she could borrow that would not hold any significance. They were not the same size, but Jeanna knew Camille kept a closet full of clothes she'd outgrown. Jeanna curled up her fist and knocked lightly. She knocked several times more, but there was no answer. Finally, she pushed the door open and walked in.

"Camille?" She looked around the room, and then went to check the bathroom. It was empty. Worried, she rushed back downstairs. First she ran into the family room, but when she didn't find Camille there either, she ran to the kitchen. "Camille's not in her room," she said breathlessly.

Jackson looked up from his plate of food. "Are you sure? Did you check her bathroom?" he asked.

"Yes, and I checked the family room. I can't find her," Jeanna said. Her voice was filled with concern and tension.

"I'm right here," Camille said.

They all turned around as Camille and Danté walked through the back door.

Jackson stood up from the table. "Camille, where have you been?" He suddenly noticed the bruise on her cheek. "What happened to your face?"

"It's a long story, Uncle Jack. I'm home and I'm fine," Camille answered.

Jackson turned his attention to Danté. "You're that thug I saw her with the morning she came home high. What did you do to my niece?" he screamed.

"He didn't do anything, Uncle Jack. He saved me. Leave Danté alone," Camille said. She stepped in front of Danté, blocking Jackson as he charged towards them.

"Saved you from what?" Jackson demanded.

"I'm sorry, Sir. Camille came to my apartment last night and one of my neighbors attacked her. She spent the night there," Danté said. He stopped speaking as he watched Jackson's lightly tanned face growing darker in color due to his anger. "Nothing happened. I swear it. I just wanted to make sure she got home safely."

"He's telling the truth, Uncle Jack," Camille said.

"Where is this apartment?" Jackson asked.

"My sister and I live in Sand Poole Manor. It's in—"

"Bankhead!" Jackson screamed, interrupting him. "You had my niece in the projects in Bankhead?" Jackson's eyes narrowed into slits. His voice was so low it sounded almost like he was growling at Danté. "Get out! Get out of this house now!"

"But, Uncle Jack, he didn't do anything. I went there on my own," Camille whined.

"Shut up, Camille! I want this trash out of this house now!" he bellowed.

"Uncle Jack, just listen to him," Camille pleaded.

Danté backed up toward the door. "It's cool, Camille. I'm leaving. Just promise me you'll think about what we discussed in the car."

Camille nodded her head.

"I'm sorry to cause so much trouble. Later," Danté said. He walked out of the back door and closed it behind him.

As soon as he was gone, Camille turned to Jackson. "Why did you do that? You had no right! This isn't your house!" she yelled.

"Don't you dare speak to me that way, young lady. You had no business sneaking out in the first place to meet that punk. Get upstairs and change clothes so we won't be late for church."

"But, Uncle Jack—"

"Don't test me, Camille. I'm not as easygoing as your father. Now, do as I say." Jackson sat down at the table and went back to eating his breakfast.

Camille opened her mouth to speak again, and he shot her a look that let her know he wasn't playing. She stomped out of the kitchen and up the stairs.

Jeanna was standing speechless in the corner, stunned by what she'd just witnessed. Jackson took a slow sip of his coffee then turned to her. "Move it!" he barked.

She quickly followed in her sister's footsteps.

When he got off the bus at his apartment complex, Danté saw Blue rushing in his direction.

"You broke my door. You gonna pay for it!"

"Get away from me, Blue," he said calmly. Danté walked swiftly past him.

Blue followed closely behind. "I let you borrow my Jeep to go visit that honey in the first place," he said.

"That's not your Jeep. You stole it and I could have been arrested for driving it. I'm warning you, stay away from me, Blue." Dante reached his building and began climbing the stairs.

Blue trotted up swiftly behind him. "What about my door?" He pointed to it with the knob hanging off. The wood was splintered around the sides. "Look at it," he said.

Danté put his key into his apartment door, ignoring him.

"You owe me!" Blue yelled.

Danté opened his door and walked inside his apartment. He slowly turned around and looked at Blue. "All I owe you is a beat down for what you did to Camille. Unless you are ready to collect, I suggest you stay away from me." He slammed the door in Blue's face and locked it.

Turning around, Danté looked over at Nichole. She was sitting on the sofa with the television tuned to a local minister. Her Bible sat in her growing lap. "You're late for church," she teased.

Danté smiled at her. He grabbed his Bible from the bookshelf and sat down beside his sister on the sofa.

"This ain't over!" Blue yelled outside Danté's door before walking back down the stairs to the courtyard. He kept walking until he reached the end of the complex. He ran up the stairs and knocked on the last door in the building. After several moments, a face peeked out at him.

"I need to see Rip," Blue said.

The person behind the door closed it without a word. A few moments later, it opened up again, and Blue walked in to the lavishly furnished apartment. He couldn't help staring at the long black leather sofa that sat in front of a fifty-inch plasma television. Under the television was an elaborate stereo system with CD, DVD player, and equalizer. Huge speakers hung on the walls.

The face in the doorway turned out to be a tall, thin, and beautiful black woman. Her long, straight black hair was pulled back in a ponytail, and she was dressed in only a long T-shirt. Blue couldn't help noticing that it barely covered her butt cheeks. Diverting his attention from the furnishings in the living room and from her behind, Blue followed her down the hallway, where she pushed open the bedroom door.

Inside the bedroom there was a king-sized sleigh bed with Rip sitting in it. Although his birth name was Marion Sawyer, everyone called him Rip. He was given that name because if anyone crossed him, there was only one thing left to say about them: Rest in peace. Rip was the son of a Japanese mother and black father. That ethnic makeup gave him a smooth brown complexion with eyes that slanted at the corners. Lounging in his bed, he wore a red skull cap over his slick, black hair and a matching T-shirt.

Weighing over four hundred pounds, Rip rarely left his apartment. He didn't have to, because everyone in Sand Poole Manor knew him. All of the drug dealers worked for him, and he was the unofficial king of the projects. Most people held only two emotions toward him: They either feared or revered him.

Blue felt a little bit of both. He took a deep breath before speaking. "I got a score to settle. I need to buy a gun," he said.

"You got money?" Rip asked.

Blue's eyes darted back and forth. He watched the woman who'd led him down the hallway climb into bed next to Rip. "Um, no, but I'm good for it," he answered.

Rip slowly shook his head. "You are good for nothing, Blue. Get out of here wasting my time."

Blue thought for a moment. "Give me some crack. I'll sell it for you and we can trade," he suggested.

Rip and the woman laughed loudly. "You think I'm stupid enough to give a crack head crack? You ain't gonna sell it. You gonna smoke it." Rip continued laughing at him.

"All right, I'll get some money. How much?" Blue asked.

"One hundred," Rip answered. "Oh, and bullets are extra."

He laughed some more as Blue walked back up the hallway and left the apartment.

Camille sat in church next to her sister and Uncle Jackson, intently listening to Bishop Snow preaching his sermon. Her mouth dropped open in awe as he was saying virtually the same thing Danté has said to her in the car on the way to her house that morning.

Bishop Snow began by reading a passage from Psalm 32:7: *"Thou art my hiding place; thou shalt preserve me from trouble; thou shalt compass me about with songs of deliverance. Selah."*

Camille was mesmerized from that point forward. As hard as she tried, she could not tear her eyes or her ears from Bishop Snow.

"Saints, sometimes in life we want to run and we want to hide. Life is not a crystal staircase. It gets hard and rough," Bishop Snow preached. "No matter who we think we are, we are not immune to the pain that comes with being a human being. We experience hurts, losses, and disappointments. Sometimes we need to get away from life's troubles and ease the pain. We are just like scared little children, and all we want to do is hide."

Everyone around Camille seemed to slowly fade to black and disappear. The choir members dissipated, and all of the ushers evaporated into thin air. Jackson's seat was empty, and so was Jeanna's. Sitting alone in her pew, dressed casually in her favorite green dress and black sandals, Camille suddenly felt as if she were alone in the church and Bishop Snow was boldly speaking directly to her.

"We try to hide with alcohol or drugs, but that's not the

answer," he said. "Those things don't help us hide; they tear us apart. I've heard that it actually feels good for a few moments. Satan tricks us into thinking that being high is a good feeling, but I'm here to tell you it's all a lie. Drugs defile our bodies and make us act crazy. We don't know who we are or where we're going."

Tears ran down Camille's face, and she struggled to keep from crying out loudly as he continued.

"But I'm here to tell you this morning that there is a place you can hide. There's a place you can run to any time of the day or night. It doesn't matter who you are or where you are from. There is a hiding place."

Camille held her breath in anticipation as she waited for Bishop Snow to give her the answer. Things in her life were more painful than her heart could bear. Inside, she felt as if there were a big pot of water boiling and any second it was going to boil over and cause her to completely explode.

Tell me where this place is. Where can I go hide? she thought.

"Your hiding place is in the bosom of Jesus Christ," Bishop Snow said.

Suddenly everyone that had previously been around her magically reappeared, and Camille no longer felt that she and Bishop Snow were alone in the church.

Oh, poo, that's what my mom always said, but I can't trust her. I can't trust anybody. Camille suddenly jumped in her seat, and Jeanna looked at her strangely.

"Did you say something?" Camille whispered.

Jeanna shook her head.

"Be quiet," Jackson whispered to them both.

Camille stared at her uncle, and then she looked around the church. Turning in her seat, she looked behind her. A grey-haired old woman in a big white church hat smiled at her.

"Turn around. What is wrong with you?" Jackson whispered.

Camille obeyed and sat frozen in her seat, unable to move. She had no idea who said it, or where the voice came from, but Camille was sure she'd heard it clear as a bell.

You can trust God, was all it said. Then, as suddenly as it appeared, the still, small voice was gone.

Chapter Eighteen

"This was all I could find for you," Keisha said.

Sharmaine stared at the bag of clean clothing Keisha brought to the hospital for her to wear. "Where did you find these? I haven't worn these jeans in months."

Keisha sighed. "They were hanging in your closet. So was the blouse."

The two women stood alone in the hospital bathroom, unpacking the bag.

"I've lost so much weight since I've been . . . Well, since I've been having these episodes. They don't fit anymore."

Keisha dug into the duffel bag the clothes had been in. "I brought a belt."

"Thank you, Keisha. You think of everything." She gave Keisha a quick hug then walked into one of the bathroom stalls to change clothes.

"How's Rodney?" Keisha called to Sharmaine over the wall.

"There's been no change since we spoke last night, but they let me and Leon see him for a few moments."

"And?" Keisha waited for an answer as she heard Sharmaine sniffling.

"He looked so small and frail with all those tubes and wires. It was the worst feeling. I don't know how any parent survives losing a child."

"Yeah, it's hard," Keisha said softly.

Sharmaine suddenly came out of the stall and looked at Keisha. "Oh, I'm so sorry, Keisha. I didn't mean to sound insensitive."

Keisha turned her back to her without answering. Sharmaine slowly backed into the stall to finish dressing.

A few moments later, Keisha's hand appeared at the top of the wall. "Hand me your dirty clothes. I'll take them home and put them in the laundry."

Sharmaine quietly obeyed. When she was dressed, she came out of the stall and went to the mirror. Before she had a chance to ask, Keisha handed Sharmaine a washcloth and her makeup kit.

"The blogs are going crazy with this story. Sandy Thorne has reported Rodney has cancer, and another one claims it's the swine flu. Do you want me to put out a statement to dispel all the rumors?" Keisha asked.

"No. I don't care what they think. If you have to say anything at all, just state that our family appreciates the well wishes and we ask for privacy." She took out her compact and began to apply her foundation.

"I'll say it, but it's going to be hard to get it. There are reporters camped outside. Hospital security has their hands full keeping them out."

Sharmaine reached for her eyeliner and put it on. "I understand they want their story, but sometimes they can be such vultures. He's just a little boy. He's no celebrity."

"You're right, Sharmaine, but you are a celebrity, and the reporters work for the public, your public. It's the same public that sent you tons of flowers and presents when Rodney was born. Many of them have sent stuff for Rodney in the past few days. They care about what happens to him."

After taking a paper towel to blot her lipstick, Sharmaine turned to Keisha. "I understand what you are saying. It's just that over the past several months, my public has been a lot less than adoring. I want to protect the children from that. I always have."

"Of course you do. I'll prepare a simple statement without any details."

Keisha gathered Sharmaine's makeup and dirty clothes and placed them into the duffel bag then the two of them left the bathroom and began walking down the hallway back to the waiting room.

"Are you hungry?" Keisha asked.

Sharmaine shook her head. "I can't eat anything."

"You need to keep your strength up. The last thing you need is to get sick while you are here taking care of Rodney."

"I guess you are right," Sharmaine said.

Keisha perked up. "I brought you a homemade smoothie. It's in a cooler in the waiting room."

"No. I think those things are giving me the runs. I've had diarrhea for days. Can you go to the cafeteria and get me something? I want to eat something solid."

As they entered the waiting room, Sharmaine lowered her voice when she noticed Leon had fallen asleep in a chair in the corner. "Bring me a sandwich and get something for Leon too," she whispered.

Ignoring her, Keisha walked over and reached into her cooler. She pulled out the plastic bottle she'd filled with the arsenic-tainted smoothie and put a straw in it. "It's right here,

Sharmaine. Besides, I don't have time to stand in line at the cafeteria."

Sharmaine looked at her with a puzzled look on her face. "I'm sorry. I didn't realize you had something to do."

"I put off all of my errands yesterday so that the kids could come over. I really need to take care of them today."

Sitting down in a chair near Leon, Sharmaine curled her feet under her. "You're right. I'm so sorry. Go ahead and take care of your errands."

Keisha held the bottle out to Sharmaine and she took it. Then Keisha gathered up the duffel bag and cooler. "I'll call you later," she said. Then she walked out of the waiting room while waving good-bye.

Sharmaine looked lovingly over at a sleeping Leon. His head was leaned back against the wall with his mouth hanging wide open. She giggled softly as she noticed a small drop of drool falling down his face.

"I miss you so much," she whispered.

Turning her attention back to the bottle of smoothie that Keisha had given her, Sharmaine put the straw up to her mouth to take a sip.

"Good afternoon, Sister Cleveland."

Surprised, she set the bottle down on the table and warmly greeted her guests. Bishop Snow and his wife Yolanda walked into the waiting room and enveloped her into their arms.

"Thank you so much for coming." Sharmaine politely offered each of them a seat.

Hearing voices, Leon suddenly awakened. He looked around confused for a few seconds before realizing where he was. Sharmaine handed him a tissue and tried to discreetly point toward the drool on his mouth. He felt embarrassed as he wiped it clean. When he was done, he politely reached his hand out to Bishop and Mrs. Snow.

"I'm sorry. I'd been awake for over twenty-four hours. Please excuse me," he said.

"You don't have to apologize, Brother Cleveland. We understand," Bishop Snow answered.

"We just dropped by to give you some encouragement, a word of prayer, and to make sure you had something to eat."

Mrs. Snow held out a paper bag toward Leon. There was a delicious aroma coming from inside the bag.

"What is this?" he asked.

"We stopped at Vonnie's Soul Food and picked up a couple of plates," Mrs. Snow answered. "We knew you probably had not had anything to eat."

Leon took the bag from Mrs. Snow and handed it to Sharmaine. "Thank you so much. We really appreciate this," he said.

Bishop Snow smiled broadly as he looked back and forth between the two of them. "It does my heart good to see you two together. I'm so sorry that it's under these circumstances, but it's a good thing. You need each other's strength at this time."

Unsure of how to respond, Leon glanced over at Sharmaine and then down at the floor. Stalling for a few extra seconds to think, Sharmaine peeked inside the food bag. "This sure smells wonderful," she said.

They all nodded in agreement.

"How is your son?" Mrs. Snow asked.

Before she could answer, Sharmaine noticed Rodney's doctor walking into the room. She looked over at him expectantly.

"I've got good news," he said. "Rodney is awake and talking."

"Oh, thank you, God!" Sharmaine said. She jumped up from her chair. "Can I see him? I need to talk to my baby."

"Of course you can, but don't stay too long. He's dehydrated and still very weak."

Bishop and Mrs. Snow stood to their feet, along with Leon. "Praise God," they said in unison.

Sharmaine rushed excitedly out of the room, following the doctor. Leon politely said good-bye to Bishop and Mrs. Snow then he joined her. When he walked into Rodney's room, Sharmaine was hugging him tightly. Leon smiled at them both.

By the end of the week, the doctor felt confident enough to allow Rodney to be released from the hospital. Sharmaine was ecstatic that he was better, but she felt sad at the same time. While they had sat with Rodney at the hospital, she'd felt a closeness with Leon that she desperately wanted to hang on to.

It didn't make sense to her why, but during the week, she'd noticed that she actually felt better physically than she had in a while. There was no confusion or headaches, and she didn't black out even once. The diarrhea had ended by that Wednesday. All of this had occurred without her taking any of her medicines. Keisha made sure to bring the pills to the hospital, but Sharmaine was too busy attending to Rodney to think of her own health. She'd promised to do it, but then put the thought to the back of her mind. Attending to Rodney and other things kept her occupied.

Briefly, she remembered the pills and was about to take one, when Rodney asked her if she'd read to him. Sharmaine sat by Rodney's bed reading a comic book when a nurse asked if she'd like to give blood.

"Giving blood can save a life," the nurse said. "Besides, we have to take your son down for more tests. It's a good way to pass the time."

Sharmaine agreed, and followed the directions the nurse gave her in order get to the blood bank in the basement. When she returned, she'd completely forgotten about the pills.

Now that Rodney was going home, she was reminded of how much she had truly missed her family. Whenever the girls came to visit their brother, Sharmaine wished she could continue to see them daily. Sitting in his room together, they seemed like a family again. It was a feeling she wished she could freeze-frame forever.

As she leisurely packed Rodney's bag while he got dressed in the bathroom, Sharmaine slowly brushed away a tear.

"Is he ready to go yet?" Leon asked as he walked in. He pretended not to notice that she'd been crying.

"Almost. He's in the bathroom," she answered. Sharmaine put the last of his toiletries in the bag and handed it to Leon. "Everything's in here."

"What do I do with this hospital thingy?" Rodney said as he walked out of the bathroom. He held up the white-and-blue hospital gown he'd been wearing.

"You can just leave it here, sweetheart," Sharmaine answered.

He tossed it onto the bed. "Okay, I'm ready to go."

Leon held the door open for the two of them to exit. As

soon as they entered the hallway, a blonde nurse walked up to them, pushing a wheelchair.

"I'm sorry, Rodney, but it's hospital policy. I have to take you downstairs in this chair," she said.

He didn't really want to, but he sat down. The nurse pushed the chair, while his parents followed closely behind.

When they reached the back entrance, she helped Rodney out of the chair and into the limousine Leon had waiting with Otis behind the wheel. The nurse gave Rodney a high five then returned inside the hospital.

Leon and Sharmaine were left alone. They stared at each other awkwardly like two teenagers on a first date. Each of them struggled for something to say.

Finally, Leon spoke. "We can give you a ride back to Keisha's if you like. It's no trouble."

She pointed down the alley behind the limo. "She sent a cab for me. You know Keisha. She thinks of everything."

"Yes, she sure does. I'm sorry that you can't come by the house, but I promise as soon as he's up to it, I'll bring Rodney to visit."

Sharmaine nodded her head. "That's fine."

Unable to prolong the moment any longer, she leaned into the limousine and gave Rodney a hug and a kiss. "I love you, sweetie."

"I love you too, Mommy," he answered.

Leon got inside the limo and closed the door. With tears streaming down her face, Sharmaine stood on the curb and watched it until it disappeared. Then she got into her cab and told the driver to take her home.

***

After dinner, Leon helped Rodney get settled comfortably in his room. At Rodney's insistence, Leon fluffed his pillows, smoothed out his blankets, and put a movie into his DVD player. He sat in a chair beside the bed as the movie began. Shortly afterward, he looked over and noticed that Rodney had fallen fast asleep. Leon turned off the television and then the light before he quietly left the room.

He trotted down the stairs to the family room. Jeanna and Camille were seated on the couch, looking bored, while Jackson watched a basketball game on television. "What are you guys up to tonight?" Leon asked casually.

Jeanna shrugged her shoulders. "Will you take me to the video store? I want to get a new movie."

"Didn't I tell you that you couldn't get any new movies until you cleaned up that filthy room? Don't think that because your dad is home you can undermine my authority," Jackson said.

Leon looked at them both strangely. "Jeanna, you haven't cleaned your room? That's odd."

"I'll go do it now," she responded. She shot her uncle a dirty look then got up and went upstairs.

"You need to be tougher on these kids," Jackson said. He threw a handful of popcorn into his mouth and turned his attention back to the game.

"What about you, Camille?" Leon asked.

"My room is clean," she replied.

"No, I meant, what are you planning to do tonight?" He sat down in his easy chair.

Camille looked over at him. "Am I still grounded?"

Jackson answered before Leon could respond. "Yes, you are. You sneaked out again last weekend."

Camille ignored him and turned to Leon. "Can I have a friend over?"

Leon thought for a moment. His brother was correct in that Camille was still grounded. Her behavior had improved, but she was still somewhat of a problem; however, his family had just endured a very trying week. He decided to show some leniency. "All right, you can have a friend over."

Camille squealed and jumped into his arms, hugging him.

"Wait a minute. There are a few rules."

Camille sat back down and looked at him. "What?"

"You have to keep the noise down. Your brother is upstairs resting. And your guest has to leave by midnight. If you can agree to that, I have no problem with it."

"Thank you, Dad!" Camille hugged him tightly. She ran to the phone in the kitchen to call Danté.

"You never learn, do you?" Jackson asked.

Leon pushed the arms on his chair, causing it to recline backward, propping his feet up. "Learn what?"

"You let these kids run all over you. Jeanna is not as bad, but Camille has you wrapped around her little finger."

"What are you talking about, Jack?"

"I'm talking about how Camille just conned you."

"If she has a guest over, I know what's going on in my own house. It's not a big deal."

"But the girl is grounded. What's the point of doing that if you are just going to give her extra privileges?"

Leon sighed. He wasn't in the mood for an argument, but he knew once Jackson got started, he would be difficult to stop. While Jackson spent eighteen years in the military, he'd raised his own two sons with an iron fist. He'd never told his brother, but Leon felt it was his hard approach to discipline that led to Jackson's divorce. It was also the reason he only saw his sons at holidays and special occasions. Of course they loved their father, but Jackson could be very difficult to deal with sometimes. While Leon believed in discipline, he also felt that it had to be tempered with love; however, he wasn't in the mood to explain that to Jackson.

"It's not an extra privilege. Being grounded means I don't want her out of the house. I don't think inviting one of her girlfriends over is a problem." Leon leaned over to the popcorn bowl and grabbed a handful, stuffing it into his mouth.

"I'm sure you don't see a problem, because you don't even realize that the biggest problem with these kids is that they lack discipline. They've got a maid who cleans up after them and cooks whatever they want. Otis drives them around wherever they want to go. And this house is full of every toy and gadget on the market. I know you love them, but you are spoiling them."

"We have a lot of nice things, but my children do have boundaries and limits."

Jackson leaned forward on the couch. "They don't have enough boundaries or limits. What they need is more discipline and chores. That's the only way to build character."

Still munching on his popcorn, Leon tried to keep his cool. "Thanks for the advice, but this isn't the Marine Corps, Sergeant Cleveland. It's my home. I'm not going to treat my children like a bunch of recruits."

Jackson picked up the remote control and turned off the television. "Let me tell you something, baby brother. While you've been at the hospital all week pining over Sharmaine, I've been here running this house."

Leon suddenly did not feel like relaxing anymore. Putting

his feet back onto the floor, he sat straight up in his easy chair. "What are you talking about? I was at the hospital because of Rodney."

"I know Rodney was sick and you were concerned, but I saw the two of you together. I walked in one day and she was asleep with her head in your lap. The two of you were acting as if the past six months never happened."

Leon shook his head. "You don't understand. We were both worried about Rodney, so we leaned on each other a little bit. There's nothing wrong with that."

"That's exactly what I mean. You are soft. You were soft on Sharmaine even after what she's done, and you are the same way with these kids. I know you love them, but it's time you cracked the whip."

Slowly, Leon stood up from his chair. "Jackson, I really appreciate you staying here this week and helping to take care of the girls. I don't know how I would have managed without you. But I'm home now. You can get your stuff from the guest room and go on home."

Jackson was stunned. "Are you asking me to leave?"

"No, I'm just telling you that you are free to go if you want to."

"Fine, man . . . whatever." Jackson walked swiftly out of the family room and up the stairs. He returned a few moments later carrying his bags. Leon walked with him to the front door.

Jackson momentarily set his bags down beside the door. He reached out and hugged his brother tightly. "I love you, bro,'" he said then picked up his bags.

"I love you too," Leon answered before closing the door behind him.

***

Danté's palms were sweating profusely as he rang the front door bell. He'd almost fainted when Camille called and asked him to come over.

"Are you sure about that?" he had asked.

"Yes. I asked my Dad and he's fine with me having company. I really miss you."

Danté quickly agreed then hung up the phone so that he could shower and change. Now, standing on her front door step, for the first time he felt his stomach doing flip-flops. After what seemed like an eternity, the front door finally opened. Consuela smiled at him.

"Um, I'm here to see Camille."

"Come in. Miss Camille is waiting for you in the family room."

As soon as he walked into the room, Camille ran up to him and hugged him tightly. He kissed her gently on the lips then looked around. Although he'd been there for the pool party, there were strict restrictions that did not allow any of the teens inside the house. He looked around at the elaborate setup of the family and game room. There was a huge television that was almost as large as the wall. On shelves nearby, he noticed they seemed to have every DVD ever released. On the other side of the room, there was a pinball machine, a movie theatre–sized air popcorn popper, a round card table for games, and a pool table.

Looking around at everything, he felt both impressed and intimidated. "Where is everybody?" he asked.

"Jeanna's in her room, probably watching another movie. Rodney's asleep. He just got home today. My dad is doing some work in my mom's office."

Danté smiled. Then he kissed her again, holding the kiss much longer. They broke apart when Consuela cleared her throat behind them.

"Miss Camille, would you or your guest like something from the kitchen?"

Camille turned to Danté. "Are you hungry? Consuela can heat us up a pizza or something."

"Yeah, sure, pizza's cool." Danté walked over and sat on the huge sectional sofa, while Camille gave Consuela their food and drink order. When she was done, she came over and snuggled close to him on the couch. He stiffened up and shifted in his seat, moving away from her.

Camille looked at him strangely. "What's wrong?" she asked.

"I'm sorry, Camille. I'm just nervous being in your house, especially since the last time I was here your uncle threw me out."

Camille laughed. "Uncle Jack has gone home. You don't have to worry about him. You can relax."

"What about your dad?"

"He gave me permission to invite you over. We are not sneaking around. It's okay." She grabbed his arm and pulled it around her then snuggled under it.

Danté finally allowed himself to loosen up and pulled her closer. They sat talking about the end of her school year and their plans for the summer, until Consuela brought in the pizza. The two of them got up from the sofa and went over to the card table to eat.

"You eat a lot for such a small girl," Danté remarked. Camille had just swallowed the last bite of her third slice of pizza.

"I just love pepperoni pizza." She laughed.

Danté took a swig of his root beer. "Did you think about what we talked about the other day?" he asked.

"We're having fun. Do we have to talk about that now?"

"I'm sorry. It's just that we have another meeting on Monday. I was hoping you'd come with me."

Camille laid her fourth slice of pizza down and leaned back in her chair. "I'm not some addict. I don't think I need drug counseling."

"It's not just about being an addict. You smoke because you are trying to escape your problems. The counseling sessions give you a chance to open up about those problems. Once you open up, you can find better ways to deal with them."

"You mean like turning to God?" she asked sarcastically.

He nodded his head and took another bite of pizza.

Camille suddenly giggled. "When we met last summer, I never thought you'd turn out to be a church boy."

Danté looked serious. "Why? Did you think I was a thug, or trash, like your uncle called me?"

"Oh, no, I'm sorry. That didn't come out right. I just never met anybody like you before. Please don't be offended."

"I know I come from the streets, and I've done some things in my life that I'm not proud of, but right now, my only focus is keeping a good job so I can take care of my sister and her baby when it's born. Maybe when Nichole is older and can take care of the baby alone, I'll go to college or something. I'm not rich like you, Camille, but don't look down on me because of where I'm from."

Camille reached out and touched his hand. "I don't. I'm sorry. I just meant—oh, I don't know what I meant. Please, just don't be mad."

Danté looked over and smiled at her. "I'm not. You know,

that's the good thing about God. He doesn't care where you come from or what you've done." He winked at her. "Now, that's the end of my sermon. Just think about the meeting on Monday."

Camille nodded and picked up her pizza, taking a huge bite.

When they were done eating, Danté challenged Camille to play pool. He won the first two games, but she had him on the ropes for the third. He was leaning over the table, positioning his next shot, when Leon suddenly walked into the family room.

"What's going on in here?" he demanded.

"Dad, this is Danté," Camille said. She smiled proudly.

"What is he doing here?"

They both suddenly noticed that Leon was upset.

"You said I could have a guest over." Camille stared at Leon, confused.

"I thought you meant one of your girlfriends. I never said you could have a date—and certainly not with the boy you've been sneaking out getting high with."

Danté laid the pool cue down on the table. "I think I'd better go," he said.

"That's a good idea. I'm sure you can find your way out," Leon answered. He turned his stare angrily toward Camille.

Danté walked to the door then turned back to look at Camille. "Call me about Monday," he said before walking out.

Leon turned to his daughter. "Whatever Monday is, the answer is no!"

"Why are you acting like this? You said he could come over."

"You never said that he was your guest."

Camille stormed over to the couch and plopped down.

"You never asked. All you do is yell and refuse to listen to anything I have to say."

"I think you've said enough. Go upstairs and get ready for bed."

Camille stood up and stalked toward the door. She stopped before leaving. "Do you know where he wants me to go on Monday?"

Leon sighed. "Where, Camille?"

"A drug rehab counseling session. He understands that I started smoking because something was wrong. Something has been wrong for months, and you didn't even see it or care. All he wants to do is help me and you . . . you threw him out for no reason."

Camille turned and left the room, leaving Leon speechless.

Chapter Nineteen

Keisha sat in her bedroom, slowly thumbing through a photo album as tears generously flowed down her face. As she flipped through the pages, she picked up each photo lovingly and stared at it for several moments as she wept. As she did every evening, Keisha began with her wedding album. As she stared at the happy couple, she still found it hard to believe that it was all over because of Sharmaine.

Keisha and Gerald's meeting should never have turned into a love connection. She had been out shopping for Sharmaine and was in a hurry to get back to the house. Sharmaine had called several times because she was running late. As she stood behind him in line at Kroger, Keisha impatiently asked the cashier what was taking so long.

Gerald turned and scowled at her. "I'm trying to get this cashier to ring up my items correctly without overcharging me," he said. "I know this asparagus is on sale, and so are the tomatoes. Be quiet and wait your turn."

Keisha groaned loudly. "Can you speed things up? I'm on an errand for my boss, Sharmaine Cleveland. She has to fly out in a few hours for the Grammys."

Gerald was completely unimpressed. "Then you should have left the house sooner." He turned his back to her and continued closely monitoring the cashier. He made her rescan several items before he was finally satisfied with his total.

"See ya later, errand girl," he yelled over his shoulder at Keisha as he walked out.

When she left the market several minutes later, Gerald was standing in the parking lot waiting for her. Keisha frowned, but he smiled as she walked past him to her car.

He trotted over to her. "Hey, I was rude back there. I just wanted to apologize. It's been a stressful day."

When he spoke, Keisha actually looked at him for the first time and noticed that he was quite handsome. He had a full beard that covered the bottom half of his dark chocolate face. Looking up at him, she guessed he was at least six feet, four inches tall. His build was big and husky, like a teddy bear. Being short and petite, Keisha had a passion for big, strong men who, she felt, could sweep her right off her feet.

Over the next few months, that's exactly what Gerald did. They had chatted in the parking lot for several minutes before Keisha's cell phone began ringing again. She suddenly realized that she had to leave in order to get Sharmaine to the airport in time. They exchanged phone numbers and she rushed off.

On their first date, Gerald told her that he'd moved to Atlanta hoping for a chance to play for the Falcons as a walk-on. He'd failed and been cut on the first day. His second passion after football was food, so he took a job as a chef in a local restaurant. Within two years, he'd been promoted to head chef, and by the third year, he was part owner of the restaurant. The afternoon they met, he'd just signed the paperwork to purchase his own restaurant. It was just a bit overwhelming, and he was sorry he'd taken his stress out on her.

Keisha listened to his life story intently before realizing she didn't have much of a story to tell. She'd traveled around the country and stayed at some of the best hotels and resorts. She'd eaten at the classiest restaurants and mingled with many of the world's biggest stars; however, she'd done it all while working for Sharmaine. Seeing Gerald so full of dreams and accomplishments, she felt inadequate.

None of that mattered to Gerald. He thought Keisha was bright and captivating. The two of them dated steadily for the next six months before he proposed.

It was the opening night at his new restaurant, and as everyone gathered to offer congratulations, he bent down on one knee to ask for Keisha's hand in marriage. She'd hugged him so tightly, saying yes, that they both tumbled onto the restaurant floor. When they finally stopped laughing, he had placed the ring on her finger.

On a sunny spring day in late May, they'd exchanged vows in the garden of Sharmaine and Leon's estate. Only seven years old at the time, Jeanna had been the flower girl, and four-year-old Rodney stood in as ring bearer. Of course, Sharmaine was Keisha's matron of honor.

Now, staring at the photos, it seemed to Keisha that day had to be a million years before. After thumbing through her wedding album, Keisha moved on to the photo album that contained the pictures of her beautiful children.

Keisha had conceived Gerald Jr., affectionately known as Junebug, on their honeymoon. When he was just six months old, she'd discovered she was pregnant again. Five months later, they welcomed Lily. It seemed that they had the perfect life and family. But all was not as it seemed—because of Sharmaine.

Gerald had asked Keisha to scale back her duties after they

were married. He insisted on it during her pregnancies. Reluctant to let Sharmaine down, she'd told him she could handle it. He approached her again after the children were born. Keisha tried to convince him that he was being overprotective. As her babies grew older, it became a constant source of discord for them.

As she sat on her bed late one evening, taking off her shoes and rubbing her feet, she had tried to explain it to her husband.

"Honey, please try to understand that Sharmaine needs me. I'm her manager, publicist, and personal assistant all rolled into one," Keisha said. She had just returned home after another twelve-hour day spent with Sharmaine. They were gearing up for promotions on Sharmaine's first movie. There were tons of things that needed to be done.

"Your family needs you, Keisha. You've got Junebug and Lily in daycare, while Sharmaine's kids have a nanny. Several times a week, you don't get home in time to tuck them into bed. This has to stop."

Exhausted and not in the mood for a fight, Keisha thought for a moment, trying to find a solution. "I can bring the kids with me to Sharmaine's. I'm sure she won't mind if they all share the nanny."

"But I will mind," Gerald huffed. "It's not that I don't want you to work. I know I married a career woman. But things are out of hand. She depends on you entirely too much. I mean, she acts as if you don't have a life of your own."

Keisha knew that he was right. Working constantly had not been a problem when she was Sharmaine's dutiful single friend. There was no reason Keisha couldn't drop everything and run to her at a moment's notice. When she lived alone, working long hours did not interfere with anything but her television schedule. That was easily solved by purchasing a TiVo. Before she was married, if their work ran late into the night, she would follow Sharmaine upstairs and sleep in the guest bedroom. The next morning, they'd start fresh.

But as soon as Gerald, and then the children, had entered the picture, things changed. Keisha had a tough time trying to juggle Sharmaine's appointments between her dates with Gerald. When they became engaged, they decided on a small wedding, as Keisha did not have the time to plan an elaborate ceremony like she did when Sharmaine and Leon married. The most difficult times were during her pregnancies, when she'd gone home so tired she often fell asleep in a chair or on the sofa. Keisha barely had the energy to make it to bed most nights.

Shortly after Lily was born, Keisha began to feel totally overwhelmed. As much as she hated to admit it, there was no way for her to be a wife and mother while working for Sharmaine. Both were full-time jobs, and it was getting harder each day to do both. She went to Sharmaine's office to discuss scaling back her duties, and she was shocked by the answer Sharmaine proposed.

"Why don't you just quit? I can easily sign with a new management firm with a staff publicist. Then I can hire a college intern as my assistant. Your family should come first."

Sharmaine had the best intentions when she made the offer, but Keisha did not see it that way. After all she'd done for Sharmaine, she couldn't believe she'd just dismiss her without a second thought.

"You want me to quit? I've worked for you for all these years and now you just want me to walk away?"

"No, I don't want you to quit, Keisha, but I want you to be happy. I know that Gerald doesn't appreciate the long hours you work. You have two beautiful children that need their mother."

"I'm a good mother," Keisha protested.

"Of course you are. I didn't mean to imply that you aren't. I'm only saying that they could benefit from more time with you."

Keisha sighed. "I love Gerald, but I'm not cut out to be a housewife. I'd go crazy sitting at home all day."

"You don't have to be a housewife. There are other jobs you could hold that wouldn't take up as much of your time. You are the most organized person I know. If you want to, I bet you could start your own public relations firm."

"Not right now. We are deep in debt because of the recent improvements Gerald made to the restaurant. It will be at least two years before I could even think of something like that. Besides, if I'm the boss, I'd still be just as busy."

"I know, honey. I wish I had the answer, but I don't."

"Just let me work for you part-time," Keisha suggested. "I could work from home a few days a week, so I could spend more time with the kids. And if I could just get done by six in the evenings, I'm sure Gerald would be happy. I just need you to work with me."

Sharmaine sadly shook her head. "I'm sorry. My career is too busy right now. I have to have someone full-time. But if you decide to quit, there would be no hard feelings. We'd always be the best of friends."

Keisha left the office feeling disappointed and sick. She had tried, but she could not think of a logical reason why Sharmaine would not meet her halfway. The only possible reason she came up with was that Sharmaine was selfish. Keisha had made all sorts of sacrifices in her lifetime for Sharmaine. Keisha had wanted to attend Howard University in Washington, DC, but chose Spellman College in Atlanta because that was where Sharmaine had received a scholarship. They'd both pledged the same sorority, but Keisha had to turn down her first choice after they refused to accept Sharmaine also. She'd even stayed up late nights tutoring Sharmaine in economics and calculus so that she could graduate on time.

After college, Keisha began managing Sharmaine's career, and the sacrifices only increased. It was Keisha who had met Shawn Reeves at a Jack and Jill function. She'd promptly introduced him to Sharmaine. She was the first gospel artist Raga Records had ever signed, but Keisha convinced him it would pay off. After all of that, all she'd wanted from Sharmaine was some time to have a life of her own. It infuriated her that she had said no.

Feeling that she had no other choice, Keisha continued with her duties to Sharmaine, working twelve- to fifteen-hour days and most weekends. It put a strain on her marriage, but Gerald loved her. He did his best to juggle his duties at the restaurant to give him more free time and to make up for her absences.

As she sat staring at the photo album, Keisha realized she wasn't there the first time Lily took a step, or when Junebug said his first words. There weren't many milestones in her children's short lives, but Keisha had missed the majority of them.

It was a cold day in February, probably the coldest Atlanta had experienced all year, when Junebug reached his third birthday. Gerald made plans to close the restaurant to the public so that he could throw his son a spectacular birthday party. They had rented balloons and hired a clown. As his staff decorated the restaurant and put the finishing touches on the birthday cake, Gerald was at home dressing the children for the party. Keisha, as usual, was with Sharmaine.

Once both kids were dressed, he decided to call her once more. "Where are you? You said you'd be home hours ago. If we don't leave soon, we'll be late for the party," he said.

"I'm sorry. Jeanna wanted a new dress for Junebug's party, so Sharmaine and I went shopping. Now I just have to fax this paperwork to Shawn Reeves, and I'll be done."

"Don't you see how ridiculous it is that you are helping Sharmaine's kids get ready for your son's birthday? You should be here."

"I know, baby."

Gerald didn't have to tell her. She'd felt that way all day as they trudged from store to store in the freezing cold. Because it was Junebug's birthday, she'd planned to take the entire day off, but Sharmaine had called early that morning, advising her that Shawn needed the final copy of her acknowledgments for the next CD. Keisha offered to fax it from home, but Sharmaine wanted to make some changes. Keisha left their apartment, promising to be back in an hour; however, when she arrived, Sharmaine insisted on going shopping before working on the acknowledgments.

Gerald sighed loudly. "When are you coming home? The kids and I are dressed."

"I'm leaving now," she said.

Then Sharmaine walked into the room. "Keisha, will you iron these jeans for me before you leave?"

Her jaw dropped in awe. "Can't you ask Consuela to do it? Gerald and the kids are dressed and waiting for me."

"She uses too much starch and I can barely walk. Besides, it's a waste of time for you to drive all the way home when the restaurant is closer to here. Iron my jeans and then you can meet them there. It makes more sense." Sharmaine laid the jeans on a chair and went back to her bedroom without waiting for an answer.

Keisha put the phone to her ear. "I'm sorry, honey. I'll have to meet you guys at the restaurant. Please don't be mad."

"I'm not mad at you. I'm disappointed."

"Me too, baby, me too. I love you. Kiss the kids for me."

That was the last time she spoke to him. As she sat at the restaurant surrounded by decorations, children, a clown, and friends, Keisha wondered where they could be. She dialed his cell phone over and over, but there was no answer. The children grew restless, so she allowed the clown to begin his show without the birthday boy. Just as he was reaching his climax, a police officer entered the restaurant. Leon spoke to him, and then led him over to where Keisha was sitting.

To this day, the details remain sketchy in Keisha's mind. She had essentially shut down the moment she heard the words, "There's been an accident." All she knew for sure was that her precious family was gone.

As she grieved, she wished she had been home that day, just so she could have kissed her babies one last time, and felt her husband's strong arms wrapped around her. If they'd waited for her, they wouldn't have been on the highway at the exact moment their lives ended. All she could think of was that she should have been there to prevent such a terrible tragedy from happening. But she wasn't, because as always, she was with

Sharmaine. As her grief turned into bitterness, Keisha found herself unable to forgive Sharmaine.

It had taken her a few years to put all the pieces together, but she'd vowed to make sure Sharmaine lost everything that she'd taken away from her. As she'd done every night since they left her, Keisha kissed the photos of her husband and children good night and closed the photo albums. She decided the time had come to bring the scenario to an end.

Chapter Twenty

Leon stood up from his bedside after completing his morning prayers. He'd asked God for guidance with a string of issues he had to tackle head on that day.

While he was in Sharmaine's office the previous evening, Leon had discovered a key piece of the puzzle involving the video of Sharmaine. Shawn Reeves had kept his word, and the high resolution video had been delivered to his home earlier that week. Now that Rodney was home and on the mend, Leon finally took the time to take a look at them.

He had taken the videos into Sharmaine's office and locked the door behind him. As he watched, he zoomed in on the man that Sharmaine was with, and he had discovered something shocking. The man in the video was wearing Leon's custom made wedding band. It had a gold and platinum band with three small diamonds. Leon was sure because it was a one of a kind he'd designed himself.

After discovering this, Leon meticulously went through each frame, ignoring Sharmaine and studying the man. His face was slender, with round eyes and a big nose. Leon also noticed the man's face was the color of roasted almonds, but his body was much lighter. The man's back, chest, and arms were a light tan color, just like Leon's.

Stunned, Leon was positive that the man having sex with his wife in the video was him. *This can't be. That's not my face.*

Leon froze the frame and studied the area leading from the man's chin to his chest. That's when he realized that while they had assumed that someone put Sharmaine's head on another woman's body, the truth was that someone else's head had been placed on his.

Leon stopped the tape for several moments so that his mind could process the new information. It was the only logical explanation for his wife being involved in a sex tape; however, this revelation did not answer all of the questions. He and Sharmaine had never taped themselves having sex. That meant that unbeknownst to them, someone else had. The questions Leon could not answer were who, when, and why. He knew that before he could reveal what he'd discovered to anyone else, he had to have all of the answers.

Needing a moment to clear his head, Leon had gone out to the kitchen and had a drink of water before returning to the office and the video. His next order of business was to study the room in the video. Leon felt that it looked familiar, but he couldn't quite remember why. It definitely was not a bedroom in any of their homes. During their marriage, he was sure he and Sharmaine had stayed in several hundred hotels. He knew the room could be any one, or none of them.

After several hours, Leon had grown weary of studying the video and decided to turn it off and start fresh the next day. As he left the office, Leon momentarily considered calling Sharmaine and telling her what he'd discovered; however, he realized that this wasn't exactly good news. For months, Sharmaine had maintained that she wasn't in the video, and now he had proof positive that she was. They both were. Someone had violated the sanctity of their marital bed and made it public. He realized this was not something that should be shared. Not until he knew more.

Instead, he had decided to go into the family room and say hello to Camille's friend. As he walked in, he was livid to find Danté leaning over the pool table.

After Camille stormed out, he sat down and thought about what she had said, realizing that once again, she was right. Not only was there something wrong with Camille, but with all of his children. He'd recognized it, and prayed about it, but Leon realized he'd never done anything about it.

Taking a deep breath, he left his bedroom and decided to start with Jeanna. He knocked on her door and waited for her to answer. When she did, Leon was stunned by what he saw. Jeanna's once immaculately clean bedroom looked like a bomb had gone off inside. Slowly, he walked in, wading through the clothes on the floor.

"I'm sorry, Dad. I . . . I'll finish cleaning it later," she stammered.

Leon stepped over several items on the floor to reach the television, and turned off the movie Jeanna was watching. Then he waded over to her bed. After moving three teddy bears, a stack of magazines, and more clothes so that he could sit down, he turned to Jeanna.

"Honey, we need to talk," he said gently.

Jeanna sat down in the chair at her desk. "Okay."

"I know that I've avoided it for a long time. I've avoided it for too long." He looked around the room. "Honey, something is wrong. Please, tell me what it is."

Jeanna stared at him. "I'm fine, Dad."

"I know that you think you are, honey, but you are not. I mean, just look around you. This isn't like you at all."

"I'll clean it up, Dad. I promise."

On a hunch, he decided to try a different approach. "What movie are you watching?"

Jeanna stood up to get the DVD cover, and Leon stopped her.

"No, I want you to tell me."

Her eyes darted back and forth as Jeanna panicked. She had no idea what movie she'd been watching. She rarely paid any attention to the movies. Instead, she sat and stared at the screen.

"I don't know," she finally admitted.

"That's okay. Can you tell me why?"

She shook her head. Leon realized that Jeanna was too young to understand what she was doing, or even why. He stood up and reached onto the floor, picking up a dirty pair of jeans. As he tossed them in the basket, he asked Jeanna about school.

"It's our last week. There's not much left to do," she answered.

Leon picked up some socks and tossed them into the hamper also.

"How did you do in Mrs. Niles' class?"

"I think I'm getting a C." Jeanna began picking up clothes and tossing them into the basket beside Leon. "I could have gotten an A if I'd done better on that last quiz."

"Oh, yeah? Was it really hard?" Leon asked as they both moved into a cleaning rhythm, picking up clothes and tossing them into the basket.

"Kind of, but I passed."

As they talked and cleaned, Leon realized why Jeanna's room had gotten so dirty. Unconsciously, she believed that if she didn't clean it, eventually he'd have to say something, anything to her. Jeanna needed something he'd failed to give her over the past few months: a little bit of fatherly attention. At that point, she'd welcome any attention at all, even if it was negative. Leon believed that his children needed Sharmaine, so he allowed them to visit, but he didn't realize that they'd lost him too, and just wanted him back.

For the rest of the morning, Leon talked with Jeanna and helped her clean her room. Leon realized he'd been out of the loop about her grades in school, basketball tryouts, and the science fair. He'd told himself that watching movies together was family time, but the truth was he used the movies to avoid talking to his children. While Jeanna rattled on and on, he deeply regretted that decision.

As they were making the bed, Jeanna grabbed a pillow and swatted Leon with it, starting a pillow fight. They swung at each other for several minutes before falling onto the bed, laughing. Leon saw a glow in his daughter's eyes for the first time in months. He thanked God that it had not been completely extinguished.

When they were done cleaning, they both looked around the room proudly and smiled. "We did a great job. I think you and I should do this every Saturday morning, just the two of us," Leon said.

"That would be great, Dad. But I promise it won't be as dirty."

"If we get finished early, then we'll just hang out." He smiled at her.

Jeanna hugged him tightly. "That would be the best."

He hugged her back and gently kissed her forehead. "It's almost lunchtime. What do you think of asking Consuela to fix tacos?" Leon asked.

"Sounds yummy, Dad. I'll be down in a few moments. I just want to take a shower and change my clothes," she answered.

Leon left her room and briefly returned to his. Sitting on his bed was the box that contained Camille's laptop, cell phone, entertainment center wires, and mp3 player. Picking it up, he carried the box to Camille's room and used his foot to knock on the door.

"Come in," she yelled.

"My hands are full. Come open the door."

Grudgingly, Camille got up off of her bed and went to the door. "What?"

"Here are your things back. You are no longer grounded."

Slowly taking the box from him, Camille stepped back so he could enter the room. She set the box down on her desk.

"What's the catch?"

Leon walked in and sat on Camille's bed. "I want you to attend the meeting with Danté on Monday."

She stood with her arms folded, staring at him. "I never wanted to go to the meeting. I told Danté. I'm not a junkie. I got high a few times. It's not a big deal."

"No one is calling you a junkie, sweetheart. The purpose of the meeting is to help you deal with your issues, so you don't turn to drugs again. There will be other kids there your age, and some adults who went through the same things as teenagers. Our church sponsors it. They even serve snacks and sodas. I think it will be really good for you."

"How do you know so much about it?" Camille's brow wrinkled up with confusion.

"I used your cell phone this morning and called Danté. I apologized to him for last night, and I asked him to tell me about the meeting."

"Who are you, and what have you done with my dad?" she said sarcastically.

Leon chuckled. "I know that over the past few months it probably seemed like I'd been abducted by aliens. Things have been crazy around here. We've had one episode of drama after the other. But with God's help, we are going to get through this."

Camille sat down on the bed next to him. She laid her head on Leon's shoulder. "Do I have to stand up in front of the room and talk at this meeting?"

"No, honey. Danté says you can just listen. They meet every week. You don't have to say anything until you are comfortable." He put his arm around her. "I just want to make sure you get the help you need. I'm sorry I didn't try sooner."

The two of them sat in silence for several moments.

"Okay, I'll go," Camille finally decided.

Leon smiled broadly at her. "Um, I have another confession to make," he said. "I sort of told Danté he and his sister could come over this afternoon. Otis went to pick them up." He glanced down at his watch. "They will probably be here soon." He looked at her sheepishly.

Camille jumped excitedly off the bed. "Are you for real?"

"Yes. I want to get to know your friends."

She hugged him tightly. "Thanks, Dad."

Leon left her room feeling content. Next he stopped by Rodney's bedroom to check on him. Rodney was lying in bed, idly flipping channels on his television.

"Hey, how are you feeling?" Leon asked as he entered the room.

"I'm bored. Do I have to stay in bed all day?"

Leon thought for a moment. "No, you don't. You can get up if you are feeling up to it."

Rodney peeled back his covers and hopped out of bed. He walked over to his closet and stood just staring at his clothes for several minutes.

"Can I lounge around in my pajamas? I don't feel like putting on clothes," he asked.

"Well, you might want to at least put on a pair of shorts and a T-shirt. I invited Danté and Nichole over."

"Really? I like Nichole. She's cool. Do you think she'll wanna play Scrabble with me and Jeanna?"

"Get dressed and you can ask her when she gets here."

Leon sat down on the bed and talked with Rodney until he was completely dressed and ready to go downstairs. Then the two of them walked to the kitchen together. Consuela stood at the counter with taco shells and cheese as she put the finishing touches on lunch. Jeanna and Camille were sitting at the table.

"I'll be back in a few minutes, guys. I need to make a phone call," Leon said.

"Dad, can we eat by the pool?" Jeanna asked. "It's all cleaned out. The pool guy was here yesterday."

"That sounds good. We'll all go for a swim this afternoon."

Leon kissed each of his children gently on the cheek; then he went into Sharmaine's office. He went to her desk and pulled out her address book. Once he'd found the number, he placed the book back in the drawer and dialed the number from the office phone.

"Hello."

"Hi, Victor, this is Leon Cleveland."

Victor was sitting in his kitchen having lunch when his cell phone rang. "Leon?" he asked skeptically.

"Yes. I'm sorry to bother you on a Saturday, but it's important."

"I don't think we should be talking. If you have some news about Sharmaine's case, you have to give it to the district attorney's office."

"Don't give me that lawyer mumbo jumbo. I need to talk to you . . . man to man."

Victor leaned back in his kitchen chair and pushed away his plate. "All right, say whatever you need to say, but I have to warn you that if you say anything that can help my client, I will use it."

"That's exactly why I'm calling. I want my family back. I know Sharmaine didn't shoot me, and I need your help so I can prove it."

"And how do you plan to do that? The D.A. has you down as a witness for the prosecution. Unless you can identify the shooter, I don't know what you can do to help."

Leon sighed. "I can't identify anyone, but I do believe my wife was framed. All we have to do is figure out who framed her."

Victor laughed mockingly. "Now, why didn't I think of that?"

Leon told Victor what he'd discovered while watching the video tapes.

"That doesn't help at all, Leon. Sharmaine has denied being in that video. If I go into court with proof that she is, her credibility will be shot."

"But she truly believed that the video was faked."

"That doesn't matter. It will make her look terrible to a jury. They will say that she's backed into a corner and now changing her story."

"I am sure the same person who made this video tape framed Sharmaine. This is not a coincidence. It has to be connected."

"Are you absolutely sure about that? I read online that some hotels have been planting cameras and videotaping their customers. Then they edit and sell the tapes online."

"I saw that story also, but surely you don't think that's happening in five-star hotels like Sharmaine and I stay in. I think someone knew we'd be there and they planted the camera. I mean, why else would they change my face but leave Sharmaine's?"

"You have a point. So, do you have any ideas on who it might be?"

"Not yet. That's where I need your help. This may take some time to figure out. Do you think you can get another postponement of the trial? I know you got one when Sharmaine—well, when she was hospitalized. Is it possible to get another one?"

"I'm way ahead of you. I applied for an extension last week when your son got sick. I'm waiting to hear back from the judge. By the way, how is he?"

"Better. He's home and up and around. Thanks for asking."

"I heard they think it was poison. You've got to keep those household goods away from kids these days. They'll drink anything."

"I agree. Listen, Victor, will you call me as soon as you hear from the judge? Oh, and don't tell Sharmaine that we talked. I don't want to get her hopes up if I can't help her."

"You bet."

Leon hung up the phone just as the front doorbell rang. When he entered the front entryway, Consuela had just let Danté and Nichole in.

"The children are out by the pool," she said to them.

"Hello, Danté." Leon greeted him and smiled.

Danté looked nervously at Leon. "Um, this is my sister, Nichole." He motioned his hand in her direction.

Leon politely extended his hand to her. "Hello, Nichole. It's nice to meet you."

Nichole shook Leon's hand as he tried desperately, but failed, not to stare at her protruding belly.

"I know. I'm pretty big. The baby's due in about a month," Nichole said after noticing him staring.

"I'm sorry. I didn't mean to be rude. The children are having lunch. Have you eaten?" Leon asked.

"No, sir," Nichole answered respectfully.

Leon turned to his maid. "Consuela, will you take Nichole out to the pool and get her something to eat? I want to talk to Danté for a moment."

"Yes, sir, Mr. Leon," she answered.

Nichole followed closely behind, and the two of them walked down the hallway toward the back door.

Danté looked at Leon apprehensively. "What's up?" he asked.

"I spoke to Camille, and she's agreed to go to the meeting on Monday."

Danté's face lit up. "That's great. I know it's really going to help her. I've been going for almost a year now. It's a great group."

"Thank you, Danté. I have been so consumed with my own problems. I knew Camille needed help, but I kept putting off getting it for her."

"Don't thank me. If it wasn't for me, she never would have started in the first place." Danté stared at the floor. "I gave Camille her first joint. But I'm so sorry that I did. I have to help her. I have to."

Leon placed his hand on Danté's shoulder. "It was a mistake. I forgive you. Besides, if it wasn't drugs, Camille would have turned to something else. It could have been alcohol, or something much worse."

"What's going on in here?" Camille asked as she suddenly came barreling up the hallway. "Dad, you aren't gonna make him leave again, are you?"

"No. We were just talking . . . man talk. Leon winked at Danté.

Camille looked suspiciously back and forth at the two of them. "Um, can Danté borrow a pair of your swim trunks? Consuela's looking for something for Nichole to wear."

"Tell Consuela to check the pool house. I'm sure there are plenty of extra suits and towels in there. Just tell her to check in the—" Leon suddenly stopped talking as something clicked in his memory.

"Have her check where, Dad?" Camille asked.

"Um, I have to do some work in the office. Just tell her to check the storage closet in the pool house."

Leon suddenly rushed off to Sharmaine's office. He closed the door and locked it behind him.

Chapter Twenty-one

Camille stood frozen at the front door of the recreation room, afraid to go inside. She'd agreed to attend the meeting for the drug counseling program, but now that they'd arrived, she was starting to change her mind. Danté grabbed her hand and squeezed it, encouraging her to walk in. Tentatively, she stepped forward into the room and looked around.

The large room had about thirty chairs arranged in a huge circle. On the other side of the room were several long tables that had white tablecloths on them. One held a bunch of cups and drinks, while the other had various snacks. There was a group of teenagers standing in the corner near the snack tables, talking casually. Most of the kids were black, but Camille noticed a few white and Hispanic teens mixed into the crowd.

"Are we in the right place? Nobody here looks like a drug addict," she whispered.

Dante nudged Nichole in the arm and they both laughed at her. "I told you before. Everyone here is not a drug addict or junkie. Some of them, like Nichole, have never used drugs," Danté said.

"Then why do you come, Nichole?" Camille asked.

"It's not easy being fifteen and facing motherhood. It's real scary, and there are plenty of times I've wanted to turn to drugs. So, I come here to talk about my feelings, and it helps me stay away from them."

"People come here for all kinds of reasons. Just relax and give it a chance," Danté said.

Nervously, Camille nodded her head and continued looking around the room. She saw a boy standing by the wall that she thought she recognized from the pool party. Then she looked to the front of the circle, where a woman stood organizing paperwork. The woman walked around and laid a flyer on each chair. Camille stared at her for a moment, trying to remember her name.

"Is that Brenetta Reeves?" she asked.

"Yeah, Ms. Brenetta is the best," Nichole said. She waddled excitedly over to the circle and gave Brenetta a big hug.

"How are you doing, Nichole?" Brenetta asked.

"I'm good, but my feet are swelling."

Brenetta looked down at Nichole's round ankles and pudgy toes that looked like sausages stuffed inside her sandals. "Did you cut back on salty foods like I told you? You need to eat plenty of fresh fruits and vegetables. Have you done that?" she asked.

"Yes, ma'am, I'm trying, but we don't have a lot of it at home."

"I tell you what. Since I am picking you up Thursday for your next doctor's appointment, how about when we're done, we'll go shopping for some good food. We want you to have a healthy baby. We'll have to tell Danté I said to stop taking you to McDonald's all the time."

Danté walked up with Camille in tow, just in time to defend himself. "Hey, she loves McDonald's. It's not my fault," he teased. He reached out and gave Brenetta a warm hug.

"Sure, Danté. I bet she begs you for it." Brenetta laughed. Then suddenly she noticed Camille. "Hello, Camille." Her voice was filled with surprise.

"Hi, Ms. Brenetta," she answered.

"Danté told me that he was bringing his girl tonight. I had no idea that it was you."

Camille blushed. "Are you in charge here, Ms. Brenetta?" she asked.

"No one's in charge. We allow everyone the opportunity to express themselves however they want, but the church requires that the group have some adult advisors. I've been doing this for about two years now."

"And she's great at it," Nichole said. "Ms. Brenetta is one of the best counselors here. If you need anything, Camille, just ask her. If she can't do it, she'll make sure it gets done."

"Yeah, she helped me fill out applications when I was looking for a job. And she takes Nichole to the doctor so she won't have to ride the bus. She won't admit it, but me and Nichole are her favorites," Dante teased.

"You know I have to look out for you two since you are all alone," Brenetta answered. She tried to hide the fact that she was blushing.

"We aren't alone, Ms. Brenetta. We have each other. But we sure are glad that you care so much about us," Nichole said. Brenetta gave her another hug.

Nichole, Dante, and Camille took seats in the circle and the meeting began. Camille watched in silence as several teenagers stood up and talked about their problems. One young woman said she began smoking weed when she was eleven years old. When she couldn't get money to buy it, she started selling drugs, and was addicted to crack cocaine by the time she turned thirteen. Just as Camille was wondering how old she currently was, she told them she'd just celebrated her sixteenth birthday. She was proud to say she'd been clean for six months.

Camille's mouth fell open in awe, and she had to cover it to keep from being embarrassed when the next young man said that he had lived in a crack house until he was eight years old. His mother was a crack addict who had been killed by her dealer. The young man didn't know how much money she owed, but the dealer felt it was worth taking her life and leaving him without a mother. Even after all of that, the young man had never used drugs himself. He joined the group to help encourage others.

Several more teens and adults told their stories and Camille and the group listened intently.

Then Brenetta stood up. "I've been a part of this group for two years, and I've never shared my story," she said. "But God placed it on my heart that I need to do it tonight."

The room was silent as Brenetta told everyone how she turned to drugs while in high school. Her mother had left her to be raised by her grandmother. Brenetta told them that she'd grown up in Sand Poole Manor only a few doors away from where Danté and Nichole now lived.

"My life was rough. We didn't have much money and I wore old clothes, so the kids picked on me at school. When I was fourteen, I was shot by a bullet that was aimed at my best friend. I had a lot of setbacks, but through it all, my grandmother was my pillar of strength. She was the only person who ever showed me genuine love." Brenetta paused to gather her words. "When I was sixteen, my grandmother passed away. It was natural causes; she was old. But I was devastated.

I dropped out of school and began running around with a bad crowd. Of course, it didn't take long for me to get hooked on drugs."

Danté and Nichole were stunned. They thought Brenetta was just another rich lady who liked doing things for people. They'd never imagined she'd come from the same place that they did, or had a life just as hard.

"Then one day, I met my future husband, Shawn Reeves," Brenetta said.

All of the kids began clapping, as they were huge fans of all of the artists on Raga Records. Brenetta smiled and waited for the applause to die down before continuing.

"Shawn and I started out as good friends. I had big dreams of having a singing career, and he was willing to help make my dreams come true. In the process, he helped me clean up my life. Years later, we fell in love and married."

One of the teens raised her hand to ask a question. "So, you married a rich guy and that turned your life around?" she asked.

"No, it wasn't quite that simple. When I met him, Shawn was not the rich entrepreneur he is today. He was an ex-con living in a halfway house. While he'd been in prison, he took college courses and taught himself to read music and play several instruments. Most people know him as a major producer, but Shawn is also a very talented musician. He began Raga Records with one artist, and he built it up to one of the largest record companies in the world."

"Yeah, Ms. Brenetta, he's the Berry Gordy of our time," Danté said.

Brenetta laughed. "I guess you could say that. What I learned from Shawn was that no matter how hard you fall, you have to pick yourself up and start over again. If you lay down in the gutter, you end up being gutter trash. But if you pick yourself up and keep going, there's no limit to what you can do with your life. If I can go from the projects in Bankhead to a mansion in Alpharetta, anybody can."

The audience burst into thunderous applause and cheers.

"Everybody loves Ms. Brenetta," Nichole whispered to Camille.

After the meeting was over, the teenagers gathered around the snack table for sandwiches, chips, cookies, and drinks.

"How did you enjoy it?" Danté asked Camille. He took a large bite of a chocolate chip cookie.

"I feel stupid," Camille answered.

"Why?"

"All of these kids had real problems, like a loved one dying, or living on the street, or even almost dying. My problems with my mom seem so small in comparison."

"You don't have to be from the street to turn to drugs, Camille. It happens for a lot of different reasons."

"That's not what I mean. It just seems like what I've been through was so trivial. I should have been able to handle it. I feel so ashamed."

"Oh, no, Camille, don't feel that way. Your problems were important to you, and that's all that matters."

She smiled at him. "No, I understand that. I'm glad I came. It just shows me that if they can survive all of those things, then I can learn to deal with my mother."

"Danté, I told you this wasn't over!"

Everyone one in the room suddenly gasped and screamed in terror as Blue walked into the recreation center pointing a gun. The crowd panicked, and people began running in all directions. Danté grabbed Camille, and they ducked down behind the snack table.

Three shots rang out before the security guards were able to tackle Blue to the ground.

"Are you okay?" Danté asked Camille.

She nodded her head just as they heard Brenetta let out a wailing scream. Nichole lay motionless on the ground as blood trickled out of her mouth.

Chapter Twenty-two

It was early Monday evening when Leon began to think he had finally put all the pieces of the past few months together. It was hard for him to believe, but he was sure Keisha was behind it all.

On the previous Saturday, when he had told Camille to have Consuela check the pool house for extra swimsuits, he'd suddenly realized why the bedroom in the video was so familiar. The ugly blue-and-burgundy paisley wallpaper that Sharmaine hated so much was the clue he'd needed. The two of them had often talked of redecorating the pool house, but they'd never gotten around to it. It was rare that either of them was inside it. He was certain the wallpaper in the video was the exact same pattern.

While the children swam, he had rushed to Sharmaine's office to view the video for confirmation. As he watched, he recognized not only the wallpaper, but also the furnishings that were in the bedroom of the pool house. The video had been tweaked, and things retooled, but there was no doubt in his mind that the video had been made while he and Sharmaine made love in the pool house.

There was only one night that he and Sharmaine had spent there, and he realized it was at Keisha's insistence. The children were away visiting Leon's parents, and when he and

Sharmaine returned from dropping them off at the airport, Keisha met them on the front steps of their estate.

"I'm sorry, but you can't go in the house," she had said.

"What's going on, Keisha?" Sharmaine asked.

She grinned sheepishly and asked them to follow her around the house to the backyard. When they arrived, they saw that Keisha had decorated the entire pool area with hanging Chinese lamps and candles. She had also set up a table with a romantic dinner for two.

"Surprise!" she yelled. "The kids are gone, and I just wanted to make this a special night for the two of you. You guys deserve it."

Inside the pool house, they found that she had lit more candles and spread rose petals on the bed in the shape of a heart. It was one of the most beautifully romantic nights he could remember. Thinking back on it now, he couldn't believe how Keisha had perverted it with the video.

At the time, both he and Sharmaine had thought it was a wonderful gesture, but he now realized it was a setup that Keisha had planned. He wondered why she would do such a thing. They'd been friends for so many years. None of it made sense to him.

In order to confirm his suspicions, Leon decided to inspect the pool house. Behind a picture in the bedroom, he'd found a drilled hole that was large enough to hide a camera lens. There was no other evidence, but he was sure that's where she'd hidden the camera.

After inspecting the pool house, Leon had spent all day that Sunday trying to figure out why Keisha would choose to videotape him and Sharmaine then release the tape. By Monday morning, he'd convinced himself that she wasn't responsible. Perhaps she'd made the video, but someone else had found it and leaked it to the press, he told himself.

Later that day, he had received a phone call from Victor. "Leon, I've got some news. It may not mean much, but I thought you'd want to know."

"What is it?" he asked anxiously.

"I finally got a call from the gun store that registered the gun used in your shooting. Although the paperwork has Sharmaine's name on it, they found a video tape of the day of sale. The person who signed for and picked up the gun was actually her assistant, Keisha Williams."

Leon had to struggle to keep from falling over on the floor. "Do they have a photograph of her?"

"Yes, but like I said, it may not mean much."

"What do you mean? It proves that Sharmaine never purchased the gun." Leon was ecstatic.

"Keisha Williams is her personal assistant. She makes purchases on your wife's behalf every day. It's no proof."

Leon suddenly realized Victor was absolutely right. The photos of Keisha could not clear Sharmaine's name. And although he knew she set up the date in the pool house, he'd found no evidence to support his theory that she videotaped them. He needed more.

"Thanks, Victor. I appreciate your call," he said before hanging up.

Later that evening, Camille left to attend her drug counseling meeting with Danté, while Leon, Rodney, and Jeanna sat around the kitchen table, finishing up dinner. They were chatting casually about nothing in particular when Leon received a phone call that convinced him that Sharmaine was in grave danger.

"Mr. Cleveland, this Dr. Winslow. I'm sorry to call so late in the evening, but we have your son's test results back. We have reason to believe his poisoning was deliberate and not accidental. He consumed a large amount of arsenic, normally found in rat poison."

Leon was shocked. "But how? I don't understand."

"There's more, Mr. Cleveland."

Leon took a seat and braced himself. "What is it?"

"We tested your wife's blood when she donated at the blood bank. We were unable to use it because she also had a significant amount of arsenic poisoning in her system. It wasn't nearly as high as your son's, but it was high."

"Could it have been something they ate or drank?"

"We aren't sure, but under the circumstances, we had to alert the police. I'm sure there will be an investigation."

"Thank you, doctor."

As soon as he hung up the phone, Leon turned to Rodney. "When you got sick, did you or your mother eat something? I mean the same thing."

Rodney shook his head. "I didn't see Mommy eat anything, and all I had was a smoothie that was in a pitcher in the refrigerator."

Leon decided that he needed to speak with Sharmaine. After the children finished their dinner and went to their rooms, he dialed her from the kitchen phone.

"Hello," she said.

"Hi, Sharmaine, this is Leon. I just got a call from the hospital about Rodney's test results."

Sharmaine sat up on her bed, where she'd been lounging, watching a movie. "What did they say?" she asked.

"It appears that he ate or drank something with rat poison in it."

Sharmaine gasped. "How did that happen?"

"I don't know." Leon paused. "They also said that you'd consumed it too. When you gave blood, the poison was in your system too."

Sharmaine was stunned. "But I didn't get sick like he did. There must be some mistake with the tests."

"They said your level of poisoning wasn't as high, but there was poison in your bloodstream. Rodney says he drank a smoothie he found in the refrigerator. Is there any way it could have been accidentally contaminated?"

Sharmaine held the phone as she thought. It had occurred to her that the smoothies were making her sick, and she had not drunk any since returning home after Rodney was released from the hospital. She had to admit she felt better than ever. "Keisha makes homemade smoothies for me. I thought they were giving me diarrhea, so I stopped drinking them, but there's no way it could have poison in it."

Leon sighed. It seemed that Keisha had something to do with every crisis. He wondered if she'd really try to poison Sharmaine. "Sharmaine, I have to tell you something about Keisha." He paused, trying to find a way to break it to her gently. "Victor found out that she bought the gun that I was shot with. She registered it in your name."

"Why would she do that?" Sharmaine asked. Her voice was filled with confusion.

"There's more. I also found out that it really is you in the video that is circulating."

"You have got to be kidding. That is not me! There is no—"

He interrupted her. "Yes, it is. It's you and me. Keisha videotaped us together that night we spent in the pool house. Then she edited the tapes and released them. Honestly, it's the truth."

Sharmaine stood up from the bed and began pacing around the room. "Leon, this doesn't make sense. It sounds as if you are saying Keisha was out to get me. That's ridiculous."

"I know how it sounds, and I am having a hard time believing it myself, but it all fits. Keisha made the video. She bought the gun, and she made the smoothie that Rodney drank. What other answer could there be?"

"Leon, you have to be mistaken about all of this. Keisha is my dearest friend. Why would she want to hurt me?"

"I don't know. I agree that it doesn't make any sense, but I think you need to get your stuff and leave there. Go to a hotel or something until we can figure out what's going on. You could be in danger."

"There's no way I can go to a hotel. My assets are frozen. I have no money. Keisha has been supporting me all this time. I can't believe these things you are saying about her."

"I'll pay for the hotel. You can use any of the credit cards from our joint account. Please, just do it. I'm worried about you."

Although she was touched by his concern, it took several more moments of talking before Leon was finally able to convince Sharmaine to leave.

"Fine. I'll have Keisha take me to a hotel tomorrow," she said.

"You haven't heard a word I've said," Leon said anxiously.

"You need to leave now. Otis and I will come get you. Just pack a few things and we'll be right there."

Still feeling unsure, Sharmaine hung up the phone and began packing. She'd just placed a few pieces of underwear in her suitcase when there was a knock at her bedroom door. Keisha opened it without waiting for an answer.

"What are you doing?" she asked. Keisha stared at the open suitcase lying on the bed.

"Um, I'm going to a hotel. Leon offered to pay for it. I've imposed on you long enough." Sharmaine went to her closet and began putting pants and blouses in the suitcase.

"Who says you are imposing?" Keisha asked.

"No one said it. I really appreciate you letting me stay. It's just time that I leave."

Keisha began to panic, realizing it would be more difficult to complete her plan if Sharmaine moved out. "You're no trouble, Sharmaine. Stay here with me. I enjoy the company. Stop packing, and I'll put this stuff away for you." Keisha walked over to the suitcase and began putting Sharmaine's things back in the drawer.

Sharmaine watched her in silence as Keisha put away all of her clothes and slid the suitcase back under the bed. "I'd better call Leon. He was on his way to pick me up," she said.

Keisha looked at her strangely. "What's really going on? Why is Leon suddenly offering to pay for a hotel and pick you up?"

Sharmaine sat down on the edge of the bed and sighed. "I may as well tell you. Leon has this ridiculous idea that you are behind everything that has happened the past few months. He thinks you videotaped us having sex, then edited and released it. Victor has convinced him you bought the gun that shot him. Worst of all, he thinks you tried to poison me and Rodney. Isn't that the silliest thing you've ever heard of?"

Keisha didn't answer, as her eyes grew wide with surprise and fear. She had the look of a trapped animal who was seconds away from gnawing off his own foot to escape.

As soon as she looked at her face, Sharmaine realized that Leon was absolutely right about everything. "It's true?" Sharmaine asked.

Without a word, Keisha bolted from the room and rushed down the hallway to her own bedroom. Sharmaine ran after her, and then realized it was a big mistake. Keisha came out of her bedroom carrying a gun. She pointed it at Sharmaine.

"Get in the living room!" Keisha ordered.

Frightened, Sharmaine quickly obeyed. She walked to the living room and sat down on the sofa. Her whole body trembled with fear as she watched Keisha pacing back and forth around the living room. Sharmaine noticed that she was fidgeting, mumbling to herself, and acting more erratic by the second.

She tried to divert her attention. "Keisha, put the gun down and just talk to me," Sharmaine pleaded.

"Shut up! I need to think."

"There's no way you could have done any of this. Just talk to me, please."

Keisha paced back and forth, ignoring her.

"Listen, Leon is tripping. How could you be responsible? You were gone with the kids when he was shot, right?"

Keisha stopped pacing and stared at her for several seconds. "Fine. You wanna know how? I drugged all of you. We were in North Carolina before the kids ever woke up again. I'm amazed that you idiots will eat or drink anything I give you.

That was the easy part. Dragging you around was hard. You are not as slim as you appear with airbrushing and a good girdle, Sharmaine." Keisha laughed loudly.

"What are you talking about?"

"I had to drag your fat behind out of bed, so that Leon would think you were in the shower. Then I had to put you back in before you woke up. Take my advice: If you care about your career, give Jenny Craig a call," Keisha cackled.

Suddenly, everything began to make sense to Sharmaine. Everything she'd experienced physically for the past few months was the result of Keisha drugging and poisoning her. She wasn't having blackouts or memory loss. They were all orchestrated by the woman she considered her best friend. Stunned, she realized that Keisha had been feeding her pills, poison, and lies every day for more than five months.

"So, my suicide attempt?" she asked.

"Yep, that was me too. So what? I didn't let you die. I just needed you to believe you were slipping. It worked beautifully, don't you think?" Keisha sat down in the chair facing Sharmaine. "You know, I almost felt sorry for you. Then I realized if you weren't so stupid, I would never have been able to do it. So, if you feel the need to place blame, you can blame yourself."

Sharmaine's insides were bubbling over with a mixture of anger, fear, disappointment, and hurt. After years of friendship, she still could not fathom what could have possibly driven Keisha to hurt her so deeply. As she sat fighting back tears, she suddenly realized that talking seemed to calm Keisha. She was no longer pointing the gun at Sharmaine. It was resting in her lap.

Just as she was about to ask more questions, they heard a

knock at the front door. Keisha jumped up from the chair and rushed to Sharmaine. She put the gun to her temple.

"Don't say a word or I'll blow your brains out," Keisha threatened.

The knocking continued as Sharmaine sat trembling with the cold steel next to her skin.

"Sharmaine, it's me, Leon," he called.

He knocked louder, and Keisha realized that he wasn't going to go away. She grabbed Sharmaine by the arm and forced her up off the sofa. "Let's go," she whispered.

She led Sharmaine through the kitchen and out of the back door of the apartment. There was no elevator, and only one stairwell door that led up to the roof, or down to the parking garage. Keisha poked the gun into Sharmaine's ribs and ordered her to start walking down the stairs.

Sharmaine obeyed, and silently prayed as she slowly began the walk down from the sixteenth floor. A few times, she stumbled, and Keisha cursed her, urging her to get up. Feeling out of breath, she momentarily stopped.

Keisha poked the gun deeper into her back. "Move it, Sharmaine," she ordered.

Weeping, Sharmaine continued to stumble down the stairwell. "I'm going as fast as I can," she cried.

"Just keep moving and be quiet."

After several minutes, they finally reached the parking garage. Looking around, Keisha noticed that the building security officer was sitting in his booth. There was no way out. Quickly, she pushed Sharmaine back into the stairwell and ordered her to walk back up the stairs.

Panting and out of breath, Sharmaine continued climbing stairs until they reached the top of Keisha's twenty-story building. She continued poking the gun in Sharmaine's back until she opened the door and stepped out onto the roof.

Terrified, Sharmaine stared out at the Atlanta skyline. She turned to look at Keisha with her knees shaking. "You're not acting like yourself, Keisha. Let's go back downstairs and talk for a while. You can tell me anything and I'll be there for you. I'm your best friend."

Keisha suddenly began laughing hysterically. "You are not my friend, Sharmaine. You are my boss. All you ever do is boss me around and tell me what to do. Is that what you call friendship?"

"I . . . I don't understand," she stammered. "Where is all of this coming from?"

"You really are stupid, aren't you?" Keisha said.

Sharmaine stood frozen with fear as tears streamed down her face. "I . . . I don't know. I thought we were friends. Remember we met in Miss Crain's third grade class?"

"We used to be friends, Sharmaine, but all of that changed when you became a gospel diva. The funny thing is you never would have made it without me. I've read every contract and negotiated every deal. I set up meetings, tours, and interviews. No matter what needed to be done, it was me who did it. I made you, Sharmaine Cleveland!" she screamed.

Sharmaine's head nodded rapidly. "You did. You worked really hard for me, and I am eternally grateful."

"Don't try to play me, Sharmaine. You are the most ungrateful person I know. You've never cared about anybody but yourself."

"No, that's not true. I care about you. We're family."

Keisha suddenly pointed the gun directly as Sharmaine's forehead. "I should kill you for even saying that word. I'm not your family. My family is dead. My husband and my babies are dead because of you."

Sharmaine's entire body trembled. "No, it was an accident. I had nothing to do with it. You and I were together when it happened."

"That's just how dense you are. You don't even realize that we should not have been together when it happened. I should have been with them. It was my son's birthday, and I should have been with my family, but you said no. All you ever cared about was your career, your family, and your needs. What about mine? What about me?" Keisha lowered the gun as she wiped away a tear.

Sharmaine began to cry harder. "Oh, Keisha, I am so sorry."

"Sorry? You're sorry?" Keisha laughed loudly. "Are you sorry that I was in New York on tour with you on my first wedding anniversary? Or are you sorry that you never gave me time off to nurse my babies? Could you be sorry that my family was lying on the highway dying while I ironed your stupid jeans? What exactly are you sorry for, Sharmaine?" Keisha demanded.

Staring at her feet, Sharmaine wept with regret. It had never occurred to her how much she'd unintentionally taken from her friend. "Everything, Keisha. I am sorry for everything. Please forgive me," she begged.

"Shut up! I'm through talking to you." Keisha looked around the rooftop, desperately trying to figure out what to do next.

"Keisha, listen to me. I was wrong." Sharmaine slowly inched closer to her. "I should have given you more time with your family. I should have given you the day off to be with your baby. I wasn't thinking, and I am so very sorry. But it's not my fault that they died."

"I should have been with them that day. I was supposed to be with them," Keisha wept.

"I know, honey. I'm so sorry. Put the gun down, Keisha, please," Sharmaine pleaded.

"No!" Keisha suddenly raised the gun again, pointing it at Sharmaine.

Sharmaine's heart ached for the pain she knew Keisha was feeling. Although she was still afraid, she desperately wanted to help her deal with some of the pain that she'd caused. She decided to continue diverting her attention. "Hey, Keisha, remember when you were eleven and I was twelve? Do you remember that we sang in Mrs. Bennett's children's choir together?"

"Shut up, Sharmaine!" Keisha continued pacing around the roof, looking for a way out.

Ignoring her, Sharmaine continued to talk. "Remember we had blue-and-white robes, and my mom put my hair in those funny-looking braids? Your mom had your hair looking cute with a bang in front. Do you remember that, Keisha?"

Keisha turned and stared at her with tears streaming down her face.

Sharmaine inched closer to her and kept talking. "I remember it so well. You and I sang a duet in the spring concert. I can still remember the song."

"I said shut up!" Keisha screamed. She held tightly to the gun and continued crying as Sharmaine began to sing:

"There is a name I love to hear
I love to sing its worth.
It sounds like music in mine ear

The sweetest name on earth.
Oh, how I love Jesus.
Oh, how I love Jesus.
Oh, how I love Jesus
Because He first loved me!"

"Do you remember your verse, Keisha? I bet you could sing it with me."

Keisha shook her head, refusing to join in. She remembered the song. She'd sung it to Lily and Junebug as they lay in bed the night before they died. They were fast asleep, but Keisha had just arrived home and wanted to check on her babies. As Gerald stood watching from the doorway, she'd gently and quietly sung it to them. It was the last lullaby she sang.

Still holding on to the gun, Keisha tried to cover her ears as Sharmaine continued to sing:

"It tells me of a Savior's love
Who died to set me free.
It tells me of His precious blood,
The sinner's perfect plea.
Oh, how I love Jesus.
Oh, how I love Jesus.
Oh, how I love Jesus.
Because He first loved me!"

Sharmaine continued to sing the first song she and Keisha sang together as children. It was still one of her favorites, and she prayed it would touch and soften Keisha's heart. She knew it was not hardened with evil, but with grief.

As she sang, Sharmaine watched tears stream down Keisha's face. Finally, Keisha took her hands off of her ears and looked around the rooftop. She appeared lost and confused. "I miss my family. I miss my babies," she cried.

"I know, honey. Everything's going to be okay. Just put the gun down," Sharmaine said gently.

Keisha shook her head. "No. No. No," she said over and over. "I should be with them. I want to be with them," she cried.

Sharmaine watched in silence as the gun slowly slipped from Keisha's hand and landed on the rooftop.

Leon and Otis knocked repeatedly on Keisha's apartment door, but no one answered.

"Didn't you say you saw Keisha's car in the garage?" Leon asked.

"I'm pretty sure it was hers."

Unable to wait any longer, Leon backed up away from the door. Then he lifted his leg and charged the door with his full force, knocking it open with his foot. Frantically, he went from room to room, unable to find anyone. As he and Otis searched the kitchen, they found the back door standing open. They rushed out of the door to the stairwell, realizing it led back to the parking garage. Anxiously, they rushed down the stairs. Once inside the garage, they looked around, unable to figure out where to go next.

"Keisha's car is still here," Otis said, pointing.

Leon rushed to the guard's booth. "Have you seen two

women down here? One of them is my wife, Sharmaine Cleveland, the singer."

"Oh yeah, they were here for a few seconds; then they went back in the stairwell," the guard answered.

"We were just at the apartment and in the stairwell. They aren't in there. I mean, they could be on any floor in this building."

"No, sir, they can't. The back doors stay locked. There's only one other way to get out. That stairwell leads up onto the roof."

"Call the police. My wife is in danger," Leon said, then ran back to the stairwell. As Otis followed closely behind, Leon began making the twenty-story climb to the top. When they reached the roof, they were too late to stop her.

Leon heard Sharmaine scream, "No!"

The three of them watched in pained silence as Keisha rushed to the edge of the building. "Please forgive me, God," she said before she jumped. Due to the height of her fall, Keisha was dead before her body hit the sidewalk.

Epilogue

One Year Later

Camille stood on the front steps of the church, impatiently waiting for Danté. Just to kill time, she looked down at herself, to be sure everything was straight and in place. As soon as she saw him pull up, she almost jumped up and down with anticipation. Her excitement overflowed, as she had not seen him since Christmas break.

On the night of the shooting, Brenetta had begged Danté to allow her to ride with him and Nichole in the ambulance to the hospital. As she lay on the gurney barely clinging to life, Nichole opened her eyes and smiled at Brenetta. "Will you take care of my baby?" she asked.

Tears streamed down Brenetta's face as she held tightly to Nichole's hand. "You are going to be able to take care of the baby yourself, Nichole. You'll be fine," she answered.

"No, I won't. I know Danté will try, but he can't do it alone. Promise me, Ms. Brenetta, that you'll take the baby and give her a good home."

Brenetta looked over at a weeping Danté then slowly nodded her head.

Nichole slowly turned her head and looked over at her brother. "I love you, Danté," she said before closing her eyes.

***

Now, a year later, Danté was arriving at the church to attend the christening of his niece, who'd been delivered by Cesarean section as soon as they arrived at the hospital. She had entered the world almost simultaneously as Nichole departed.

Danté stepped out of his car and rushed over to Camille. He hugged her tightly.

"I'm so glad you made it," she said.

"I would not have missed this day for anything. If they had not allowed me to take finals early, I probably would have just walked away from campus."

Following Nichole's death, Danté was lost and unsure what to do with himself any longer. He'd vowed to pay Blue back for killing his sister, but he'd never gotten the chance. Due to jail overcrowding, Blue had managed to make bail only two weeks after the shooting. No one was really sure where he went after being released. The next morning, his mutilated body had been found behind a dumpster in Sand Poole Manor. Blue had paid for the gun he'd used in the shooting with counterfeit bills. Trying to trick Rip had turned out to be a fatal mistake. Danté struggled between feeling sorry for him one minute, and being relieved the next.

However, Blue's death did little to ease his grief. For so long, he had been focused on taking care of his sister and her baby. He had no idea what to do after she was gone. As Nichole predicted, he wanted to take care of the baby alone, but he had to admit that he had no idea what to do. So, he followed his sister's wishes and turned her over to Brenetta and Shawn Reeves.

Their joy at becoming parents was marred by their concern for Danté. They knew that without the baby or Nichole, he was quickly slipping into depression and despair. Brenetta suggested that perhaps he just needed to leave Atlanta, and felt that it was the perfect time for him to begin college. She told Danté that she and Shawn would pay his tuition and fees. Angrily, he had refused their offer.

"You can't pay me for my sister's baby," he had said. Inside, he was still full of rage, confusion, and grief.

"That's not what we are trying to do," Shawn answered. "My wife and I have prayed for a baby for several years. We are saddened that God took Nichole, but we love her daughter, and Brenetta made a promise to Nichole to take good care of her."

"What does that have to do with me?" Danté asked.

Shawn didn't answer. Instead, he turned to Brenetta for help.

"We want to help you, Danté. This is nothing new. We've always cared about you and Nichole," she said.

"So why didn't you offer to send me to college when I graduated high school? Why are you doing this now?"

Brenetta smiled and gently took his hand into hers. "Because we knew you'd never go off to college and leave your sister. But she's in heaven now, and we are taking care of the baby. You took care of Nichole for so long, Danté, and she loved you very much, but it's time for you to take care of yourself," she said.

As he walked into the church, Danté thanked God that he had listened and accepted their offer. Sean had also given him a car. It was nothing fancy, just a used Toyota, but it was clean and ran well. Danté had just completed his freshman year at South Carolina State University. He was studying engineering and sincerely hoped that soon Camille would join him on campus as a student.

They walked to the front of the church and took their seats. Directly in front of them were Leon, Sharmaine, Jeanna, and Rodney. They looked back and smiled at them as they sat down.

It had taken Victor almost two months after Keisha's death to get the attempted murder charges against Sharmaine dropped. Although Keisha had confessed to Sharmaine, there was little evidence linking her to the crime. As executor of Keisha's estate, Sharmaine was reluctant to allow them access to Keisha's apartment and belongings. Regardless of what transpired, Sharmaine still loved Keisha and did not want to destroy her memory. She realized, however, that unless she implicated Keisha, she could not clear her own name. Sadly, she had turned everything over to Victor and the police.

Inside Keisha's apartment, they found the rat poison, as well as the other drugs she'd used in order to make Sharmaine sick. They had also gained access into her computer, which contained proof that Keisha had recorded and edited the video. Armed with this information, along with verification that Keisha had falsely obtained the gun in Sharmaine's name, Victor was finally able to get a judge to clear Sharmaine of all charges. After the charges were dropped, the judge released the freeze on her finances. She moved back into her home, and she and Leon began rebuilding their lives. It wasn't an easy transition, but they were slowly finding their way back to the family they once were.

After reconciling, Leon and Sharmaine's first order of business was a press conference, during which they admitted to being the couple in the video. They also let the press and all of Sharmaine's fans know that she was filmed without her knowledge or consent, with her husband. Realizing that she was actually the victim, her fans rallied behind her in forgiveness.

They flooded the radio stations and the record company with so many requests that Shawn Reeves had no choice but to immediately re-sign her to Raga Records and re-release her CD. It shot up the charts like a meteor, breaking sales records second only to Michael Jackson's *Thriller*.

In just a few weeks following the christening, Sharmaine was due to begin her nationwide tour. It would be her first tour without Keisha, and she was determined to learn from her mistakes. Instead of having one personal assistant, manager, and publicist, she requested that the record company hire a team of people, each with a different job. She was also insistent that no one was required to work excessive hours. Although the tour was scheduled to last three months, she'd requested that the schedule allow one week off in between shows every two weeks. This would allow anyone who worked on the tour time to relax, rest, and see their families.

Pearls of Righteousness, the movie she'd completed prior to all of the trouble, had been picked up again by the studio. It was scheduled for release on Christmas, as planned, the same as her other movies. The studio also signed her to an exclusive contract for three additional movies over the next five years. Her career was destined to become even larger and more successful than it had been before.

Sharmaine still deeply missed her friend. After planning her funeral, she'd buried Keisha in the same plot with her husband and children. Sharmaine took flowers to her grave often, and prayed that she'd somehow finally found peace.

Also inside the sanctuary, Shawn and Brenetta sat with their baby girl happily squirming in Brenetta's lap. After watching Nichole die, Brenetta was so grief stricken that initially she was hesitant to take the baby, as Nichole had requested; however, the events finally allowed her to look at her life in perspective. Brenetta had also been shot as a teen, but unlike Nichole, she survived. As she reflected on how fragile life can be, she realized that she had a wonderful husband and a beautiful home. She had family and friends who loved and respected her. For the first time, Brenetta realized she was truly blessed. Her hunger for a child of her own had overshadowed that.

As they prepared for the christening, she'd told Shawn that she wanted to adopt more children. He was surprised, as she'd always fought him when he'd suggested it in the past. Brenetta explained that she realized that a baby did not have to come from her body for her to fall in love and be a good mother. They agreed that there were plenty of children that could use a good, stable home with loving parents. Both of them looked forward to soon giving their daughter siblings.

Everyone in the congregation ceased their idle chatter as Bishop Snow entered the sanctuary to begin the service. After greeting everyone, he opened his Bible and began reading aloud from Luke, 18:15 "*And they brought unto him also infants, that he would touch them: but when his disciples saw it, they rebuked them. But Jesus called them unto him, and said, Suffer little children to come unto me, and forbid them not: for of such is the kingdom of God.*"

He closed the Bible and invited Shawn and Brenetta to the altar with their daughter. He took her into his arms.

"What name is given to this child?" he asked

"Shawnetta Nichole Reeves," they answered in unison.

Bishop Snow turned to Mrs. Snow, who stood holding a white bowl full of water and a white towel. He dipped his hand into the water and gently sprinkled a few drops on Shawnetta's head.

"Shawnetta Nichole Reeves, I baptize you in the name of the Father, and of the Son, and of the Holy Spirit. Amen."

Shawnetta giggled as he tenderly dried her head then handed her back to Brenetta.

Bishop Snow then requested that Danté and Sharmaine come forward as Shawnetta's godparents. He smiled at them. "As godparents of this child, I charge you both with a very important task. Live your lives as an example for this child, so that she may live a godly life. It is your duty to assist her parents in raising her in a godly fashion. Do you accept this charge?"

They both stated, "We do."

Bishop Snow then turned to the congregation. "Many of you here today may not be aware of the circumstances surrounding this wonderful little life. Church, this child was conceived in the midst of an evil act. A wicked man raped a teenage girl and she became pregnant."

The congregation gasped in unison. Bishop Snow paused as his congregation processed the information.

"Wait, church, that's not the end of this story. That poor teenage girl, while she was alone and pregnant, was gunned down by a crazed drug addict. The bullet went through her arm and pierced her heart, just barely missing her unborn child. This young girl was an innocent bystander who had not done anything wrong. That bullet cut short her life. She gave birth; then she went home to glory."

Danté wiped away a tear as Bishop Snow talked about Nichole. He stood silently at the altar next to Sharmaine.

"Oh, but glory hallelujah, that is still not how the story ends," Bishop Snow continued. "I know it sounds like a sad story. It sounds like Satan entered her life and turned everything upside down. But don't you know that God always has a plan? What Satan intended for evil, God turned into good. This beautiful baby girl that you see today has become a blessing in the lives of Brother and Sister Reeves."

"Amen, Bishop! Hallelujah," several parishioners shouted out.

"This child's life is an example to everyone here today. Her life is an example that sometimes Satan will come into our lives and turn them topsy-turvy. There will be so much drama going on that we begin to think we are losing it. But, church, that's when God steps in. He will not leave you nor forsake you. Even in the worst of times, God can and will bless you."

Danté and Sharmaine began applauding, as they both were witnesses to Bishops Snow's words. The congregation joined with them, and everyone applauded loudly.

"I charge all of you today, as well, to live as examples before this child of God. Let your light so shine that she may see the God in each and every one of you. Let the church say amen," Bishop Snow concluded.

Brenetta handed Shawnetta to Danté and smiled. Then she turned to look at the entire congregation. Suddenly, she began to sing. "*Jesus loves me, this I know, for the Bible tells me so. Little ones to him belong. They are weak, but he is strong.*"

Shawn looked over at her, stunned. Her voice was not powerful or dramatic. It certainly wasn't the best he'd ever heard. But she'd managed to stay on key, and Shawn had to admit she actually sounded pretty good. He took her hand into his and began singing along. *"Yes, Jesus loves me. Yes, Jesus loves me. Yes, Jesus loves me, for the Bible tells me so."*

One by one, the congregation stood, and each of them joined hands or linked arms with their neighbor. In unison, they lifted their voices and all stood singing together. *"Yes, Jesus loves me, for the Bible tells me so."*

Reader's Group Guide Questions

1. *Losing It* is a modern adaption of the story of Job. What are your thoughts on how Sharmaine's problems compared with those of Job?

2. Sharmaine is a celebrity falsely accused. Does her story make you take a second look at how quickly we believe rumors about others?

3. Have you ever been in a situation where you were an outcast among your peers? If so, how does Sharmaine's situation compare and make you feel?

4. What were your feelings regarding Leon's mother not allowing Sharmaine to see or speak to her children?

5. If you had been one of the parishioners at church when Sharmaine came to sing, knowing only what they knew, do you think you would have stayed or left?

6. Did you judge Danté as a bad person as soon as he was introduced, the same way Jackson and Leon did, or did you wait to get to know the character and his motives?

7. Does your local church group sponsor a drug rehabilitation counseling program? If not, do you feel that it's something that is needed?

8. Keisha's grief led her to bitterness and eventually revenge on the person she felt was responsible. Do you think grief counseling could have prevented her from feeling this way?

9. What emotions did you feel when you discovered Keisha's motive for harming Sharmaine? Did you feel she was justified or crazy?

10. Was there a character in this story that you closely identified with? If so, which character and why?

About the Author

Zaria Garrison is an award-winning author who is committed to writing and publishing literature that ministers as well as entertains. She is part owner and staff writer for EKG Literary magazine, an online magazine dedicated to being the pulse of the literary community.

Zaria also offers insight and encouragement to aspiring authors through workshops and writing classes that allow each participant to discover the craft of writing and how it can be used to effectively minister to youth, women, and all members of the community. Her first Christian fiction novel, *Prodigal*, was released in 2009.

You can find her online at www.zariagarrison.com or www. ekgliterarymag.com